SWEET VALLEY CONFIDENTIAL

FRANCINE PASCAL

arrow books

Published by Arrow Books 2011

2 4 6 8 10 9 7 5 3 1

First published in Great Britain in 2011 by
Arrow Books
Random House, 20 Vauxhall Bridge Road,
London SW1V 2SA

www.rbooks.co.uk

Addresses for companies within The Random House Group Limited can be
found at: www.randomhouse.co.uk/offices.htm

The Random House Group Limited Reg. No. 954009

A CIP catalogue record for this book
is available from the British Library

ISBN 978-0-099-55773-9

The Random House Group Limited supports The Forest Stewardship
Council (FSC), the leading international forest certification organisation.
All our titles that are printed on Greenpeace approved FSC certified paper
carry the FSC logo. Our paper procurement policy can be found at:
www.rbooks.co.uk/environment

Mixed Sources
Product group from well-managed
forests and other controlled sources
www.fsc.org Cert no. TT-COC-002139
© 1996 Forest Stewardship Council
FSC

Typeset by SX Composing DTP, Rayleigh, Essex
Printed and bound in Great Britain by
CPI Bookmarque, Croydon

For my darling daughter,
Jamie Stewart

ACKNOWLEDGMENTS

The first thank-you goes to my agent of twenty-nine years, Amy Berkower, the best agent, manager, and friend any writer could have. And to Dan Weiss, who goes back to the beginning of Sweet Valley, a partner and a friend as well. I am grateful to my excellent editor, Hilary Rubin Teeman, and to my copyeditor, Frances Sayers. And especially to Genevieve Gagne-Hawes for knowing everything there is to know about Sweet Valley and saving me from any number of memory lapses and doing it so kindly and so fast. I'm always grateful to Hilary Bloom, who for twenty-three years has run every part of my office and from time to time, my life.

And thanks to Ken Gross for the title and Molly Wenk for the pieces of current technospeak I would never have known. Thanks to Judy Adler for her wedding contribution.

My gratitude and love go out to my family, who always support me in my work: Laurie Wenk and Susan Johansson. And to Anders Johansson and all the rest of my remarkable family: the

Bigs, the Middles, and the Little. You know who you are. Thank you.

And a special thanks to Justin Timberlake and his coauthors, Nate "Danja" Hills and T.I., for quotes from "My Love." And to Beyoncé Giselle Knowles, Kenneth Brian Edmonds, Mikkel S. Eriksen, and Tor Erik Hermansen for their beautiful song, "Broken-Hearted Girl."

1
New York

Elizabeth had turned the key in the Fox lock, releasing a heavy metal bar that scraped across the inside of the front door with an impressive prison-gate sound, and was about to attack the Segal lock when the phone in the apartment started to ring. By the time she had opened the second lock and was sliding the key into the last one—this was New York, after all—the phone was on its fourth ring.

At almost midnight, it had to be the West Coast calling.

She could still grab it in time, but Elizabeth didn't hurry. Slow, with purpose. Slow, giving the internal anger and hurt time to shoot from zero to a hundred. It needed only seconds, like the start-up speed of a Maserati. Except it was never at zero. Not anymore. Hadn't been for the last eight months. And she couldn't imagine a time when it would ever be there again.

As always, the hurt overpowered the anger, and what welled up in her throat came with tears that choked her.

"You going to get that?" David Stephenson, the young man standing next to her, asked as he stretched his arm over her head to hold the door open. David was six-three and at her five-six it was way over her head.

"That's okay," she managed, quickly ducking her face away from him, stealing a sliver of extra time as she put the doggie-bagged pork chop she was carrying carefully and more precisely than necessary down on the hall table. It gave her enough time to catch her breath and let the tears slide back down her throat.

And with that momentary respite came an irresistible, nasty need to satisfy the anger physically. All she had was her purse. It would do. She flung it as hard as she could into the hall chair and watched as the Prada knockoff hit the upholstered back, bounced off, and came to rest on the edge of the chair. A little dumb, but it was a surprisingly good release.

Like that embarrassing time a month ago on Broadway, when the fury escaped her mind into her mouth and she said, out loud, really loudly, "I hate you!" People turned, shocked and then interested; she quickly put her hand to her ear as if she were on a cell phone, and it became ordinary and they lost interest.

David had already walked into the living room, missing all the action behind him. "You have a landline? And an answering machine?"

"My mother. A going-away gift. She said it made her feel that I was safer. How, I don't know. I think it made *her* feel safer."

Elizabeth could hear her own calm message playing in the background: "Please leave your name and number, and I'll return your call as soon as possible. Thank you."

"I'm just going to throw this in the fridge," she said, scooping up the doggie bag, back in control. "Would you like a glass of wine?"

By now she was halfway through the narrow, sparsely furnished living room, heading into the safety of the very small jerry-built kitchen, with its squeezed-in mini refrigerator, two-burner stove, tiny oven, and an outsized, badly chipped, probably prewar like the rest of the building, porcelain sink deep enough to wash babies as well as dishes.

"Sure. Okay. With a couple of ice cubes, please."

"Lizzie. Pick up." The woman's voice on the machine was plaintive. "Please. I really need to talk to you."

Of course, Elizabeth could hear it from the kitchen. Could she ever miss that voice? Now so sweet, so seductive, pleading softly, spreading out the vowels, almost songlike. Liz . . . zie . . .

That voice, so heavy with love. Love me, it said, forgive me, so I can put you out of the way and get back to my own life.

"I forgot to fill the ice tray, but the wine's really cold."

Elizabeth's voice was so calm David thought maybe she hadn't heard the message.

"It sounds important. Don't you want to get it?"

Now Elizabeth was back in the room carrying two glasses of chilled white wine. David was sitting on the small low couch, so low his knees almost obscured his face.

She answered him completely composed, as if she were reciting dialogue in a play. "Actually, no."

It had everything but the English accent.

David's cheeks creased in a slightly embarrassed smile that pulled in his breath with a little hiss; he was politely uncomfortable, knowing he had stumbled into something too personal. "Sorry."

"That's okay. Forget it." She brushed it off, but there was no way to hide her flushed face.

"I have to tell you. It's really weird," he said.

"Because I didn't take the call?"

"No, because the voice . . . it sounded just like you."

No wonder. How many times over the years had she herself been fooled by a recording? For just a flash she would think, Was that me? Or worse, when she had to pick herself out of a family picture. How pathetic is it not to recognize yourself?

Elizabeth handed David his wine without comment, put hers down on the low table next to her least favorite chair, comfortable but covered in a scratchy plaid fabric.

Normally, she never sat there, but the choice was either next to David on the loveseat, which would surely be more intimate than she felt right now, or the scratchy chair. She wasn't in the scratchy chair two seconds before she bobbed up and reached for the stereo which, because the room was so small, was within arm's distance.

"You like Beyoncé?"

"Really," he said. "I mean, you could have fooled me. It was identical." He wasn't going to let it go so easily.

Instead of the scratchy chair, Elizabeth sat back down next to David on the loveseat, making the only move that could detour the direction of the conversation. A direction she seriously didn't want. Certainly not with this semistranger, a guy she'd barely spoken to before tonight. Her boss.

It worked. He turned to her, delighted, a little surprised at the possible gift he was not expecting, all thoughts of the telephone message wiped out of his head.

They worked together at the online magazine *Show Survey: Off Broadway in New York*, a weekly struggling along with only a smattering of sponsors and even fewer paid advertisements. It was put out by a passionate staff of three dedicated theater lovers and the newcomer, Elizabeth Wakefield. The printed copy left at hotels was not much better than a throwaway, but Elizabeth was grateful to be part of the venture. Not having much experience in theater, she'd lucked into the job eight months ago after two frantic days in New York, one of which, the worst, was her twenty-seventh birthday. She celebrated alone, then lied to her parents that she'd spent the day with a couple of old friends from Sweet Valley who had moved to New York. Her mother asked who they were, but when Elizabeth sidestepped the question, she very kindly and wisely didn't pursue it. In fact, her parents had been very gentle and understanding. Never asking the wrong questions. Even the two times they came to see her in New York, they only talked about her work.

Actually, it was David who had hired her. He and his partner, Don Barren, both in their early thirties, both trained accountants who hated the confinement of numbers, both theater enthusiasts, had self-financed *Show Survey* about two years ago as a kind of Zagat ratings guide for Off Broadway. No critics, just audiences. Elizabeth was hired to interview people coming out of the theater and write up paragraph descriptions of shows, just as Zagat did for restaurants.

There wasn't enough staff money for Elizabeth to see all the shows, so they had arranged to buy tickets the day of the show at the TKTS booth on Forty-seventh Street, and only the cheapest ones at that, and only for shows without an intermission. If there was an intermission, Elizabeth would sneak in free for the second act. Though she worried in the beginning, she never once got caught. She had a story ready about how her brother was in the cast and had told her just to use his name. Of course, she always found an ensemble name in advance for her "brother." So far, she hadn't had to use it.

All printed copies of *Show Survey* were free, given away at hotels and restaurants, but it was beginning to catch on, and they had picked up a few more online sponsors. Recently they had added interviews with everyone involved in the theater—actors, writers, producers, directors, even ushers. Just this week David had given Elizabeth her first interview assignment: a playwright named Will Connolly.

Tonight wasn't a real date with David. It was more like, Hey, you eat yet? No? How about we grab a bite at McMullen's? Hence, the leftover pork chop. It was okay, but somehow Elizabeth had gotten stuck with the tip. David was attractive enough—tall with a very good body, every muscle well worked out at least five times a week at a local gym—but the tip thing was a turnoff.

Additionally, sleeping with the boss was a famously bad idea. In her four years at the *Sweet Valley News,* Elizabeth had never done it. Well, of course, Todd was in her life then.

Still, David did have a great body, and maybe the tip thing was accidental. Right from the start Elizabeth could tell he was attracted to her. It had probably helped in the hiring, though she had decent credentials, but a little gratitude wouldn't hurt. He was, after all, a nice guy.

A nice guy she didn't feel like sleeping with.

On the other hand, in the eight months she had been in New York she hadn't slept with anyone but Russ Klein, a friend of the rental agent for the building. With Elizabeth's permission, the agent had given Russ her e-mail address. They e-mailed back and forth for a couple of days, and he seemed like a nice guy. Like Elizabeth, he was new to New York; he had come four months earlier for a job as a trader on Wall Street. Coffee turned into a three-week miniaffair spread out over two months. Definitely rebound stuff. She cried after every orgasm. How embarrassing, but he pretended not to notice. Russ was not a man to complicate a good thing with feelings.

Elizabeth had thought maybe they'd stay friends after—not that they had such a great connection—but she was in the market for new friends, people with no association to Sweet Valley. Whenever anyone asked where she came from, she said California. They immediately thought L.A., and she didn't disabuse them.

But it didn't happen, the friendship with Russ. His sister was in the middle of a divorce, and though Elizabeth thought she was good at hiding her own problems, he sensed another sad story and got out of the way.

She could feel David staring at her while she feigned deep involvement with her wineglass. Eventually, she would have to turn toward him. That would be the moment. The turn would be a Yes, let's have sex, or a No way.

Beyoncé was having her heart broken in soft sounds. "*. . . don't wanna love you in no kind of way, no no.*"

A little more of this and she would cry *before* the orgasm.

"That was my sister. I mean, on the phone." At the moment

it seemed the lesser of two evils. Elizabeth stood, reached out, hit the Next button, and Justin Timberlake was in love, ". . . *holding hands, walking on the beach . . . toes in the sand.*"

She had to remember to change the CDs.

"We had a little something, nothing important. You know, sisters . . ."

Now she was standing, safe, having made the decision not to have sex with him. "I'm doing the Will Connolly interview Thursday; how long do you want the piece?"

David hesitated for a moment, adjusting to the loss, then spoke. "Seven hundred fifty words should be enough. Don't go more than a thousand." He finished his wine.

"Another glass?"

"No, that's okay. I'm running early tomorrow morning."

Pushing himself off the low couch was like doing a bench press, but he did it flawlessly.

There were a few awkward seconds when Elizabeth opened the door, but they pulled it together, and by the time David said, "See you tomorrow," and patted her head, they were back to business.

Elizabeth leaned against the closed door. A faint hint of regret was wiped out by relief.

"Stupid!" she said to the stereo as she clicked Timberlake off, walked to the kitchen, and refilled her wineglass.

Almost one in the morning. But really only 10:00 P.M. She always did that—went back to real time. Eight months and she was still taking off those damn three hours. Would she ever truly be free of Sweet Valley?

That was minor compared to being free of being a twin. How to explain something as natural and unlearned as seeing or feeling when you've never known anything different? It was always that way with a matching half: You only knew it by its absence.

She remembered a poem they had found when they were about ten called "The Twins."

In form and feature, face and limb,
I grew so like my brother,
That folks got taking me for him,
And each for one another.

They both loved that poem, especially the ending:

And when I died, the neighbors came
and buried brother John.

Would anyone else ever delight in that silly poem?

Like the twins of that poem, Elizabeth and Jessica Wakefield appeared interchangeable, if you considered only their faces.

And what faces they were.

Gorgeous. Absolutely amazing. The kind you couldn't stop looking at. Their eyes were shades of aqua that danced in the light like shards of precious stones, oval and fringed with thick, light brown lashes long enough to cast a shadow on their cheeks. Their silky blond hair, the cascading kind, fell just below their shoulders. And to complete the perfection, their rosy lips looked as if they were penciled on. There wasn't a thing wrong with their figures, either. It was as if billions of possibilities all fell together perfectly.

Twice.

Elizabeth finished the last of the wine in her glass, undressed and slipped into her oversized SVU T-shirt, and curled up on the couch.

The outside noises of a New York apartment in Midtown Manhattan were a constant: garbage trucks, standing buses spewing the sounds of endless pollution, an occasional police siren, a vagrant nut screaming obscenities, and now and then Con Edison digging. But in the last eight months it had become white noise for Elizabeth Wakefield, barely registering as more than background, never disturbing the silence of the apartment enough to keep her from feeling alone.

Especially tonight.

Bereft and abandoned, Elizabeth was overwhelmed with feelings of loss, with the ache that had been chewing at her insides day in and day out. The betrayal. Without trying, she'd become the lyrics to every sad love song.

That he didn't love her anymore should have been the most important part, but it paled next to his deceit and betrayal. Elizabeth winced when she thought how blind she'd been, what a fool she must have looked like all that time.

And all that time may have been years.

When the light finally came, she'd followed her first instinct and fled. And now here she was, self-exiled, stranded alone in strange territory.

Everything about New York was unfamiliar. Yes, she had been here before. In her freshman year at SVU she had won a competition to have her one-act play produced in New York during spring break.

It had been one of the most exciting times in her life, in fact, so exciting that she'd barely noticed where she was. And then to make it even more fabulous, she'd gotten some good reviews that turned into raves when Jessica took over the lead.

But this was a different New York. Now she was really living here and alone and miserable. And she knew every ugly detail of the apartment.

To begin with, it was old. Growing up in Sweet Valley, nothing was old. Old was more than thirty years. And nothing seemed to have more than a couple of coats of paint. Not enough so that you could see it. Here, the old paint, maybe eighty years' worth, was so thick it looked like plaster but bumpier and more uneven. No sharp corners anywhere. And no matter how much she cleaned, the dirt seemed painted in. Nothing had that bright, crisp feeling of home and what used to be.

She didn't even have any real friends. Sure, she'd gotten to know some people, even a woman in her building, but there was no one she trusted. Good. About time she learned not to trust.

It was still early enough to call her best friend, the only friend she still had from Sweet Valley, Bruce Patman. It still made her smile when she thought of that impossibly arrogant and conceited boy of high school. Actually, she could hardly remember him that way anymore.

She could call. It wasn't even eleven there. Not that she hadn't called him a lot later than that. In fact, there were a few three-in-the-morning beauties when she first arrived in New York—whiny and complaining—she was almost too embarrassed to remember them.

She could call him now. But she wasn't going to. Not when she was feeling so low. He took it too seriously, like a good friend would, and she just didn't want to upset him. Bruce Patman upset by someone else's trouble? That almost made her smile.

But she didn't call and she didn't smile.

The room was still. And silent. Until she hit the Replay button on the answering machine.

"Lizzie. Pick up. Please. I really need to talk to you."

Never!

*P*lease, Lizzie. I really need to talk to you."

Exactly the same words. Only it's eleven years earlier and Jessica and I are sixteen. And it's not on an answering machine, it's face-to-face.

"No way, Jess," I tell her, "Daddy said no car for the whole month, and I'm not giving you the keys."

"You'd think I totaled the whole car. It was just a tap on a way ugly little mailbox."

"And half the rear fender."

"That really sucks. You can't even see it from the front."

"Forget it. I'm *so* not giving you the keys."

But Jessica is not one to give up, and for the whole ten-minute ride from home to Sweet Valley High, she pleads with me, nags, cajoles, bribes, and finally threatens, but I don't budge. My parents have given instructions and, unlike my twin, I follow instructions.

When Jessica sees that it's hopeless, she resorts to punishment.

"Todd called."

I bite. "Todd Wilkins?" Now she has my complete attention. "For me?"

"No way."

"For you?" I can feel my voice creeping up about two octaves from my normal tone, like a squeak from a disappointed eight-year-old.

"Like you're surprised that the captain of the basketball team would call the captain of the cheerleaders? Can't you see we're a natural?"

"I guess."

For a flash, I think I see Jessica feeling a tiny prick of guilt, but it's gone in a flash. Maybe it was never there. Truth is they are a natural, she and Todd, and besides, he's a jock, and everyone knows I'm not interested in jocks.

Except for this one.

Ever since I first saw him in kindergarten hanging on to his ratty baby blanket with the pulled-out fringes, his face shiny with big fat tears because his mommy was leaving him. I try not to remember that his nose was running right down to his lip.

Are there pheromones at five?

And *coups de foudre*?

I tried to give him a tissue, but he threw it on the floor. Was that a portent of the future that I was too love-blind to see?

And just in case any shred of hope lingers, Jessica jolts me back to reality. "He called to wish me luck with Pi Beta today. I think he's going to ask me to the Phi Epsilon dance."

"Cool," I say as my stomach drops. A stomach can drop even if it doesn't really go anywhere. The sliding sensation, along with what feels like a whoosh of empty air, is absolutely physical. Especially when, as in my case, that person is struggling with an important crush.

Jessica gets quiet, so deep in some kind of plan—she is a planner, often devious—that she doesn't even notice that I've stopped the car to pick up Enid Rollins, whom Jessica refers to as Wuss of the World.

Enid jumps into the backseat.

"I have to talk to you about something," Enid whispers to the back of my head.

Enid is my dearest friend, and I really love her, but the jealousy between Jessica and Enid sometimes makes things very uncomfortable: divided loyalties, but not really. No one could be closer than my sister. I wouldn't know how to do that.

"What?" I don't quite hear what she's saying.

"Later," she says.

Jessica sticks her head between us. "I am so not interested in anything you say. Especially anything about boring Ronnie Edwards."

Enid lets out a yelp. "Who told you? And he is *so* not boring!"

"Yes, he is. Ask Caroline Pearce."

Caroline Pearce is Sweet Valley's major gossip.

What Caroline doesn't know she simply makes up, so she can always be counted on for some kind of information.

"Jessica!" I try for the mommy tone, but it comes out with a little giggle. "You're horrible!"

Admittedly, Jessica is incorrigible. After all this time, sixteen whole years of life, it still fascinates me that identical twins could be so different. When I'm not the subject, I admit it tickles me.

But it doesn't tickle Enid at all. "How can you, like, stand her?"

"Oh, who cares anyway." Jessica has completely lost interest in our conversation. She's too busy trying to wave down Bruce Patman's Porsche, which is idling at the light right alongside us. "Let me out here," she says, already halfway out the door.

"Hey, Bruce!"

Bruce smiles and motions with his movie star head for her to hop in. Simultaneously, he reaches over and flips open the passenger door; Jessica runs around our car and jumps in.

Bruce Patman is the male Jessica but a whole lot richer, as rich as Jessica's best friend, Lila Fowler.

What Enid was trying to tell me was how much she likes Ronnie Edwards and he'd just asked her to the Phi Epsilon dance.

I know I should be listening to my best friend's problems, but I can't get my mind off the disappointment. Todd and Jessica.

Most people think I've escaped big crushes so far—that's what it looks like to the outside world—but the secret is simple: Since that day in kindergarten, I've had a crush on one boy—Todd Wilkins.

For the longest time, right through grade school, he didn't seem to even notice me or—and I was watching carefully—any other girls.

But at the start of high school, there was a change. He was still more interested in basketball, but there were times when I felt he looked at me in a special way. Though he was friendly, he never asked me out.

I watched in teenage agony when he seemed interested in a couple of other girls, but it never lasted.

At least, I comforted myself, he had never asked out Jessica, either. Until now. And that's the one that really hurts. So close and yet about as far away as possible.

Even though my best friend is talking about the boy she likes, I am no longer reachable. Jessica and Todd. The nightmare of my life.

That's the way it stays all day, through all my classes. In fact, I am so distracted that in English, my favorite teacher, Mr. Collins, takes me aside and asks if anything is wrong.

I convince him that I'm fine; it's only a little headache. That it's the size of a twin sister, I don't mention.

That night Jessica wants to borrow everything of mine for her date with Todd. Even my new blue button-down shirt. But for one of the rare times, I'm not lending. My clothes aren't going out with Todd, not unless I'm in them.

Jessica doesn't press. In fact, she looks a little uncomfortable. Maybe she does suspect that I might be interested in Todd. It's like that: Just when Jessica seems most heartless . . .

Oh, who am I kidding? She is a heartless bitch, and I hate her!

2
Sweet Valley

"Did you get her?"

Jessica shook her head. "No."

"But you left a message?"

"I always leave messages. All over. I text, I e-mail, I everything. It's hopeless. She's never going to answer."

"What about Facebook?"

"She ignores me. She'll never let me be a friend. She doesn't even answer. And she's never going to answer you, either, is she?"

Todd shook his head. "I don't know."

Jessica Wakefield was sitting on the couch, curled up in one corner with the phone in her hand. There were no tears, but her mouth was twisted in a silent sob.

"You know she's gotten your letter by now, but she's never going to read it."

"She will when she's ready."

"She'll never be ready for either of us."

It was evening, almost nine o'clock in California, and Jessica and Todd were in the living room of their rented two-bedroom townhouse apartment. With Jessica's natural good taste and the help of Alice Wakefield, her decorator mother, it was furnished in sunny colors, soft and comfortable, if a touch feminine. But Todd didn't mind at all. Whatever Jessica wanted, he wanted, and taking that extra step of a man in love, he came to think he actually liked it.

Todd Wilkins was a real talent and beginning to be recognized. His sports column was regularly picked up on the wire and sometimes ran in up to ten other papers. He had an agent, and syndication was a strong possibility.

He still looked like the high school basketball star he had been, tall and well built, with a sweetness to his face that overruled handsome and made him very accessible and well liked. Until now.

Like Jessica, he, too, suffered criticism—deserved, yes, but still painful. A criticism that he could find no way to answer. But since it was never to his face, he didn't have to. But, by God, could he feel it.

In the back of his mind was the possibility of leaving Sweet Valley. He could do it, but Jessica wasn't ready yet.

In many ways, Todd was still that same boy from their school years, with the straight brown hair silky enough to keep sliding down over his eyes and be whipped back with his signature sweep. In those days Elizabeth used to imitate him. Now Jessica did. But he would never tell her that.

Yes, he was the same boy, yet in many other important ways

he was quite different. Difficult circumstances had challenged him, and he had risen to that challenge with a maturity that belied his twenty-seven years. But there was just so far he could rise with the weight of such transgressions. There were days he was tempted to abandon everything. And everyone. Until he looked at his greatest challenge and knew he could never leave her.

Todd sat down next to his love and took her in his arms. "She'll call. Give her time."

"That's what my mother says," Jessica said, pulling away. "And it doesn't help. It's like what you say to a child. It's been eight months; that's time, isn't it? She hates me!"

"She's angry."

"What do you know? She's not your twin. Not your flesh and blood. Do you know what it's like to be hated by someone you desperately love?"

"I know Elizabeth. She doesn't hate you."

Todd truly believed that—despite all that had happened—because, twin or not, he knew Elizabeth was unique.

When he'd first noticed her—and it took him a long time, almost to high school—he knew she was different. And then there was the Phi Epsilon dance business. He had summoned the courage to call to ask Elizabeth out, but Jessica answered the phone. When she said Elizabeth was in the shower, he got flustered and hung up. Later when he'd thought Elizabeth had gone out with bad boy Rick Andover, he asked Jessica instead. He remembered thinking, Well, they are identical twins. . . .

But he soon realized his mistake. They were nothing alike. And after staring longingly at Elizabeth the whole dance, and discovering it was really Jessica who had gone out with Rick, he and Elizabeth had finally gotten together. To this day, Todd wasn't sure what had happened, and now, he never wanted to.

After that dance, he knew Elizabeth was going to be his first real girlfriend. She was beautiful; everything about her was soft and fragile and perfect. Her hand in his was silky, and he remembered holding it as gently as one would a small bird. She made him feel big and clumsy, just what he'd need to be to protect her.

It would be a relationship that he could count on. Something he could grow with. And where it would grow he couldn't even begin to imagine.

There was a connection between them he never knew he could have with a girl. Girls had always seemed a pole apart from him, like another species, deeply desirable yet intimidating, which made them even more desirable.

Even though Elizabeth was as kind and tender as anyone he had ever known, and he could feel that she really cared for him, the idea that a stranger, a girl at that, would become part of his life was probably the most exciting thing that had ever happened to him. Excitement always carries with it a touch of fear, of danger, and this one did as well.

Still, it was nothing like it would have been had it been Jessica. Instinctively, Todd knew that she was the true danger. But he planned never to get close enough to find out how dangerous she really was.

And then, during senior year at Sweet Valley University, for that one night he forgot his own warning and found out everything about danger. By then it was too late.

And now?

Now it was too late, too.

If Jessica hadn't married Regan Wollman, would it have been any different? Would Todd have gone through with the marriage to Elizabeth? He was still struggling with that answer. He knew it; he just didn't like it.

The answer was he probably would have. Jessica despised him. She'd told him five years earlier and after that had never missed a chance to show him. And never more so than the time eight months ago when she was staying with him and Elizabeth.

And he'd begun to hate her, too. It was his only protection.

Yes, though he would never admit it to anyone but himself, he would have gone on with the wedding. He would have married Elizabeth because he loved her and she loved him.

He would never have betrayed her again.

It was the only answer he could live with.

"She hates me! And she hates you, too!" Jessica shouted, interrupting his thoughts. She was near tears.

Todd got up and started toward the kitchen.

"Where are you going?"

"Nowhere. The kitchen. I don't know," he said, walking out of the room.

Jessica was alone. The expression of misery turned to anger.

"I don't want to go tonight," she called to the empty doorway. No answer. "You have to call them and make some excuse. I don't care what you say. Tell them I've got the flu."

Todd reappeared, a beer in his hand. "Come on, Jess. I can't do that, Lila's expecting us."

"Well, I am so not going. Besides, she doesn't really want me. She's just hoping for some gossip."

"Hey, I thought she was your best friend."

"Right, like all your best friends."

"What does that mean?"

"It means everyone hates us. We have no best friends anymore."

"Hey," Todd said, kneeling down in front of Jessica. "Come on, Jess. I'm not saying it's easy or that we don't deserve a lot of what's happening, but if we're going to stay here—"

"I *am* staying here!"

"Then we have to find a way to live with it. I love you, and there's nothing I wouldn't do for you, but this is no good and getting worse."

Now the tears came and Jessica reached out and put her arms around Todd's shoulders and held on tightly, burying her face in the crook of his neck. He rose, taking her with him, still in his arms, and they stood together, two people together, painfully alone.

The phone rang. Both pulled away, alert, a shock of excitement electrifying them.

Jessica grabbed for the phone. "Hello," she said, breathless, her eyes meeting Todd's, alive with hope.

And then, "Oh, Mom . . . Can I call you back? I can't talk now, I'm just out of the shower."

Jessica put down the phone. "I hate to do that, but I can't talk to her now."

"Come on, baby, it's going to work out."

"No, it's not. You know what's going to happen eventually? I'll end up hating Elizabeth for hating me. It's a natural defense.

And then I'll even find a good reason. Something like, she knew you didn't really love her, so why was she hanging on? Maybe because she knew I loved you."

"You're wrong. That's not what's going to happen. What's going to happen is that Elizabeth's going to find someone she really loves the way I love you, and then she'll know she and I weren't right together."

"And then she'll say, 'So really Jessica helped me by sleeping with the man I thought I loved but didn't. How lucky I am to have such a wonderful sister.'"

ust like when I do her another great favor way back when we're six-teen and Todd calls for the first time and asks for her. Well, he doesn't exactly ask for her, it's more like a guess.

"Elizabeth?"

"Liz is in the shower."

I don't know why I do that since I never was particularly interested in Todd Wilkins, but he sounds really sexy on the phone, and I'm thinking maybe I should give him a chance. Especially now with the Phi Epsilon dance coming up.

I have three invitations already, but not one is even a remote possibility. Winston Egbert. That's all I need: to be stuck with someone named Winston Egbert who actually looks like a Winston Egbert. And two other nonentities I just said no to without bothering to make up an excuse. What were they thinking?

"This is her sister, Jessica." Like there's no one in Sweet Valley who doesn't know "the twins."

I can hear his frustration, so I jump in. "Can I help you?"

I can practically read his mind. He's thinking, They're identical twins, so how different can she be from her sister?

"I don't know. . . ."

I can tell he's stuck. So I help him out and say, "I have to go. We're finding out whether we were picked to be Pi Beta Alpha pledges today."

"I'm sure you won't have any trouble, but good luck anyway."

I'm actually doing Liz a favor. Everyone knows she would never go out with a jock. Why put her through actually having to say no, which is always especially difficult for her? Besides, I'm doing him a favor, too—saving him the pain of rejection.

I'm good at convincing myself, and since it's me telling me, I believe it right away. Rejection is very painful. So I hear.

Even without rejection, life is harder for me. I always have to spend a lot of time planning, which might look like manipulation, but I can't leave anything to chance. If I did, I would have nothing. Like this morning, with Todd. If I hadn't moved things around a little, I wouldn't have a chance of going with him to the Phi Epsilon dance.

And it isn't like I was taking anything away from Elizabeth. I know her better than anyone else does, and she so doesn't care about things like that.

Elizabeth has always had everything under control. Without being conceited, I know I'm pretty but not nearly as gorgeous as Elizabeth, who like never has to do anything to look absolutely flawless. Oh, sure, she has to comb her hair and do the ordinary things, but that's it. I'm stuck blow-drying forever, straightening endlessly, and spending most of my allowance on makeup and creams. Still, I so never feel like I come near my sister.

It's like unfair to have to compare yourself constantly to someone so perfect and always come in second. Outside of twins that just doesn't happen.

I so truly hate being in second place all the time. It's not something I could tell Elizabeth because I know her, she's so caring and sensitive, especially about me, that she would feel guilty. So even though I know that sometimes I probably come off looking self-centered, I don't defend myself.

But this is the way it has to be as long as I have that kind of competition in my life, which, of course, will be forever.

No matter what, even if I am always stuck being second, I love my sister more than I love anyone else in the world. It's a love I never fell into; a love I was simply born with, like it was fused to my DNA.

This phone call fiasco happens the week after I had this little accident with the car, a so-nothing dent, but my parents go berserk and say I can't drive for a month, which is like practically forever if you live in California, where there's nothing that isn't at least a car ride away, so I'm stuck having Elizabeth drive me to school today. And because she's the driver, she can pick up the Wuss of the World, Enid Rollins, a girl I totally hate. It's like she thinks she owns Elizabeth.

Lucky for me, Bruce Patman pulls up alongside in his Porsche and saves me from more wuss stories about some creep she's crazy about. Caroline Pearce already filled me in. Bor-ring . . . But as soon as I get in Bruce's car he starts with, "So, who's your sister going to the dance with?"

My head actually snaps around to take a hard look at Bruce. He's the same great-looking guy as ever, all perfect black hair and dark blue eyes. Maybe I'm missing something about Elizabeth. Did something happen in the middle of the night, some magic-wand stuff that suddenly made Elizabeth so desirable?

This is the second guy today asking about Elizabeth. Why is everyone suddenly so interested in my sister? Lizzie is the same old Lizzie: serious and sensible, reliable and comfortable, sort of like nurses' shoes. Definitely not hot. So what's going on?

And then it comes to me. They must be confusing Elizabeth with me. People do that all the time, get our names mixed up. They know who they want but simply have the names switched.

"I don't know. She has, like, a million invites," I tell him.

"Like who?"

"Mostly older college guys. Why?"

"Just curious."

Then he drops it. College guys are too much competition for a high school junior, even Bruce Patman. It's working, so I do a kind of riff on what I did with Todd earlier, insinuating how busy Elizabeth is.

"Just drop me on the next corner. I'll walk the rest of the way."

"Whatever," Bruce says, and pulls the car up to the curb. I can see he's ticked off, but so what. Obviously, he's not going to ask me to the dance, and that's where I am right now.

Sometimes I feel like people don't really understand me. To bottom-feeders like Winston, I might look like I'm selfish or even a little conceited, but that's just on the surface. I have to look that way because I can't let anyone know that inside, where it really counts, I'm vulnerable and insecure and total mush, always worrying that I'm doing the wrong thing or sounding dumb. It's so unlike Liz, who never seems to doubt anything and always knows exactly what to say and do.

Elizabeth is like those people who never have to study for a test— they just know it all—whereas things don't come as easily to me. I have to work at anything I want. And yeah, I want a lot, which is why I can never rely on things coming naturally.

Just thinking back about those early days and the awful things she did to Elizabeth made Jessica squirm. Why were all her worst times with Elizabeth always connected to Todd? Jessica knew Elizabeth thought she was going out with Todd that night, and she just let her.

How could she be so cruel? Well, it was a choice, Elizabeth or her. And sadly to say, in pure Jessica sound and form, there was like *so* no choice.

In truth, she was sneaking out with Rick Andover, a true piece of garbage her parents would never let her date, which was why she had to pretend it was Todd. She'd always had this fascination with danger. And Rick was danger.

Not telling Elizabeth the truth afterward—that she wasn't really with Todd—was the meanest part, but she felt as if she'd suffered enough from her mistake with Rick, who turned out to be *really* dangerous. He wouldn't let her go home. It was truly frightening, a horrendous night with a bar fight and the police and Caroline Pearce catching her when they dropped her off in a patrol car, that she went easy on herself. It was actually all a lot of nothing anyway, but it did cause trouble and endanger her position as captain of the cheering squad. Besides, she made up for it by not making a fuss when Elizabeth started dating Todd even though Jessica had gone wih him to the Phi Epsilon dance. And it did make Elizabeth very happy. She couldn't remember ever seeing her sister so excited about a boy. She felt that she had made Elizabeth so happy that she was able to forgive herself completely.

And even added another proud moment by not taking credit for fixing everything.

As if that made it all right.

Nothing would ever be right with Elizabeth again.

Todd interrupted her misery. "Come on, Jess, I'm not saying it wasn't horrendous what we did, it was a terrible betrayal that we'll have to live with. Nothing is going to change that. So what should we do now? Break up?"

This was the point they always got to, over and over and over again: how to punish themselves for what they'd done. And the worst pain they could think of was to break up. That's where the conversation always stopped.

"I never want to lose you," Jessica said.

"You won't," he said.

But Jessica worried.

Ultimately, Todd talked her into going to Lila's party; if they continued to hide from everyone, he told her, they might as well move away. The idea of being driven out of Sweet Valley, even if they themselves were party to it, was off the boards for Jessica, and so she agreed to go.

But with great trepidation.

For the ten minutes it took to drive over to Lila's house, she sat silently in the car. Actually, it was Lila and Ken's house, but they were separated and working on a divorce. Except he was there most of the time. Even Caroline had trouble explaining that. But Jessica said Ken just loved Lila, no matter what. Some people are like that.

"Hey, Jess." Todd reached out and took her hand. "I'm here. I'm always here."

Jessica squeezed his hand and smiled, but she said nothing.

Until they got to the house, and then miraculously, she turned back into Jessica the adorable.

Lila Fowler was no different than she had been in high school. Still the same light brown wavy hair—only now it was ironed flat and streaked blond—hazel brown eyes, a perfect little figure, and just as rich and snobby as ever. Lila had never really changed, never grown, and now all she had left was her old cheerleader uniform. She'd done nothing with her life so far other than drop out of college in her third year. She'd spent a few months trying to get work as a model, but when the agencies didn't scoop her up immediately, she gave up and went back to plying her natural talent as a shopper and a flirt. It was like the good old days, and Elizabeth said it made her feel popular, just like in high school.

Lila, her perfect body delectable in the shortest shorts possible and a salmon-colored silk halter top loose enough to slide lightly over her just right, slightly augmented, perky braless breasts, answered the door with shrieks of delight and surprise. Surprise mostly because they were there at all. Unbeknownst to Todd, Jessica had called in the afternoon with some preparatory excuses in advance of the not being able to come one.

"They're here!" she called behind her, as if they were the special guests everyone was waiting for. Which, of course, they were. That's the way it was anytime they went anywhere in Sweet Valley. Here come the freaks, as Jessica liked to describe Todd and herself.

And pulling Jessica along, with Todd following, Lila took them through the magnificent two-story entrance foyer into the living room, a stunningly decorated room with good antiques, all done in monochromatic beige with occasional blasts of black lacquer.

And there they were, sitting and standing, Sweet Valley at its most successful. Lila's almost ex-husband, Ken Matthews, was playing host. Still the NFL star, as handsome as any football quarterback should be, he was truly happy to see them and not because of any gossip thing, just because he really liked his old friends whom he, like the rest of Sweet Valley, saw little of lately.

Caroline Pearce, Sweet Valley's most successful real estate broker, a cancer survivor, and still gossip supreme, looked at Jessica like a ravenous raccoon with the good luck to spot a newborn kitten. She wasn't drooling, but she did lick her lips a couple of times before she charged in for the big hug. She was the Perez Hilton of Sweet Valley.

"Jess! I've missed you. I call, but you're never home."

Jessica manufactured enough enthusiasm to return a limp hug. "Miss you, too." And, pulling away, went on to greet the others, starting with the easier ones like Jeffrey French, who had moved back to Sweet Valley after leaving for the East Coast with his family in the middle of high school, and who now had a thriving dental practice; his wife, whose name Jessica never remembered; and A. J. Morgan, who was her competitor for status as the hottest gossip item.

Enid Rollins had known A. J. Morgan since high school, when he was Jessica's boyfriend. She was secretly crazy about him then, but, of course, she didn't stand a chance against Jessica.

A.J. had made some changes since high school—unfortunately none for the better—but happily, he now seemed to be as wild about Enid as she was about him. If she had actually been his girl-friend in school, she probably would have dumped him by now, and if she met him today she wouldn't look twice, but those un-requited desires of school years tend to hang on well after matu-rity should have used them up. Unfortunately, A.J. wasn't the best thing for Enid's image as a serious doctor, hard enough with being a recovered alcoholic, so she kept their relationship very private. Thanks to Caroline, though, not that private. In fact, Enid and A.J. had made gossip headlines for months, though ev-eryone pretended for Enid's sake not to know about their affair.

Enid wasn't really Jessica's competitor anymore, since her best friend relationship with Elizabeth had ended long ago when the "Wuss of the World" turned into Doctor Arrogant.

Jessica felt she had been right about Enid all along. Under-neath that humble, self-effacing, best-friend disguise, there was a pretentious, egotistical shit who wanted only to steal Elizabeth from her. Well, they didn't have to compete anymore. They'd both lost her.

"Hey, how're you doing?" Jessica took the initiative since they were equal gossipees and she knew she was on safe ground. Enid was not likely to ask her any personal questions.

Jessica looked around for Bruce Patman, but fortunately, he wasn't there. She dreaded seeing Bruce. Not only did he know too much, but he was still Elizabeth's best friend.

She was surprised and actually happy to see Robin Wilson there. She looked terrific, having gained back only a tiny bit of that lost weight from her high school years, which was amazing since now she was a successful food caterer and restaurant critic, chin-deep in delicious food every day. She was with her new husband, Dan Kane, a lawyer from Jessica's brother Steven's office. It was a wedding Jessica and Todd, armed with some elaborate excuse, had managed to miss.

"Congratulations," Jessica said. "You look great."

"Thanks," Robin said. "I feel great. How are you—" She cut herself off. "You look terrific, too."

"How about a drink? A Bellini?" Ken offered.

Jessica said, yes, and Todd asked for a beer.

The group seemed to settle down into a normal gathering, nibbling on guacamole and little sausage bites, drinking this and that and chatting among themselves. When the subject moved on to some boring thing about a planned pocket park downtown, Jessica began to relax.

She took a sip of her Bellini and thought maybe this wasn't going to be so bad. And it was nice being with old friends. But she didn't count on Caroline.

"So," said Caroline, "any word yet?"

Jessica looked at Caroline, a person she had known since kindergarten and never liked. Always matronly, even as a little girl, she was consistently taller than most of the other girls, and for a while, most of the boys. Plus, she was squarish. Even after puberty, when she had breasts and she wasn't fat, she had no real waistline. No curves, just straight up and down, up to about five-ten. And she always looked hungry, leading with her nose, smelling out gossip fodder to chew on. And she usually found it. So people were a little afraid of Caroline, who was not always fair. Or as a lot of people said, never fair, certainly not if it interfered with a good story.

"Oh, yeah, lots of words," Jessica said.

Incredibly enough, Todd, who was on the other side of the room, heard his beloved, heard her tone, and spun around and crossed the fifteen-foot room in about three steps.

Meanwhile, Caroline's face lit up like neon. Was she really going to hear it right from the villain's mouth? Wow!

Over the years there had been lots of scandals and gossip in Sweet Valley, but this one, the Todd and Jessica story, was far and away the winner. And it was going to be hers. Of course, all the other people listening would cut down on the embellishments. If only she could pull Jessica over into a corner. But, still, when word spread, she would be the go-to for inside information. Her head was spinning with anticipation.

"Jess!" Todd called out, waving his hand. "I have to show you something."

Jessica didn't even look at him. Her eyes were boring into Caroline's eager face. She took a step closer and now she was but inches from Caroline. Close enough to bite her nose.

"Yeah, lots of words." Jessica looked around. "For everyone . . ."

She slowly turned back to Caroline. ". . . but especially for you."

Todd wondered how Caroline could not see the bloody sledgehammer coming. But she seemed not to.

"I've known you for over twenty years," Jessica said in a very soft voice that belied the words, "and like most people in Sweet Valley, I don't like you. You're malicious and you never mean any good. Most people are too afraid of your vicious tongue to tell you, but I'm not. Not anymore."

Caroline just stood there, nailed to the spot. It was rare anyone ever attacked her, and she was too stunned to move.

Then Jessica turned on Lila. "Why did you invite me when you knew this pig was going to be here? For entertainment? Thanks, best friend. Let's go, Todd."

Todd, grateful that it was no worse, took Jessica's arm, and together they walked out of the living room, down the hall, and out the front door. No one followed.

Once out in the car, Jessica said, "What?"

"You did good."

"Do you think any of them will still come to the wedding?"

"Every one of them."

"Caroline, too?"

"Are you kidding?"

"Right."

Jessica looked at Todd, the anger gone. "Will it ever not be painful?"

3
New York

The theater was on Forty-fourth Street on the west side of Manhattan, in a converted loft building between Ninth and Tenth avenues. Elizabeth had Googled the theater and found out the building had been converted to a hat factory in the thirties and stayed that way until hats bombed out in the late sixties. For a time, it became a storage space. For the last five years it had been an Off-Broadway house that still felt like a storage space storing, instead of hats, rows of tacky, incongruous plush red velvet theater seats probably picked up cheap when some old movie palace was torn down. The seats were inconsiderately placed one directly behind the other, and with no incline in the floor, it was almost impossible to see comfortably from anywhere but the first few rows. However, for a first-time playwright like Will Connolly, the idea of having a play anywhere in New York City, especially a theater with this kind of proximity to Broadway, made it almost magnificent.

Green-and-yellow-striped banners hanging from a flagpole outside announced *The Follies of 1763,* a new play with music that revealed the love triangle of the venerable lexicographer, essayist, and poet Samuel Johnson; his biographer, James Boswell; and the object of their affections, Mrs. Hester Thrale, written by the same Will Connolly. Posters bordered the entrance with photos of actors in eighteenth-century costumes in the midst of what had to be a serious argument: angry faces with heads jutting turtlelike at each other in attack mode. Somehow, it had a comic feel.

Not an autobiographical first play in the kitchen-sink style, Elizabeth guessed. Since getting the job at the magazine eight months ago, she'd been enjoying the hubris of being something of a theater insider, the result of endless catch-up play reading and watching hours of American Theatre Wing interviews and other theater panel shows. No, not autobiographical at all; in fact, an unusual and risky choice for a debut play. Not a musical, but a play with music. She had asked to read the script but was told the author had refused. It made her even more curious.

Elizabeth tried each side of the double front doors, but they were both locked. And there was no one around to ask how to get inside. A tiny wisp of panic at the thought of screwing up her first interview by not finding something as stupidly simple as the stage door entrance hit the theater insider, adding more discomfort to the heat of the late July day. And then she saw the blessed smoker, an older man, his face creased from years of cigarettes, looking very theatrical in his jeans and wifebeater worn under a suede vest. He was sitting on the stoop in front of the brownstone next door, smoking away.

"Excuse me," she asked. "Are you from the show?"

"I am." Just those two words gave away his Irish accent. "What can I do for you?"

"I have an appointment with the playwright and I'm not sure how to get inside."

Elizabeth was hot enough to move the man into action. He pushed himself up from the step, crushed his cigarette with his shoe, and walked over to Elizabeth.

"Follow me," he said, leading her to another door a few feet down from the front entrance. "You're here for the auditions, right?"

"Sort of."

The man hesitated and turned to Elizabeth, now suspicious. Was this one of those nutty fans or an actor without an appointment? Actors would try anything. "What do you mean, 'Sort of'?"

"Well, it's more like a magazine. Do you know *Show Survey*?"

"No."

"You're an actor, aren't you?"

"Stagehand's union."

"Well, it's like a Zagat for Off Broadway, and I write for it." She hated that description, felt it denigrated the magazine, but it led to instant understanding. Despite her own disapproval, she found herself using it more often than she wanted.

"Ah, so you're a writer."

Immediately, her credit rose from lowly, needy actor, one step below everyone, to intellect. Elizabeth loved that fringe benefit, though she still didn't think she deserved it. She had been writing professionally for close to five years but still felt like she was in on a pass.

"Follow me," he said, pulling open the heavy metal door. "See that door at the end? That's the theater part. They're all in there."

He watched as she walked down the hall to the doorway, turned, waved him a thank-you, then pushed open the door and disappeared inside.

Elizabeth stepped into the theater and was blinded momentarily by the darkness, which was cut only by the dot of light way down front on stage. With the exception of a piano, the stage was empty. When her eyes adjusted to the darkness, she could make out the outline of four people sitting in the first few rows of the audience. Three were sitting together and one was sitting a couple of rows behind on the aisle.

The light from the briefly opened door made the lone sitter turn.

"Who's there?" he shouted.

"Elizabeth?" It was so tentative it sounded more like a question than an answer.

"Elizabeth?"

"Yes."

"Get out!"

Her first instinct was to flee, but before she could, one of the other three, a large square figure, jumped up. From the back of the theater Elizabeth could see from the outline what was kindly referred to as an ample woman.

"Easy, Will," the woman said gently to the man who had shouted, her voice softened by a pleasant Texas accent. She called out to Elizabeth, "Are you from *New York* magazine?"

"*Show Survey*?" Another question, not answer.

"Not *New York* magazine?"

"No. *Show Survey* . . ."

"*Show Survey?*"

"You know the Zagats . . ."

"The giveaway," the man next to her said.

"Well, actually we don't give it—"

"That's okay, honey. You come on down here." The woman took a few steps over to the shouter, leaned over, and whispered something in his ear. Elizabeth could see him put his feet up on the seat in front of him. He was the only one who didn't turn when she got closer.

"I'm Bala Trent," said the big woman, putting out her hand. "I'm one of the producers, and the man with the big welcome is your subject, Will Connolly, the writer. You're Elizabeth, right?"

Elizabeth shook the producer's outstretched hand and smiled at the others, who stopped talking and turned to greet her. No one else got up.

Pointing to the two seated men, the producer said, "That's Bob Ross, our director, and Neil Quest, our music director."

Both mumbled a pleasant How do you do, and turned back to their conversation.

"Elizabeth Wakefield," Elizabeth said to their backs.

"Why don't you sit here, next to Will?" The producer pointed to the empty seat next to the writer, but Will didn't move his legs, effectively blocking Elizabeth from his row.

"That's okay," said Elizabeth. "I'll just sit here." She moved into the seat just behind the writer.

The producer stepped over Will's legs gracefully, considering her girth, and took a seat one away from him.

Elizabeth was dressed properly for the outside summer heat

but very underdressed for the chilly theater. Everyone else, professionals knowing what to expect, had on sweaters.

"Sean!" the producer called out. From the wings, Sean, the same stagehand Elizabeth had met outside, stepped onstage. A thin, awkward-looking young woman came on behind him. With a birdlike nod to the spectators, she creased her cheeks in a quick smile, walked to the piano, and sat down. And didn't look up again.

"Let's have the next one." Sean waved to someone backstage, and a dark-haired, handsome man of about twenty-five stepped out, walked over to the piano, and handed the pianist some sheet music.

"Hi." He turned to the audience of five. "I'm Mark Evans."

"Hey, Mark," one of the two men sitting in the front called out.

Mark shielded his eyes, squinting as he peered out into the audience.

"It's me, Bob. How're you doing?"

"Pretty good . . . up to now."

Bob and the man next to him chuckled. "What are you going to do for us?"

"'The Colors of My Life.'"

"Great. I love *Barnum*."

The young woman at the piano played the intro and Mark Evans sang.

Someplace around the fifth bar, Bob stopped him and asked for a few bars of another song, something lighter and faster; the actor obliged. There was a little chatter, and then the director turned to Will and Bala and with an imperceptible shake of his head made the decision. The producer thanked Mark Evans, and the next actor came on.

In the few moments it took to set up the new music, Elizabeth squeezed up enough courage to speak to the writer.

"Excuse me." Elizabeth leaned over and said to the back of Will Connolly's head, "Could I ask you a few questions?"

"Hey, can't you see I'm busy," he said in a nasty tone without even turning.

"Well, maybe when there's a break . . ." She braced for the unkind response.

And got it.

"I said I was busy. Jesus. Get her off my back, somebody, huh?" Without waiting for an answer, he went back to checking the papers he had on his lap.

Bala Trent leaned over from the row in front and smiled at Elizabeth.

"We'll stop for lunch in about an hour and then he's all yours."

"Thanks," she said, adding a new dread, the lunch break.

Another actor came on and sang a few bars of some song Elizabeth didn't recognize, then most of another from the same musical, which Elizabeth planned to Google as soon as she got home.

"That was nice. Thanks," Will called out in a very friendly voice, so warm she didn't realize that it came from the same man.

Again, the director nixed the actor and another auditioner was called.

This went on for ten more actors. Elizabeth was amazed at how good some of them were, but no one seemed to make the cut.

How did they stand the rejection? And it wasn't just a comment on their talent. It could be their appearance: too tall, too short, not good-looking enough, too old, anything. They would never know what it was, so how could they ever fix it? Most of it couldn't be fixed anyway. She would die being judged like that. It was bad enough having all those rejection slips from *The New Yorker* for her short stories, but at least that wasn't face-to-face and not because she wasn't pretty enough or young enough or thin enough or whatever. It was just that she wasn't talented enough. Oh, my God!

Between the miserable rejections she had been watching for the last hour and her own lack of talent, Elizabeth's day was ruined. Additionally, Will Connolly was obviously a prick.

Just then the houselights went up and everyone stood for the lunch break, including Will Connolly, who stretched his arms out, palms pushing the air as he rotated his shoulders, and turned around to Elizabeth.

She gasped.

The prick was a doppelgänger for Todd Wilkins.

When it first happened, when she first found out she had been betrayed, Elizabeth fled. Ran like a whipped dog. But in these last eight months, the pain of hurt had solidified into anger. Anger that left the ugly taste of metal in her mouth. And sometimes it became fury.

All directed into thin air.

It was mostly silent, but sometimes her fury erupted into voice, and the voice was loud and hoarse with rage, the words vile and threatening.

All directed into thin air.

Other times, she played with the idea, What if she hadn't found out? Would they have gotten married? And then she tried to remember whose idea it was to get married. Maybe it was hers, but why did he go along with it? Weak asshole!

Would he have married her and still been in love with someone else? If he really *was* in love with Jessica and not just pushed into it when he got outed. What was the matter with him that he just kept going on with their relationship when he should have ended it?

Who knew and didn't tell her? Winston for sure, but he had a loyalty to Todd. Still, he was Elizabeth's friend, too, and he had to have known it would explode one day and ruin everyone's life. Maybe that's what ended their friendship—his and Todd's.

And what about Bruce? By that time he was her best friend, if he had known he would have told her. There would be no reason she could think of for him to keep such a secret. She decided he couldn't have known.

What if it was all a big mistake? A momentary lapse. Like some crazy thing that happens only once and you regret it for the rest of your life? Could she ever forgive him?

A nauseating thought.

No argument in Todd's defense would matter. The head had lost control and her heart would rule. And her heart could never again trust; suspicion would corrode it.

Suppose they had gotten married and then later, maybe after they had had children, she had found out?

Another nauseating thought.

Then would she have left him?

Absolutely.

What if she never found out? That would be like it never happened. Except it did.

But when? When? When?

At night, in bed, alone, Elizabeth went over her years with Todd, always looking for clues, hints that she had missed. So many questions she couldn't ask. Too late to ask. Now every time she remembered him going somewhere without her was suspect. She didn't even know how long it had been going on.

And she would never read his letter to find out.

All she could remember now was how much they had hated each other, Jessica and Todd. They hardly spoke. They weren't even Facebook friends. If Elizabeth was around, it would be okay, but otherwise, there was no interest at all. She'd tried to push them together just because it made it difficult to spend time with her sister when Todd was around. And, of course, as premier boyfriend, he was around a lot.

She remembered that time in her senior year at SVU when she was sick with the flu or something and had promised she would show up with Todd at Jim Regis's party and then couldn't go. When Todd heard, he announced that he wasn't going alone. Elizabeth had to practically force Jessica to go with him.

⌒

I'm shivering under mountains of quilts, begging her. "You have to do it for me, Jess."

Jessica and I have been sharing an apartment since the end of our sophomore year. Our bedrooms are on the second floor of a small, two-story, white clapboard house about two miles from the school. The house is one of fifty originally built in the seventies to house faculty.

Mrs. Schriker, our landlady, had taught psychology for twenty years and was now retired and letting out the two bedrooms on the top floor to students. Simply but neatly furnished in flowery prints and beveled blond woods, the apartment has the quiet and order of someone's childhood home in the Midwest. And—with the exception of Jessica's room—it is impeccably kept.

"You know Todd's never going to go alone." I'm almost pleading. "And I owe Jim; he picked me up every single day for two weeks when my car broke down."

"Is that supposed to be a dig at me because I didn't?" Nobody could get hurt faster than Jessica. Except maybe the people she hurt.

"No, I understand perfectly." And the truth is I do. No matter how many justifications I have to invent, no matter how many rationalizations I have to twist into shape, I always end up understanding Jessica. Because I love her unconditionally. Or maybe just uncontrollably.

"They're counting on me to bring Todd. I promised. He's, like, the star of their whole party."

After Todd's magnificent performance at the basketball game the night before that snatched the state championship away from UCLA and gave it to the long-shot SVU, he wasn't just king of the court; he was king of the school.

It was something of a redemption for Todd, who had botched up his college career for a while, losing his scholarship and dropping out.

Besides, an Elizabeth Wakefield promise was gold. On the other hand, getting a favor from Jessica on a Saturday night was diamonds. If I thought I owed Jim, it was nothing to the debt I would owe Jessica.

Today, with the shades pulled down, the normally sunny, cheerful bedroom is sickroom dark. It might have been a bit of a sympathy ploy, but I was desperate.

"Listen, it's got to be better than sitting around all night watching me sneeze and fixing tea."

I don't think it had actually occurred to Jessica that she would have to babysit her sick sister. In fact, she'd just gotten off the phone after making plans with her friend Lila Fowler. They were going to try a hot new club that had just opened.

"Jim Regis is short and dumpy and has terrible parties with other short and dumpy people," she said.

"You are so cruel I can hardly believe you're my sister."

"Just honest. Hey, maybe Winston would go with him?"

Todd's roommate, Winston Egbert, had been his best friend since grade school.

"He can't. He's going down to San Diego for I forget what. Besides, Winston would not be a draw. As it is I'm going to have to talk Todd into going with *you*."

"Really. Well, he doesn't have to do me any favors."

"Oh, Jess, you know what I mean. He's just not that big on parties, but he would go if I asked him to do it for you."

"For me? Like I'm dying to go?"

"I can hardly swallow. Why are you making me talk? Just go with him for a couple of hours. Wear my favorite beige sweater."

"The cashmere?"

"Yes, the cashmere. And take anything else you want, like you don't already anyway."

"Well, all right. I'll do it for you."

I know the price has just soared.

Actually, Jessica looks like she's beginning to warm to the idea; it has to be better than staying home playing nurse, a part she could not be less suited for. In fact, now that she's safely out from under her medical responsibilities, Jessica lets her caring gene take over. If it could be found.

"Are you sure you're going to be all right? Alone, I mean. Should I call Mom?"

Our parents still live in the same house in Sweet Valley not twenty minutes away.

"On pain of death. Do me a favor and just go get dressed. Todd'll be here in an hour."

Certain that I would be able to bribe her, I had already arranged with Todd to pick her up. And that wasn't easy, either. He gave me an unusually hard time. Now, I'm wondering.

"Maybe I'll wear your new suede skirt."

"I haven't even worn it myself yet."

But Jessica is already deep in my closet, pulling out the skirt, helping herself to a pair of black boots and, for good measure, grabbing my purse.

"You're taking my purse, too? It's got all my stuff in it."

"That's okay," Jessica says, dumping the contents on my dresser. "I'll put it all back later."

"Yeah, right." And she's gone.

Why was she fussing so much over a party she couldn't have cared less about? I know why: Jessica has to have her triumphs. Even if they were only over short, dumpy people.

Or was she wrong? Had Jessica been fussing over her "date" with Todd?

It was the first time they had ever gone out together without Elizabeth. And afterward, Jessica hadn't stopped complaining about how she'd hated being with Todd without Elizabeth. And it had never happened again.

To her knowledge.

But after that, she remembered that the relationship between her sister and Todd was even worse. Jessica never seemed to have a good word to say about him.

Or, methinks "The lady doth protest too much."

Elizabeth tried to think of other times like that, but there were none she knew of. And she and Todd were together for that year and more than four after that. And nothing was really different.

Well, maybe a little. Senior year was strange. The end of one life, the protected school years, and into another, the big world without the safety of parameters; that was more than a little scary. They were both sort of preoccupied with their own plans, but they didn't argue or anything like that. Additionally, that year was hard for Todd; he and Bruce seemed to grow apart, and he had a falling out with Winston that had nothing to do with her. At least that's what he had said and there was no reason to doubt him.

Maybe that was her problem: She should have doubted him more. And that took her right back to her pain.

How would it ever go away?

By turning the other cheek?

By offering forgiveness?

In these last eight months Elizabeth hadn't come close to either of those possibilities. Maybe she was looking on the wrong side.

What about revenge?

That would take away the metal taste and replace it with the sweetness of triumph.

The thought alone made her feel stronger.

But how?

By not going back for the wedding?

So Elizabeth. So lame. Even putting a curse on them would be better.

Except she probably had been doing that all along and obviously, it didn't work.

How about getting married first?

Unrealistic. She hadn't found anyone in eight months; four weeks certainly wouldn't be enough time.

But if she hurried she might be able to go back with a fiancé.

Even in her misery that made her smile. Unfortunately, she'd seen that movie. Besides it was too cute for what had happened to her. What had happened to her was the most horrible, gouging pain in her whole life. And it wasn't only emotional. Her heart hurt, physically. She could feel it in her chest. It was really so bad for the first month she was in New York she'd considered going to a doctor, but then, after a couple of weeks, and after starting the new job, the physical pain started to go away.

The heartbreak stayed. And it was still there.

Elizabeth felt as if she would never get over it, and she was never going to let anyone else get over it, either. There was just enough hatefulness in that thought to be the start of a true revenge.

Many nights when she couldn't sleep, whether she wanted to or not, she played scenarios over and over in her head. They were hardly ever complete; there would be a beginning and a middle, but rarely an ending.

And no matter what the story was, it always stopped at the same point, just when she was about to confront Jessica and Todd. Sometimes it happened on the street, or in her childhood home, or even in an anonymous apartment in New York. And sometimes in her dreams. The setting was always different, but the anger and bitterness were the same, burning hot and fierce, strong enough to take them down, but she never stayed long enough to do the deed. Instead, it would jolt her awake and leave her staring at the darkness, consumed with unexpressed rage.

If anyone could peek into her mind they would be shocked. She wasn't the Elizabeth anyone knew. Her anger was taking her places it would have been inconceivable to imagine for herself.

She'd always thought of herself as moral, ethical and compassionate, and—possibly somewhat immodestly—as one of the better people. No way. When it came right down to it, revenge was all she could think about, and there was nothing very moral or ethical about that. And compassion? Thank goodness no one could look into her head and see the tortures she thought up for Todd.

But even those gave only momentary respite. She needed true revenge, big-time. She needed something so that instead of stupid, whiny tears, she could feel the straight back of strength, hard enough to wipe out the loser feeling she had whenever she thought of the two of them.

Sometimes her personal revenge scenes would go wild. One would take place at her parents' country club. They would be playing the "Wedding March" and Jessica, ethereal in her white silk taffeta gown and on the arm of their father, would be standing at the top of the aisle waiting to take that first step. Todd would be waiting at the altar.

And to make it real, in true Jessica form, she would stand there until she had everyone's complete attention. And when she felt she had it, she would take her first step.

That's when she, Elizabeth, the uninvited guest, would appear out of nowhere and shout at her betrayers, "You vile, miserable, lying cheats!"

That's all. Then she would turn and walk out.

Yes, it would be horrible, and both of them would be hurt and embarrassed, but it would not be nearly as cruel as what they had done to her.

Yes, the wedding would go on, but it would be blackened and shamed forever, never forgotten. It would always be the talk of Sweet Valley. It would stain their lives as they had stained hers.

Dumb and childish, and far too brutal a scene for Elizabeth to enjoy.

But there were other scenarios.

In one of Elizabeth's favorites, she would write a letter to Jessica describing her intimate times with Todd while he was cheating with Jessica, which would be like he was cheating on Jessica with Elizabeth.

Maybe that was too much of a reach, but it would certainly hurt. Lots of tears. Even more childish.

Or . . .

Another letter reporting all the horrible things Todd had said about Jessica through those many years. And there were plenty. They'd have a big fight, and Jessica would be in tears.

Jessica's tears. Was that the best she could hope for? Not nearly enough to avenge what they had done to her life.

By the time Elizabeth got through all these scenarios, she would have drifted off, somewhat satisfied until the morning, when she would wake up miserable again. She still hadn't found the perfect revenge.

But she would.

4
Sweet Valley

That night, as on so many agonizing nights in these past months, there was no way Jessica could find sleep. Elizabeth was waiting in every corner of her mind.

Was it worth it?

A question answered with one look at Todd's sleeping face and an involuntary rush of love. His face was relaxed and untroubled, softened by the safety of sleep—a rare sight these last several months.

There was a sweetness on his face, just like the look she remembered from that night, five years earlier, when she first saw him.

She was taking a little liberty there. Yes, she had known him since kindergarten, but she'd never really seen him until that night. The night of Jim Regis's party; that terrible night in their senior year at SVU when Elizabeth was sick and Jessica did her another of her fabulous favors.

Since then, Jessica had rearranged the real events of that evening a thousand ways, but it always came out the same. Truth was too powerful to lie to. And that something so precious as their love, hers and Todd's, should have had such an ugly nascence was an unalterable truth, and no matter how far and how gloriously it had transformed, there was no escaping its beginning.

She remembered every minute of that beginning, starting from her standing in front of Mrs. Schriker's house, their college rental, that night, waiting for Todd to pick her up. She was dressed almost entirely in borrowed clothes. Everything belonged to Elizabeth, including Todd.

R ight from the first, when he pulls up in his black Audi convertible, it feels slightly strange. And when I open the door and slide in, it's more than strange; it's weird. I've been in his car hundreds of times but always in the backseat. The front seat is Elizabeth's place, but now here I am.

"Hey," I say, pulling the door shut.

"Hey."

Straining to make normal chitchat proves so too much for both of us, and after two blocks the little wisps of attempted conversation drift down like snowflakes into a blanketing silence. The discomfort is like excruciating, forcing me to make another effort. This time I aim for the smallest talk: weather. Except that in Southern California, unless you have storms or earthquakes or mudslides, none of which are expected, there is no weather. It's all like sun. And more sun.

More silence. We are two very uncomfortable people. The evening that could have been like a fun idea isn't turning out to be as easy as it sounded. Or, maybe, it's just me. Todd probably doesn't even notice.

When we arrive at the frat house the party is already going full blast. I excuse myself and take my jacket to the bedroom. Lianne Kane, the host, Jim Regis's girlfriend, is there.

"Hey," she says. "Jim was worried that you two wouldn't make it. Todd is with you, right?"

"Absolutely. Come on, I'll introduce you."

And Lianne and I go out to the living room and over to where Jim, who wasn't all that dumpy, though maybe a little short, is digging into the cooler to get a beer for Todd.

"Todd," I say, "this is Lianne."

"Great to meet you," says Lianne. "I've watched you play every game this season. You're fabulous."

Of course, Todd is flattered, and Lianne, at almost six feet, is not just a fan; she's a player, too, and has to hear all about the fabulous last game.

Meanwhile, I talk to Jim. Naturally, I expect that Todd will have explained about Elizabeth being sick. It doesn't occur to me that he hasn't and that Jim probably can't tell the difference. Even though I know it happens more often than not, I still can never understand how people aren't able to see the enormous difference between Elizabeth and me.

Mostly Jim is talking about how hooked his girlfriend is on basketball; she was captain of the girls' team at Sweet Valley High. She was there after us, he explains.

Jim excuses himself to greet some people who have just come in, and since Todd is still deep in conversation with Lianne, I wander around looking for cute guys.

After a few minutes I decide that even though the short and dumpy accusation wasn't exactly fair, Todd is probably the cutest one there, so I

stop looking and drift over to the cooler to get myself a beer. The bartender, a frat pledge, is too young but totally hot, so I stay and talk to him.

At some point Todd breaks away from Lianne and finds me. We're
standing together when Jim comes over and introduces us to some of his
frat brothers.

That's like when it first happens.

"Hey, guys," Jim says. "You saw that game Saturday, right? This is
the big scorer, Todd Wilkins."

Lots of hand shaking and happy talk about the win and then Jim says,
almost as an aside, "And this is Elizabeth Wakefield."

Before I can object, they all give me a quick, rather perfunctory
hello, and the conversation moves back to Todd's last game. I'm not
even sure Todd hears the mistake. The moment passes, and I feel like it
would be awkward and unimportant to correct them. I can see they
don't really care who I am, so I just let it go.

A girl standing next to me asks where I live, and after I answer, introduces me to her boyfriend. "Hank, this is Elizabeth."

By now Todd has turned back to me and hears the error. He smiles.
"I don't think so."

But it doesn't seem to register with anyone else.

Except me, and I smile, too.

"Elizabeth?" Hank says. "You go to Sweet Valley U, too, don't you?"

"Yes, but I'm not—"

"Yeah, I've seen you around."

"Lots of times, I'll bet." Todd winks at me, and I smile back.

"Yeah," Hank says. "I see you around all the time. I think we even
met before. At the newspaper."

"Right." Now like I'm playing along, too.

From there on it just grows. I become Elizabeth and begin to love the fun of it. Todd does, too. Now we're beginning to get outrageous about it. Holding hands, being affectionate with each other; we become the perfect couple.

As the night wears on we dance, joke around, and make lots of new friends. We're having a great time. Both of us. And in the process we have a few too many beers. At least I do, but it's okay because I'm not driving.

For the first time I'm beginning to see why Elizabeth is so crazy about Todd. He is totally sexier than I'd realized and, now that he's relaxed, is fun and warm. Maybe I hadn't ever really taken a good look at him. Additionally, it feels good being a couple, even if it is only pretend.

When it comes to committed relationships, I'm a moving target. No boyfriend has ever managed to hold me in his sights for like longer than half a term; and it isn't because they don't want to. Sometimes it bothers me that I lose interest so quickly. What seems sexy and exciting in the beginning becomes ordinary and then trying and finally annoying, and I can't get away fast enough. Will I always feel that way? What about marriage? And I don't mean that craziness like with Mike McAllery. I still haven't explained that to myself yet. Annulment closed the book as far as I'm concerned.

I haven't had a real relationship since I dumped my last boyfriend at the beginning of senior year. And now, with this faux one-night relationship, I'm getting a taste of it again.

Though it can be a little confining, being part of a couple has its own advantages. How good is that, owning some great-looking guy who is obviously crazy about you? Elizabeth is so luckier than she knows. Too bad it has to be Todd.

We are having like such a good time we practically have to drag ourselves away from the party, but it's getting late and Elizabeth will be waiting.

As soon as we get in the car, reality, like a jolt, shoots through the beer haze and wipes out all our easy pleasure. The very air in the car chills, and the front seat extends, like, two blocks; we are that disconnected.

And silent.

Then Todd breaks it. "That was fun. Incredible how nobody even questioned it at all."

"It's like I'm just one double person, not really an individual. Sometimes I hate that. But it was fun tonight."

"Yeah, it was."

"I loved when that guy said how much I reminded him of someone. And you said . . . who'd you say?"

"Jessica Simpson."

"Yeah. He said, 'Jessica sounds right.'"

As we warm to the subject, it becomes easier. At one point in a story, being funny, just as we stop at a light, I poke Todd in the chest and say, "Mr. Basketball!"

Todd takes my hand and holds it for a second against his chest, a second too long. Everything stops. His hand is still covering mine against his chest. And it pulls me in closer, my face inches from his, my eyes on his. Both of us are barely breathing.

That's where everything gets cloudy, not just from the beer but from the excitement. The thrill. For me, the next few moments like don't register in my mind, only in my body.

I can feel Todd's response, and then we're out of control; our mouths furiously pressing, kissing, sucking, inhaling each other. All the while I feel the weight of his body crushing me and I want more, I want him still closer. I so want him to be part of me. To keep holding me.

For the first time in my life, I don't care about anything or anyone. I don't even care about Elizabeth. All I care about is that he never lets go.

"Come back to my room," he says between breaths.

"Winston," I whisper.

"San Diego."

"Right."

We pull apart. Neither of us looks at the other for the ten minutes it takes to get to Todd's apartment in downtown Sweet Valley. When we get out of the car, we look straight ahead at the door to the house where Todd and Winston have a rented room.

On the way up the stairs to the second floor, we stop. Todd pulls me to him and we kiss. The depths and longing of that kiss are like no other kiss has ever been for me. Neither of us can pull away. Other than our lips we stay joined together for the rest of the flight, Todd like half carrying me up to his room. Racing.

He unlocks the door, pushes it open with his shoulder, and shoves it closed with his foot, all the while never letting go of me. We tumble onto the bed, ripping at our clothes, flinging them over our heads, kicking off our shoes, and not stopping until we're both naked and locked in each other's bodies.

We make love with an otherworldly passion that is so powerful neither of us would hear a knock on the door if there were one. Or any sound when it cracks open a few inches, but I do catch a sliver of light shooting into the room; then it's gone.

The affair goes on for a month. Todd wants it as much as I do. It's like a wild, out-of-control time, those thirty days that never touch the ground.

We meet in the middle of the day at the same diner, a banged-up metal imitation bus in a sparsely populated industrial outskirt of Sweet Valley. A safe time in a safe place where it is almost impossible to be lovers; where an unforgiving sun beats down, blaring through the grimy windows, lighting up every mark and tear of the red plastic seats. Unable to compete with a McDonald's half a mile away, Shirley's Diner limps along with never more than a handful of customers, none of them likely to be anyone Todd or I would know.

Every day I swear to myself that I won't go. All through the morning I feel in control; the decision has been made. It will never happen again.

But the longing grows, and by noon no sacrifice is too great. Everything and everyone fall by the wayside, and I'm gasping and my heart is pounding and I think I will stop breathing unless I see him, touch him, feel him next to me.

Jessica wasn't aware of the sounds she was making, tearing at those excruciating memories, but they were audible enough to wake Todd, who, seeing her pain and knowing exactly what was torturing her, reached out and took her out of her dark thoughts and into his arms.

"I was there again, in that month, destroying my sister."

"Jess, what can I do to help you?"

"Nothing. Nobody can. I'm going to lose you, Todd. And I so deserve to." She wept.

"You'll never lose me," Todd said. "I'm not going to let that happen."

But he, too, had his tortures. Starting with that first wild month, torn in a million directions, he'd been filled with shame and misery and passion, and one other torture he remembered too well: every day thinking he had lost her.

⌣

I'm always there first, inside the diner, each time certain Jessica won't show. But then she does, and I watch with relief and excitement as her white Ford sends up a dry cloud of dirt in the parking area. I can see into the car, see her leaning over for a last-minute check in the rearview mirror, fluffing her hair once quickly, then opening the door.

Then comes the best part: the moment before she slides out. First come her feet spiking the air, flip-flops dangling, then the long, naked legs—naked because her skirt, short to begin with, has pulled up around her bottom in the slide out. Last is her slim body and beautiful face. I memorize every move of the ritual and each one thumps a separate beat somewhere in my chest.

I lose sight of her when she walks around to the door and see her again only when she's inside the diner. That first sight without the dirty windows separating us is raw, sending a rush of heat to my head.

Never once does she look like Elizabeth to me.

It doesn't matter that we made love only that first night. Each time we see each other after that is the equivalent of making love again, so powerful is our connection.

⌣

"I love you, Todd," Jessica said, and held on to him tightly, burying herself in his body. She'd lost him once and it was nearly unbearable, though she had done it herself. But then that time, caught in the throes of that terrible month, drowning in the agony of guilt, there had been no choice. Even the day she saw A. J. Morgan's car in the parking lot outside the diner. She gasped and though she had already pulled in, she swooped around without slowing down, hung a U and drove out.

But instead of leaving, getting out of there, her chance to get out of everything, she drove around the block. Twice. On the third time, A.J.'s car was gone.

*D*aily, I like beg myself to do it, to end it, and finally I just shut my eyes and do it. That's when all the passion turns vicious. It is the only way for me to break away and to eradicate some of my guilt.

I tell him it was a terrible mistake, which is true, and that I don't love him, never loved him. In fact, now despise him. Which is not true.

He tells me the same, and I believe him.

Not three days after that last meeting, we have a scare. Elizabeth is with me at the bookstore, picking up some textbooks for her psychology course, when we run into Todd and Winston. As usual, Winston is being his goofy self, hopping up on the ladder, pulling erotic titles down from the shelves, and suggesting he read them to me.

"That reminds me, I'm gonna need Thursday night . . ." he says to Todd in a fake confidential voice, ". . . alone."

"No good, man. I have that physics final Friday," Todd says.

Winston climbs down from the ladder and hands the books to Elizabeth, who starts to put them back on the shelf.

"Come on. Wasn't I nice to you a few weeks ago?" Winston gives Todd a kind of leering smile. "Remember, San Diego?"

Elizabeth is busy with the books, her back to Winston and not really listening, but the reference to San Diego grabs my attention.

"You probably didn't even know that I got back Saturday night." Looking at Elizabeth, he says, "I knocked, but you guys were very busy."

At that point, I like deflect the action, quickly handing a book to Elizabeth, who automatically takes it and turns to find a place for it on the shelf.

"I had to crash at Bruce's pad that night. And man, he wasn't happy. You owe him one. Me, too."

"What are you talking—" Then it hits Todd what night Winston is referring to, and his face freezes.

I catch his change of expression and know my own face is like registering the same shock. Winston, who is momentarily confused, sees Todd's expression, then mine, and to my amazement, he seems to read it right immediately. All the while, Elizabeth is busy trying to squeeze a fat edition of Havelock Ellis back onto the shelf.

It is only the strange silence that makes her turn around.

"Huh? What's up? Something wrong?"

Strangely, it's Winston, the insensitive clown, who so saves the moment for us by doing a really funny bit about mistaking his girlfriend for her dog. He like tells it so fabulously that Elizabeth practically falls off the ladder, and even Todd and I can't help laughing despite the horror of the situation. Rescued just in time, but too late for their friendship.

When someone knows a terrible secret about you, and you can't in good conscience kill them, you get them out of your life. And that's exactly what Todd does that very day. With some clichéd excuse about like needing his own space, Todd moves out and finds an apartment on the other side of town.

Time passes and only a few people notice that the relationship between the best friends has dissolved. Of course, I'm one of them. Elizabeth like sort of notices and I hear her ask Todd a few times where Winston is, but he always has some reasonable-sounding excuse. She even mentions it to me a couple of times, but I say I don't know anything.

After awhile Winston's absence becomes as natural as his presence had been and for us, the ex-lovers, the betrayers, senior year, like the longest year of our lives, crawls on toward the relief of graduation.

5
New York

Even on pain of losing the best opportunity she'd had, it still took two days for Elizabeth to work up the courage to come back to the theater. Her return was inauspicious, to say the least; dressed in black, she slipped in, keeping her back against the wall and taking advantage of the darkness. She found a seat on an aisle twenty rows back in the orchestra, well away from the clot of the hierarchy, i.e., producers, director, and, of course, the monster playwright.

During that first week of rehearsals Elizabeth became an unnoticed fixture sitting quietly, silently actually, in the back. She spoke to no one.

Without the warmth and bubble of an audience, the atmosphere in the darkened theater was grim. Its rows of empty seats were outlined only by the dim work lights from the stage, which gave no cheer. Nor was there any cheer from its only occupants: the unfriendly, clannish producers, the angry writer, or the kinglike director. Onstage, nervous actors bumping into new lines lent an unmistakable air of desperation.

No theater magic here. And if there was any hint of the legendary passion, it was not obvious.

Even though Elizabeth had been writing about theater for eight months and seen lots of shows, this empty theater with its unique population made her realize that she had been looking in from the outside. Now she was inside, and even though she wasn't in the line of fire, she felt nervous and edgy. Everyone was edgy.

By the end of the first week of rehearsals, Elizabeth had mastered the uniform: sneakers, jeans, and a heavy black sweatshirt she could throw over her black T-shirt as soon as she got into the empty theater that, no matter how hot it was outside, never felt above fifty.

She thought it strange that no one else seemed bothered by the constant sharp draft of air-conditioning; these were not people who held back complaints. She'd heard the actors, desperate though they were for the work, stop everything to whine about minor inconveniences like a dressing-room bulb that wasn't bright enough or a dripping faucet. Ultimately, no matter their age or how valid their complaints, they were infantilized by the director, whom they were encouraged to call Bob but treat like Mr. Ross, and nothing changed.

Except when Mr. Ross himself complained, and he never held back. That's when everyone listened. It was rare that he wasn't quietly disappointed, so quiet as to be almost martyred. In the pecking order, he, Bob Ross, was the top, and everyone else stepped gingerly, more than a little careful not to be the cause of his unhappiness. Even the producers cowered under his rule. This show business was nothing like the song. It was scary.

Needless to say, Elizabeth, tucked away in her hiding place, was almost faint at the prospect of being noticed by either the director or, as she thought of him now, the shithead writer, who was no slouch when it came to projecting his own air of discontent.

One couldn't be certain whether director or writer would come out on top since they hadn't clashed yet, but it was coming. Elizabeth could see from the hunch of Connolly's shoulders that he was strung tight and crouched to spring.

Elizabeth wasn't about to risk the chance that he might spring at her. She hadn't renewed her request for an interview; she had decided she would just be an observer and write what she wanted. If her subject, Mr. Connolly, didn't like it, too bad; he shouldn't have been so rude. All she wanted was an interview. What an asshole.

She'd started off on his side; he was a young, first-time playwright, big chance and all that. At least before he turned around and she saw that face. The shock of the resemblance to Todd was like a whack in the stomach.

That very first day, when the casting session was over, she'd just sat there in a sweat and stared.

Connolly had twisted around to see her. "What?" he'd said in an impatient tone, more comment than question.

He'd waited a couple of seconds, and when she didn't answer, shrugged and left.

Bala Trent, the nice producer, had tried to make some excuses, but when Elizabeth still didn't respond, she just smiled and said, "Y'all come back tomorrow and you can have a nice long chat with Will. All right, sugar?"

Elizabeth finally managed to nod and form something like a smile before she picked up her papers, hurried up the aisle, and ran out the door. She didn't stop running until she got to Seventh Avenue. Instead of going to the office she went straight home.

That night she rehearsed how she would tell David, her editor, that she didn't want to do the interview. Then she decided she did, and then she didn't, and by morning she understood she was being ridiculous. The interview was a plum, something she could maybe work into a monthly column. She'd have to be really dumb to give up this chance because Will Connolly looked a little like her ex-boyfriend.

It was probably just the bad lights in the theater. She was definitely doing the interview. That was it.

But all that week, it got worse. Even though she kept her distance she couldn't miss the resemblance to Todd. It was striking; he even had the same brown hair. At least he didn't do that awful sweeping-it-back thing, but it was straight, and if it were a little longer it would fall over his eyes. And then he might push it back and she didn't know how she would handle that.

At the theater, Elizabeth had developed a routine of disappearing just before they called a lunch break. She perfected an exit using the side door into an alley; from there she'd shoot down the street across Seventh and Broadway and up to a small coffee shop on Fifty-second Street a little too far out of the way for anyone from the cast to go.

As she did on all the other days, she'd wait until everyone

else was back before slipping into the theater and sliding into her seat.

Today, she was a couple of minutes late, and they had already started working on an early scene where the young James Boswell tries to sell himself as a biographer to Samuel Johnson, who has no interest at all in having his biography written. He has too many things to hide.

"No!" Will Connolly, the playwright, stood and spoke directly to the actor. "There's no way Johnson's angry. He's only playing with Boswell. You are the great Samuel Johnson. With your words and wit, you're over-armed; there's no need for anger."

Everything stopped. Elizabeth could feel the shock in the room, but she didn't know where it was coming from. It seemed like an insightful criticism.

Obviously the actor knew what was wrong. He panicked and looked to Ross, the director, for help.

Bob Ross didn't move.

Everyone was looking at the playwright. Will Connolly felt the message and sat down. But he didn't slink; he sat down with resolve, alert for an attack, without his natural slouch of remove.

Ross walked up to the stage manager, who leaned down at the edge of the stage to hear the director.

The stage manager turned to the cast behind him. "Take ten, everyone."

A major faux pas had been committed, but Elizabeth couldn't imagine what it was.

The cast moved reluctantly offstage, unhappy to miss what surely would be an interesting contretemps.

To say that the producers fled would be overstating it, but

they did get up almost instantly and move out and up the aisle without a word.

Normally, Elizabeth would have slipped out, but she was baffled and sensed this was an important part of the story that she had to know. She was, after all, a journalist.

Sorta.

Besides, if she slunk down a little lower in her seat, and with the cooperation of the dim lights, no one would see her.

"Hey, Will." Elizabeth heard Ross, but she couldn't see him well enough to catch the expression on his face.

But Will could, and it obviously wasn't warm. It wasn't even the usual disappointment. It was almost hostile. Something was wrong. Being a novice, he didn't know what it was, but he did know it was his fault.

"Yeah, what's up?"

"It's probably better to check with me first if you have any problems with the actors. Then, if I think it has merit, I'll deal with it."

"I'm not going to sit here and watch him do it wrong."

"It's better my way," Ross said softly, almost kindly.

"Last time I checked, I was the writer," Will said, falling right into Ross's trap.

"And I'm the director." Ross didn't wait for Will's response. Gathering up his papers, he started up the steps to the stage. On the last step he turned to Will. "You might want to check that with Bala before you come back."

"Thanks. I will," Will said to an empty stage. Ross had already disappeared into the wings. Will added to no one, "Asshole!"

In a fury, Will swept up his script and charged up the aisle out of the theater. If he saw Elizabeth as he passed, he gave no indication.

Elizabeth waited a couple of minutes to give Will a chance to be gone, got up, and walked out into the lobby. Rich Meaninfeld, an assistant stage manager, was there.

"What was that about?" Elizabeth asked him.

"It's an unwritten rule: Only the director talks to the actors. If a producer or a writer has something to say, he's got to send Ross a note. If Ross thinks it's valid, he talks to the actor himself."

"That seems like a long way around. I mean, Connolly is the writer."

"Yeah, but that's the way it is."

"So what's going to happen?"

"Bala or somebody will talk to Will. And then it won't happen again."

"I don't know; Connolly is pretty strong."

"So are Sondheim and Herman and Mamet. . . ."

"Mamet sends notes?"

"Right."

This was the real theater, not her little spring break experience. And it could be hard. Even brutal.

"So when is this going to happen? The talking-to?" she asked.

"Pretty soon."

"Where?"

"I don't know. Maybe in the bar across the street. Don't worry; they'll find him."

"Thanks. See ya!" And out she went, straight to the Wicked

Teapot, the Irish bar facing the theater, happily enjoying the warmth of about twenty seconds of sunshine before she was back in another dim, chilly place.

Connolly was there. At the bar, in front of an empty martini glass, which rested next to a full one. Quietly, Elizabeth took a seat a couple stools over from him. His head was down, studying the script on his lap, his fingers pushing the pages, fast and angry. If he looked up he would see her in the mirror behind the bottles, but he didn't, not even when he took great gulps of the second martini.

Now he was making notes, scrawling words over pages. Elizabeth could see from his hand motions that he was making lots of exclamation marks, punctuating the script with dots that hit almost hard enough to break a pen point or at least tear the page. He was obviously furious.

The bartender, a young Irishman who was so incredibly handsome that Elizabeth almost forgot why she was there, asked for her order in that soft, gentle-on-the-ears Irish accent.

"A dirty martini," she said.

"On the rocks?"

"No, straight up."

He hesitated for that nanosecond that spoke of more than bartending interest. But gorgeous as he was, he wasn't Elizabeth's type. Now Jessica . . . she'd have gone nuts for him. No matter who he was with, she'd have scooped him up in a minute. She always had a thing for dark hair and blue eyes. Black Irish, she called them.

In fact, the bartender was undeniably the best-looking man Elizabeth had seen in New York. Movie-star material, probably an aspiring actor. It looked like all waiters and waitresses in New York really were out-of-work actors.

Elizabeth remembered a cartoon of a couple sitting in a restaurant in New York: The man wants to call the waiter, who is across the room. He lifts his hand and calls out, "Actor! Actor!"

Elizabeth watched the bartender pour a healthy portion of Stolichnaya vodka and just the tiniest splash of olive juice into a glass of ice and stir, eyes fixed on her all the while, mixing the drink by feel. Even without the alcohol, she was beginning to cheer up, though he was definitely wasting his time on her.

"Olive?" he asked, pouring the chilled liquid into a martini glass and making the single word sound positively loving, flashing a dimple that was almost overkill.

If he wasn't an actor he should have been, especially the way he was playing this scene. She had to ask.

"Just curious: Are you an actor?"

"How'd you guess? Are you?" he asked, snapping out of romantic lead and right into hungry actor.

"No. I'm a writer."

If he loved her before, he loved her even more now.

"A playwright?" he asked, pressing his luck.

"No, reporter."

Elizabeth was beginning to enjoy the afternoon. If only she didn't have to deal with Connolly, who at his best was hostile, now probably psychopathic.

"What paper?" the bartender/actor asked.

Fortunately, she was spared the Zagat explanation by a customer at the other end of the bar motioning to him just as Connolly, who had caught sight of her in the mirror, was turning to face her.

For Elizabeth, not that much of a martini drinker, two

swallows was enough to smooth the outside edge, the rehearsal edge that had been making her crazy nervous every day for the past week. Two more swallows smoothed out all the other edges. She was starting to feel very warm—first toward the bartender, who was filling an order at the other end of the bar, and then down the row of stools to the asshole.

Who was looking right at her.

Elizabeth smiled.

Will looked confused, like he couldn't place her. But then he had seen her only briefly that once in the dark theater. She'd spent this whole week out of sight, hiding in the back.

"Hi," she said, and then to jog his memory, she added, "Elizabeth, *Show Survey* . . ."

"Yeah, right, the Zagat thing. . . . So what do you want?"

Instead of being intimidated, as she had been this whole week, martini-fortified Elizabeth lost the smile and attacked. "What makes you think I want something from you?"

"Then what are you doing here?"

"What does it look like I'm doing? Hint hint," she said, holding up her glass. It felt good, not groveling. In fact, it was just what she needed. "You have to forgive me; I didn't realize you owned this bar."

Now there was no stopping her. And it was about time. In fact, maybe it was eight months about time.

"You know you've been a real pain in the ass," she said. How nice it would be if she could just fling her whole drink in his face, but then she wouldn't be able to drink it. To sustain her new personality, she probably needed it.

Will had touched the magic button, and it was all coming

out. And maybe it helped that he looked like Todd. Probably just what he needed, too, a little taste of intimidation.

It worked.

"Hey, sorry, I—" he started, but she didn't give him a chance.

"I was here to give you some publicity. How about being grateful instead of nasty?"

"Please, cool it. I've got enough stuff happening. I don't need more from you," he said. The portentousness of his demeanor announced that he had regained his writer position.

"Arrogance without portfolio," Elizabeth said right in his face, and then without waiting for a response, turned back to her martini.

Will didn't say anything; he just looked at her. The slightest crease of a smile played on his lips.

"That's not bad," he said.

Elizabeth didn't look back, continuing to sip her drink as if she hadn't heard him.

"Arrogance without portfolio. Mind if I borrow it?"

Elizabeth didn't answer. The feeling of not catering to someone was decidedly new and surprisingly good, gloriously unElizabeth.

"Lizzie—"

"Don't ever call me that," she snapped.

"Elizabeth?"

"What." She didn't turn.

"Why don't we start over?"

"Not interested, thank you."

"What if I apologize?"

Elizabeth didn't feel like answering, so she didn't.

He continued. "I'm sorry. I guess I was pretty much an ass-hole. Nothing against you. I'm just nervous. . . ."

Elizabeth still didn't answer, but now she turned and looked at him, not so much with anger as with curiosity.

"Actually," he continued, "more like scared. I've worked on this play for four years. Every word counts. They're all mine, but now I'm losing it. Like what happened before. The actor's good, but he was reading it wrong. I had to tell him. I'm not go-ing to just sit there and watch Ross take it all away from me. I gave up too much for this."

"What did you give up?"

"Who's asking? The reporter or the sympathetic listener?"

"I'm working."

"Then this is off the record."

"Okay."

Will was beginning to feel the head start on his martinis; pushing his drink toward Elizabeth, he slid into the seat next to hers.

"You're not from New York, are you?" she asked.

"Almost nobody is. I'm from Chicago. Not such a second city anymore."

"I guess." Elizabeth was doing just what she felt like. And still pissed off is what she felt like. Will had made things really hard for her for no reason and now, with the help of his martinis, he was feeling warmer. And maybe a little needy. Well, she wasn't.

"Talk about not friendly," he said.

"Any special reason why I should be friendly to you?"

"Two martinis?"

It was worth the quick smile she allowed but nothing more.

"So, what did you give up?" she asked.

"Not so fast. I need a lead into it."

"Is it that bad?"

"It's not good."

Despite herself, Elizabeth was beginning to feel an interest. And she was getting excited. What could be more New York than sitting in a bar across from the theater in the middle of the day, talking to the playwright? *And* being sort of in charge.

"You feel like telling me," she said in her reporter voice, "I'm listening." Or at least it was what she thought from movies sounded like a reporter voice.

"I dropped out of law school in the middle of the term. Fifty thousand dollars down the drain."

"Student loans?"

"Nope. My father's fifty thousand."

"Well, if the play is a success, maybe—"

"And I walked out on my fiancée."

"Oh . . ."

"Big oh . . . One day it just hit me: I didn't love law or Chicago or maybe even Wendy."

Elizabeth turned back to her drink, took a big swallow, and let it burn its way down to her chest before she turned back to Will.

"What happened to Wendy?"

"I don't know. I tried to call her, but she wouldn't talk to me. I had to think she wasn't on my side. Why else wouldn't she talk to me?"

"How about 'cause you walked out on her?"

"I don't know. I'm not really in touch with anyone else back there, so how would I know?"

"You don't talk to your family?"

"Especially not my family. We had this huge argument. My father thought I was a fool to give up law for the theater, like all the years of sacrifice he'd made to save money for expensive private schools and law school were a waste. He told me hardly anyone makes it in the theater.

"Then he really lost it and asked what made me think I had the talent? He would have seen it. And he never did. I was heading for failure, and he certainly wasn't going to be a part of it. I wasn't to expect any help from him. And as far as he was concerned, I owed him fifty thousand dollars and I shouldn't bother to come around until I had the money. My mother was in tears.

"I didn't even argue. I just stormed out. Went back to my apartment, grabbed my play and some clothes, got on the bus that same day, and came to New York."

"What about Wendy?"

"I left a message where I was going. I never heard from her. I know she was hurt and angry, and I felt terrible, but I didn't feel the support from her. Maybe I didn't love her enough. Or maybe she didn't love me enough. All I know is that staying because of her would have been a mistake."

"How long had you been with her?"

"About three years. We were planning to get married right after I finished law school. Once it was decided, I guess I never did much thinking about it. Yeah, I thought about whether I wanted law or writing or what, but not about love. Wendy was great. I can't believe what I did to her."

"Do you love her?"

From the warmth on his face, a sweet memory passing by, Elizabeth thought he was going to say yes. But then his face hardened and he said instead, "I don't know."

He left it at that. Then he said, "It's been very hard to keep believing I did the right thing, and after a day like today, I really don't know. Maybe I'm not cut out for this. . . . Maybe I gave up too much. Did you see what happened in there?"

Elizabeth considered lying, but the martinis took away any concern she might have had. "Yeah, I saw it all."

"It's like I committed some heinous crime. Did you see the king's face?"

"It seems you're not supposed to talk directly to the actors. You have to send a note to the director and then he tells them. It's 'an unwritten law.'"

"Then let them arrest me."

"Yeah, but what are you really going to do?"

"I'm really going to have another martini." With that he motioned to the bartender. "Another round. Join me," he said, smiling at Elizabeth. "I'm buying."

Elizabeth felt too relaxed to keep up the angry persona. Additionally, she was delighted to see that Will's eyes were a bright blue—as far from Todd's dark brown as you could get. The alcohol was making her feel very warm inside her chest. Made her want some kind of connection, a feeling she hadn't had in a lot of months.

"Hey," she said to the bartender. "This is a real playwright. Will Connolly, meet . . ."

"Liam O'Connor." Liam wiped his hand on the towel around his waist and reached over the bar, delighted.

They shook hands and Will smiled the friendliest smile Elizabeth had seen in a week—an honest smile, not a photo smile.

"Hey," Will said.

"Liam is an actor," Elizabeth, the martini-relaxed hostess, said. "Will's got the play across the street."

"I know," Liam said.

Turned out he had showed up for an open call but didn't get the part.

"Which part?" Will asked.

"One of the servants."

"Sorry," Will said. "Too good-looking."

Which Elizabeth thought was a very nice rejection. It made her feel warmer toward Will. Really, she was beginning to feel warmer toward everyone.

Liam put the second martini on the little napkin in front of her. Meanwhile, Will, the putative doppelgänger, moved painlessly into his third martini wondering why he had been so unfriendly to this beautiful girl. He made up his mind to make her his friend.

Elizabeth's second martini was even smoother than the first. Liam was probably watering them—that was why they weren't affecting her. If she had to, she could drive home.

The thought made her giggle. She once heard that a better gauge of drunkenness than a breathalyzer was a simple test: The drunker you are the more you think you can drive. And she was certain she could drive. If only she had a car.

If this was a martini buzz, it was nice, even a little happy. Quite possibly Will was the friend she'd needed all these months in New York. But she would take her time, play it cool. Be a little mysterious, not tell him everything, let him work for it.

"My twin sister is marrying my boyfriend . . . well, my ex-boyfriend."

So much for cool and mysterious.

"That sucks."

"Yeah."

"When?"

"In about four weeks."

"Hey, that's when I have my opening."

"They want me to go."

"To the opening?"

"No, dummy, to the wedding. Unless, of course, you want me to come to your opening."

"I think I'd like that. Hey, listen, Elizabeth, I've got to get out of here before one of those producers finds me. I'm in no shape to defend myself. How about coming to my place and we can hang out and you can tell me all about your sister?"

"No way."

"Well, where else can we go?"

"Your place is fine. I just don't want to talk about my sister."

"Deal. I don't talk about your family and you don't talk about mine."

"Unless there's something you want to tell me. You don't happen to have a long-lost twin, do you?"

"Not that I know of," Will said as he stood. "Hey, Liam, what do I owe you?"

Liam handed him the bill, and Will took out three twenties.

"Nice meeting you, Liam," Elizabeth said. "I'm doing a story on Will's play, so I'll see you around."

"Great," Liam said, and turned and rang up the tab. He handed Will the change.

"Keep it," Will said.

"Thanks. And if you hear of anything, or need an understudy or whatever, I'm here."

"See you around," Will said, and headed for the door.

Elizabeth slid her purse over her shoulder, stood up, wavered a little, touched the stool for balance, got it, and started to follow Will out the door. As she passed his stool she saw the script, reached down, and scooped it up.

"Hey," she said. "You forgot something." She handed it to Will.

"Thanks." His smile was nothing like Todd's. Except—on closer look—for the slightly crooked fucking front tooth.

By the time Elizabeth pushed through the front door, Will had already hailed a cab and was holding the door open for her.

She scooted in and slid over to the side. God, she was feeling good. All this time she had hated Will when anyone could see he was a great guy. It was like she had known him forever. And he seemed to feel the same way.

Even before the taxi pulled away from the curb, they had started talking; they kept at it until the cab stopped in front of a brownstone on West Eightieth Street, about half a block from Central Park.

Elizabeth reached for her wallet—she was a reporter after all, and reporters don't take favors, even taxi favors—but Will was faster. By the time Elizabeth fumbled her twenty-dollar bill out, it was done and Will was holding out his hand to help her out of the car.

She reached for his hand and missed. No more martinis.

Once she stood she felt fine, better than fine, and she had no trouble going up the stone steps to the front door. Nor any problem with the next two flights to Will's apartment.

It was neatly furnished in the manner of the west side of Manhattan. That meant a little dark, a little too much furniture, and too many rugs, but otherwise very comfortable, with a good armchair for reading. And lots of books.

"This is really nice," Elizabeth said, plopping herself down in the armchair.

"It's not mine; it's a sublet, but I was lucky the people are in Italy for another year. Would you like a drink? I'm not as cute as the bartender, but I can make a martini."

"You noticed? God, he was gorgeous, wasn't he? My sister would have gone wild for him."

"The same sister who's marrying your boyfriend?"

"I shouldn't have told you that."

"Hey, I told you too much, too. But that's okay. We're friends. So, friend, you want a drink?"

"Just a little one. Mostly ice." There didn't seem to be any reason not to continue such a good feeling. The first really relaxed good feeling she'd had in eight months.

"I may not have ice. Orange juice, okay?" he called from the kitchen. Then he said, "How about you? Did you go wild for him, too?"

"Definitely not my type." Elizabeth started to get up. It was better sitting down. "Light on the vodka, please."

She looked around the room. It was rented furnished, so there wasn't much of Will around. But it was neat, and she liked that.

"I haven't read your play, and all I've seen was the first two scenes rehearsed, but I'm fascinated with the idea. It's such an unusual take on Samuel Johnson. I mean, the triangle with Boswell, Johnson, and Mrs. Thrale?"

Will came back into the room carrying their drinks.

"Did you invent that?" she asked.

"Not really. It's almost obvious if you understand who Johnson was in Boswell's life. From early on Boswell was fixated on him. He knew that one day he would go to London and write his hero's biography. Johnson was the light of his life. And he followed that light. Left his family, left everything, and went to find Johnson in London. That's what you do when you have a passion for something or someone."

"Is that why you left Chicago?"

"I don't know if I knew it at the time, but yes. I have a passion. It's this play."

He handed Elizabeth her drink, then stopped. He looked at her and kept looking at her for too many beats. The signal was unmistakable and had nothing to do with Samuel Johnson.

"How did I not see you all this time? Am I that obsessed with this play?"

"Actually, I was hiding."

"From whom?"

"You."

Will pulled up an ottoman and sat down, rather close. "No way. I'm a really nice guy."

"Except you look too much like Todd."

"Who's Todd? Wait. Don't answer. I think I know. The ex-boyfriend, right? The one your sister stole."

"You got it. And I hate him. When you turned around that first day I thought someone had hit me in the stomach."

"Sorry."

"Then—and you might not know this—you can be a real asshole."

"Elizabeth *Show Survey*! That sucks. I'm actually one of the nicest, kindest guys you'll ever meet."

"How come when I asked you to answer a couple of questions you nearly bit my head off?"

"Hey, I'm an angry young playwright. What was I supposed to do?"

"You know I never read your play because no one would give me a script?"

"You should have asked me."

"Okay, I'm asking."

Will stood, took a script from his desk, and handed it to Elizabeth.

"Should I read it now?"

"Here?"

"Whatever."

"I'm torn."

"Between what?"

"Ego and . . ."

"And what?"

Will reached out and took Elizabeth's hands, pulling her to her feet. Very close to him. "And this."

With one hand he gently brushed an errant strand of hair back from her forehead.

"Your hair is like silk."

"If I were completely sober I would say, modestly, oh, that I haven't washed it in days. But since I'm not exactly sober or even close, I'll just say thank you."

"And since I'm not exactly sober myself I'll say this is one of the best afternoons I've had since this whole play thing started. In fact, it's the only good afternoon in four months."

"It was that bad?"

"No. This is that good."

Elizabeth could tell that Will was almost exactly Todd's height. If he were Todd her face would be just about chin-high. Just like it was now.

Up close, his features were very different from Todd's, but when he reached out and brought her close to him, his body felt just as warm and wide.

But he wasn't Todd. And that was very good.

Then his mouth was pressed against hers and she opened her lips and tasted his urgency mixed with her own and everything and everyone else fell away. And that was very good, too.

Elizabeth pulled away from Will. And smiled. "I beat you. This is my only good afternoon in eight months."

Will pulled her back into his arms. "Wait, it gets better."

But Elizabeth wasn't ready for better. Not right now. Between the two of them they had enough family turmoil to start a new HBO series. And when you ran out of those stories, there was always Wendy.

And Todd.

She could play Wendy. Abandoned for another passion. Love of theater. Does that hurt less than a twin sister?

Are you kidding?

Even in her martini-fogged brain, Elizabeth knew that. And she knew there was no way she would chance any more complications in her life. Not now, anyway. But she did like him.

"Would you mind if I took your script home with me?"

"You sure?"

"Yes. I really want to read it."

"I mean right now . . ."

"Probably a good idea. For me, anyway." Elizabeth slid Will's script into her purse. "Maybe you could find time tomorrow, after rehearsal, for a short interview."

"I have time now."

"Tomorrow."

From the look on Will's face, there was no chance he was going to say no. She could see he liked her. It was as if he were a whole different person from the one in the theater.

A person she could really like.

Elizabeth took a cab from Will's apartment and was home by late afternoon. She tried to write up some of her rehearsal notes but couldn't concentrate.

Will was on her mind. They had so much in common—bad things. They were both the runaways. Obviously she was attracted to him. Everything about him was right: He was physically desirable, not really a doppelgänger after all—certainly not in personality. Additionally, he was a talented playwright with a play about to open in New York. And he liked her.

Her first thought was what Todd and Jessica's reaction would be to her new conquest.

What an ugly first thought. Was everything always going to be distorted and twisted by her bitterness? Was she always going to have that bad taste of metal in her mouth? And the taste for vengeance that went with it?

Just as she was settling in for a deep reverie over how much she hated her sister and Todd, the phone rang. It was her mother.

"Hi, Mom. Is everything all right?"

The picture of her home in Sweet Valley flashed into her mind. She could see the afternoon sun streaming into the kitchen, where her mother was, holding the cordless, probably making coffee. Her mom was a four-coffees-a-day person, and this would be the third. After dinner she'd have her last cup, decaf please.

Elizabeth knew exactly where the sun would slice across the kitchen table at this hour. In the summer, when the sun set late enough to still be strong at dinnertime, nobody ever wanted to sit in the seat with the sun in her eyes. Even the bamboo shades didn't deflect it enough. Only now did she wonder why they didn't get proper shades.

Right now Elizabeth was longing for that seat.

What she wouldn't give for that stream of sun coming into this dark apartment. But it never happened. The only sun she ever got was secondhand, a reflection bouncing off the hotel across the street.

As usual, it was warm and comforting to hear her mother's

voice. But always a little sad. She was the banished one, even if she'd banished herself.

"Absolutely, sweetie," her mother said. "Everything is fine. I just wanted to talk to you about something."

"Not the wedding, Mom. I really don't want——"

"Not the wedding. I've told you my thoughts about that. And Dad's told you, too. We want you to be there, but it's your decision, and we will understand. I don't think there's anything more to be said now. No, this is about your grandmother's eightieth birthday."

"I wouldn't forget that."

"I know you wouldn't."

"I already sent her favorite perfume. And I thought I would send her an orchid on the day."

"Why don't you bring it?"

"I can't, Mom. I'm not ready to come home yet."

"We're making her a small dinner at the club. Just the family and a couple of close friends. You know how much your grandmother loves you. It's very important to her."

"Is everybody going to be there?"

"Yes, sweetie, of course; your sister and Todd will be there."

"I can't."

"Don't decide yet. Think about it. Will you?"

"I just can't."

"Elizabeth." Alice Wakefield pronounced Elizabeth's name in that special mother's voice that was someplace between asking and telling. "Please, I want you to think about it."

"I have to go. I'm supposed to be at the theater in ten minutes."

"Is that going any better?"

"Much." A quick picture of just how much better things would be after this afternoon shot through Elizabeth's mind. It wasn't exactly the sun seat, but it did make her smile. Close as she was to her mother, she wasn't ready to talk about Will. In fact, outside of Jessica she probably wouldn't have told anyone.

"I'm not surprised," Mrs. Wakefield said, with obvious pride. "Who can resist my fabulous daughter?"

"Obviously, some people," Elizabeth said, bringing it back to earth.

"Sweetie, like you're always saying, let's not go there. Why don't you call me later when you can talk? I want to hear all about the play."

As much as she loved her grandmother, Elizabeth couldn't stomach the idea of sitting at the same table as those betrayers. They were horrible, both of them, and she hated them and never wanted to see either of them again. She knew that was unrealistic, but for now she absolutely wasn't ready.

She definitely wasn't ready to walk in there alone.

Poor, pathetic Elizabeth . . .

Unless, of course, she were to arrive, unexpectedly, at her grandmother's party on the arm of a handsome New York playwright. *That* certainly wouldn't be pathetic.

Even though it was ridiculously early in the relationship, Will would probably understand. Without wasting a moment in sensible thinking, Elizabeth looked up his number and dialed.

"Hello," Will said. She could tell he had been sleeping off the martinis.

"Hi, it's Elizabeth."

That woke him. "You're coming back?"

"No, not today anyway, but maybe soon. Did Bala get to you yet?"

"Nope. I've been screening my calls. And I'm not answering the door."

"Actually, I'm calling about a big favor from a new friend."

"Am I the new friend?"

"I hope so. My grandmother is having an eightieth birthday party, and I'd love it if you would come with me."

"Love to. When and where?"

"Next week. In Sweet Valley."

"You mean California?"

"Yes . . ."

"I really would love to go with you and shove it to that sister and her lying, cheating fiancé, but they would never let me leave, even for a day. Dinner is hard enough. Leaving the state is impossible. Starting next week we've got a six-day rehearsal schedule. Seven for me. I'm really sorry, Elizabeth. Am I still your new friend?"

"Forever."

"Hey, why not take Liam? You said your sister would go nuts for him. Okay, it's not a fabulous victory, but it's guaranteed to catch her attention. What do you think?"

Strangely enough, the first time in eight months that Elizabeth had thought about Jessica in any kind of normal way was that afternoon at the bar when she saw Liam. When it hit her how Jessica would go bananas for him, how he was just her type. It was enough to make Elizabeth smile in the way she always used to about Jessica's antics.

Will was onto something. Todd notwithstanding, there was no way the Jessica she knew could resist Liam.

"Actually," Will said, beginning to enjoy the game, "if I were writing the scene I'd do exactly that. Get a little conflict going there."

"Not bad, playwright person. I know my sister very well, and her natural instinct would be 'I want that!' This could be fun. What else would happen in the scene?"

"The obvious, like you said. She goes nuts for him, can't keep away, fiancé catches her with Liam, and the wedding is kaput. You like that?"

Silence.

"Elizabeth? Are you there?"

"Wow. Do you know how many revenge scenarios I've gone through? And nothing is nearly as good as this one."

"I'm just fooling around. It's only a scene, Elizabeth. In a play, not real life."

"I know, but it's nice to think about it anyway. So, go back to the scene; how does the fiancé catch her?"

"You're dangerous. I'm not going to mess with you."

Suddenly, they weren't talking scenes.

"I'll remember that. Thanks anyway," Elizabeth said. "See you for the interview tomorrow. Around lunchtime?"

"Right. Tomorrow," he said. They hung up.

Ridiculous as it was, Will's idea was intriguing, and Elizabeth played with it for the rest of the evening. She was enjoying herself so much, she didn't even go out to eat. Instead she fixed macaroni and cheese from a box and ate it in front of the TV, watching the last half of a bad movie she never caught up on. Even if she'd cared, it wasn't nearly as good as Will's scene.

It was crazy, the idea of asking this almost stranger to go to a dinner in California. Still, she couldn't help enjoying the picture. Immediately, it took a prime position in her revenge scenarios.

At about eight o'clock she decided to take a walk down to the Wicked Teapot. Just for a little company. Maybe see how Liam was doing.

6
Sweet Valley

Jessica got her mother's call the same day her sister did. And when she told Todd, the first question he asked was, "Is Elizabeth coming?"

"Are you kidding? Like, there's no way. Not with us there."

"Did you ask?"

"She'd have said something if Elizabeth were coming. But, you know, I almost wish she would, I mean be there, even though it totally scares me."

"It's been eight months, maybe it's time."

"What do you think about our wedding; you think she'll come?"

"No, I really don't think she will. It's one thing to come to a family celebration, like your grandmother's birthday, but coming to our wedding? I think that would be too hard."

Jessica shook her head; she knew Todd was right, but still she felt unhappy and disappointed.

"What's going to happen with us?"

"I don't know. Maybe one day she'll forgive us. That would be like Elizabeth."

"You still care for her, don't you?"

It was a question Jessica had asked many times in these last months, but not in this context. It took awhile, but she'd come to understand that that other part of Todd's love for Elizabeth was over.

Todd didn't have to think long. "Elizabeth is someone you can't stop loving." It was good for him to be able to say it. It was an indication of how far his relationship with Jessica had come.

"I know. I can't, either."

No matter how many times Jessica tried to rationalize, to give some small iota of integrity to what she had done, she never succeeded. But she kept trying. She accepted that nothing would ever excuse the betrayal, but if only she could find some way that Elizabeth could understand the love—not approve, maybe not forgive—but understand. She would settle for that.

If only she could have some part of her sister back. She had never faced anything of this magnitude without Elizabeth's comfort and good counsel.

Eight months ago in France, when she desperately wanted to leave Regan, the only one she called was Elizabeth. That call made leaving her husband viable. Talking to her wise sister cut right through the misery of indecision, and with Elizabeth's permission, her life could start over again. She remembered the strength that conversation gave her.

*O*kay, that's decided, but don't do anything until I get there," Elizabeth says. "I can be in Nice by tomorrow morning."

"No," I tell her. "I can handle this, really, as long as I know you're going to be there for me when I get back to Sweet Valley."

"I'm waiting for you. And if you're not back in two days, I'm coming to get you."

"I'll be there. I promise. I so love you, Lizzie."

"I love you, too, Jess."

I click off my cell phone, or as the French insist, *le portable,* and feel a hundred percent better. Talking to Elizabeth can do that for me. She makes me feel safe and loved, just what I so need.

Though why anyone whose magnificent blue-and-white 149-foot yacht is sitting glistening in the dazzling sunshine of the Côte d'Azur, stocked with an ever-obliging crew of ten and a doting husband, wouldn't feel safe and loved already was a question peculiar to me. But that's the way it is.

When I don't want something, I don't want it right this minute. Like this whole marriage. And I don't want to have to sit through endless boring discussions about how we could make it work and all that. It's over, and I'm ready to move on. Even six months has been too long.

Okay, there were fun parts. Like that he is fabulously handsome—dark hair, charcoal eyes, a great body—and very young-looking for forty-two. And with his wealth and brains he's extremely powerful, which is very sexy. And I love the parties and the private planes and yachts and all that stuff.

Like, who wouldn't? But his friends are all too boring, and I know they don't like me. The age difference matters more than I thought it would.

We don't want to do the same things. I mean, I like food, but I don't want to sit around and talk about it all the time, especially while we're eating. I want to eat and then get out and get some action; I like dancing, hangin' out, fooling around. Even updating Twitter would be more exciting, if only I had something interesting to say.

I thought it would be different, more like when we were dating, when it was all about what club we would be going to or flying down to the Caribbean for the weekend. I so loved the clubs. The fun of dressing outrageously in clothes you can only wear in clubs. And I loved the dancing.

Regan never was that crazy about the club stuff. I think he was always like sort of jealous. Actually, he didn't have to be because it really was all about the fun of the music, all those colors and lights and the excitement of feeling like you're in a fantasy. It was thrilling and I thought it was great. What's so wrong with that? Nothing.

Except he makes me feel there is.

I know he loves me, but it's too much. In the beginning all that attention was delicious, but now it feels more like he's obsessed, and it's suffocating. I mean, he's every place I turn. And like I feel a bit of an edge, that same edge that was so exciting when I first met him. Now it feels like almost dangerous.

Maybe Elizabeth was right. She claimed that there was something dark in Regan, sensed it like an old brain warning, but I wasn't about to listen.

What she couldn't possibly know was the magic of not having to think about Todd for the first time in too long. Marrying Regan Wollman would lift the weight that had been crushing me since that horrendous time five years ago. Going to L.A. after college didn't do it for me, and besides, it wasn't far enough. And then wasting time in a million meaningless PA jobs for all kinds of very unimportant people who didn't really need personal assistants but had enough spare money and were just too lazy to do the work themselves didn't help, either. None of that did anything to ease the pain that haunted me.

Then I met Regan.

He didn't take me just miles away; he took me into another world. An older, sophisticated, international world, where I wouldn't have to see Todd except on those occasional family events and even then we would be like strangers with nothing in common.

The added bonus was I would be saying, See, I so got over you.

True, I had been going out with Regan for only two months, but he'd swept me off my feet with endless attention and expensive gifts: diamond studs that were each more than a carat. In fact, like one point four seven, pure white set in yellow gold. Not my favorite setting, but I figured I could change it later.

Turns out later is just about here.

Plus, he's always thinking I'm fooling around. I'm not different than I ever was. I've been the same Jessica forever. Even when I was just a little kid, I liked boys to like me. And they did, and I was happy. It's what makes me, me.

It's not like that's all there is in my life. I love my sister and my family, and I really want to do something with my life. Maybe like the PR stuff I loved in college. I know I'd be good at it, but it's not possible if I keep traveling around the world like this. Regan does his business by e-mail or phone, so it doesn't matter to him where we are.

No, it so isn't working for me.

I admit the first four months were beautiful. I was his darling and could do no wrong. Quite out of character for me, but it was nice. Around the fifth month I did my first wrong, or at least the first one Regan noticed—the actor.

It was one of those endless charity affairs. Yes, I flirted a tiny bit, harmless flirting, just me being me, but Regan took exception and like went a bit nuts. He twisted my arm a little too hard, then swore it was by accident. Turned out, my perfect husband had a flaw—he could be very jealous, with dangerous hints of physicality. I've been there before with Mike and so don't want to go back.

With all kinds of apologies on both sides, that little aberration was forgiven and we moved on to another luxurious Mediterranean port, which happens to be here, in Cannes. And that's where my second wrong occurred; in fact, it was earlier today. But this time I was like really completely innocent. Almost. All I was doing was sunbathing topless on the deck at the bow of my own boat. Well, my husband's boat. It so wasn't my fault that the captain was gorgeous and happened to be steering the boat with nothing in front of him but empty sea and my topless body. For hours. What was I supposed to do? That's where the sun was.

Again, Regan didn't take kindly to such attention directed at his wife. He summarily fired the captain and chewed me out with words a little too menacing for the situation.

Later, in our cabin, he really carried on.

I'm not a dummy, and I can see that this is on its way to becoming a very nervous-making, unbecoming habit. Something has to be done.

Of course, I called my sister immediately. And Elizabeth, always a rock, settled it. Maybe it will only be for breathing time, but for now I am going home to Sweet Valley, to Elizabeth, as soon as possible.

Unfortunately, Todd is there, and I can just imagine his reaction. But

I need Elizabeth, and that comes first. I need her desperately, need her love, her warmth, and her total understanding. When Elizabeth puts her arms around someone they just feel safe. And if that someone is me, her twin sister, there're no questions asked, no judgments made, just the bottomless love of a big sister. Only four minutes bigger, but very big to me.

Besides, I'll have like the whole transatlantic flight to worry about Todd. My first concern now is getting away from Regan, getting the Delta flight from Nice to New York. I figure if I can make an early plane tomorrow morning and arrive in New York by afternoon, I can be on my way to Los Angeles later that very afternoon. By nightfall, I'll be safe, with Elizabeth, the dearest person in my whole life.

I walk down the dock, determined to tell Regan I'm leaving him, and why. Yes, I'm younger, but I'm his wife, not his child, and I refuse to be treated like some kind of chattel.

In fact, there are a lot of things I can say to him. Like that I understand that he is used to being in charge—well, so am I. And though I admit initially I was a little overwhelmed by his world and took a more pliant position, it is time that he sees the real Jessica. It's a matter of self-respect. And more important, respect for the truth.

The decision is made: I'm telling him right now that I'm taking a plane to the States first thing tomorrow morning and that's that.

I can feel the good feeling of the right resolution. I feel like Elizabeth.

I pull myself up tall and start down the dock toward the boat. Unfortunately, my heel gets caught momentarily between the planks of the dock, which cuts the elegant walk, but I simply pull it out and continue on, head still high. Nothing can stem my determination, but I'm so busy arranging the presentation of my bombshell news that I don't even see Regan until I like nearly bump into him.

"I never saw anyone more adorable than you," says my about-to-be-abandoned husband, his hands on my hips stabilizing my balance, his dark eyes alight with adulation. "I watched you walking down the dock and thought, You are the most precious thing in my life and I'm probably screwing it up."

Before I can answer, he says, "I behaved like a jerk. I'm sorry. Please, forgive me."

For the first time since we married, I know for absolute certain that I don't love Regan. But discretion is the better part of valor, and truth can be overrated; there's no point in putting yourself in a bad position just for a little self-respect.

"Okay, you're forgiven," I tell him, and receive a big hug for my acquiescence.

"Sensational. Tell you what. Why don't we get dressed and go into Cannes for a little dinner—maybe even hit the casino later? What do you think? You like the casino, right?"

"You know I do. But I don't want to be out too late. I thought maybe I might go into Nice tomorrow morning for some shopping. I saw the most precious shoes the other day at Gucci that I so have to have. Off-the-wall expensive. That can be your punishment." I hope I'm at my most adorable.

"I'll take you myself."

I must be.

"No, it's too boring hanging around while I shop. Besides, it inhibits me. You don't want to inhibit me, do you?"

"Never. And absolutely not tonight."

I kiss him lightly on the cheek, and then more seriously on the lips.

"The driver can take you tomorrow. *On y va, ma petite amie*."

And so one happy lovebird and one about-to-fly-the-coop bird hold hands and walk back along the dock together to my husband's yacht.

⌒

'm up before six; in fact, I hardly sleep all night, planning my escape. I force myself to lie in bed until seven. In a few hours this peacefully sleeping man lying next to me is going to be my enemy. I so don't want to be around when that happens.

I can't take a suitcase, not even a shopping bag, only the things I can jam into my purse, which is a stupidly small but adorable two-thousand-dollar Judith Leiber. It's like the only one I can get to without opening the cabinet above us.

All I really need is my passport, cash, and credit cards. Everything else I can buy.

By the time I finish jamming in my makeup, the purse looks like a leather beach ball; no way it will ever go back to its shape. As long as it's ruined anyway, I squeeze in a pair of heels. It's like the first time I'll be traveling in sneakers.

Quietly—silence is not possible in a boat where every move creaks or splashes—I creep past Regan on tiptoes and slip out of the cabin. On deck, the crew is busy carrying on supplies and, except for Georges, the driver, no one pays me any attention.

"*Les magasins n'ouvrent pas avant dix heures,*" Georges tells me. Even though I don't understand all the words, I already know the stores don't open until ten, so I give him one for his English, which is, like, right up there with my French.

"*Nous allons passer l'airport* for *chercer* un package of *caoutchouc* from *ma tante*." *Caoutchouc* is my favorite French word. I'm not exact on the meaning, but I know it's something to do with rubber. He gets "rubber" and "airport" and chalks the rest up to bad translation.

"*Oui, madame.*"

I get that. I follow him to the Rolls; he holds the door open, and I get in. I'm almost smiling, the worst is over and it's not even eight o'clock and I'm going to make the Delta flight to New York easily.

Then I feel a shadow on my right side and look up and see my husband.

He opens the door.

"I owe you a beautiful present, and I'm personally coming to see that it's beautiful enough for you," Regan says, smiling as he slides in.

I don't say a word. All I can think is, Does he know what I'm planning?

"Georges," he says, "the Rue D'Antibes, *s'il vous plaît.*"

"*Oui, Monsieur.*"

The Rue D'Antibes is the grand shopping street in Cannes. All the best designers have shops there, and a nothing little black dress can easily go for thousands of euros. Under normal circumstances, I would be more than delighted; right now, I'm practically paralyzed with fear. I still haven't said anything.

"Madame," Georges says. "*L'airport?*"

That gets me my tongue. "Not *l'airport, L'air du Temps,* the perfume, Georges." Then to Regan I say, "Thank goodness you're here! He would have taken me to the airport."

"*Caoutchouc?*" asks Georges, totally confused.

"God bless you," I say, and turn to give Regan a loving hug. He doesn't know.

Georges swings the car up from the port toward the Croisette, the broad boulevard, the jewel of Cannes, that runs alongside the beach. He drives past the grand hotels and turns left at the corner of the Carlton, a white bedecked wedding cake of a hotel that dominates the Croisette.

"Pull over, Georges," says Regan. To me he says, "It's too early for the stores to be open. Let's get a coffee on the Carlton terrace."

"Love to." I grab my stuffed purse à la suitcase.

"You can leave that in the car," Regan says. "Georges will watch it."

"Never. What if I need my lipstick?"

Regan knows better than to persist in an area totally alien to him. I clutch my purse to my chest and follow Regan out of the car.

Now the big question is how do I get away from him and to the airport?

Regan, a man used to having the best seats in a restaurant, chooses a table on what is called the *bord de mer,* the border of the terrace over-looking the Croisette and the sea. Mr. In Charge orders for both of us, café crème and croissants.

Then he starts telling me about the next port and the port after that. Since I don't plan to be there for any of them, I barely listen. I'm trying to figure out like how to get away from him long enough to catch a taxi to the airport. The best possibility is the ladies' room.

"Be right back, darling." I jump up, still clutching the bag. "Ladies' room." I head for the glass doors that lead to the interior of the hotel. I see a *Herald Tribune* on one of the tables, grab it, and race back to give it to Regan. I want to keep him occupied as long as possible.

Once on the other side of the glass doors, I head straight for the front entrance. There have to be taxies there.

Happily, there are.

I jump right in the first one and the driver jumps right out.

"M. Marville?"

"No?"

"Excusez-moi, madame, ce taxi est réservé pour M. Marville."

No point in fighting this. I see another taxi just behind this one, so I get out quickly, look around to see that Georges isn't waiting, and when I see he's not here, get into the second taxi just behind.

"Nice airport, s'il vous plaît."

"Oui, Madame."

Gorgeous luck to get the cab so fast. But we don't move.

Mainly because the taxi in front of us is still waiting for the famous M. Marville.

By now I've given up any attempt at French and ask my driver in a kind of fractured English, loudly and slowly, if he can go around the first car. He shrugs his shoulders, which like means either Huh? or I can't do it.

"Plane!" I add the wings with my arms. "Please, do something!"

Again he shrugs, so I get out of the car and, without taking my eyes off the hotel entrance, ask the first taxi in my loud and slow facsimile of French if he can move just to let us pass.

He adds the outspread hands to his shrug.

He watches while I dig into my purse past all the makeup and under the heels and pull out a twenty-euro note.

Now he understands my English/French perfectly and pulls the car up onto the walkway far enough over to let us pass.

But my moron driver doesn't get it. I race back to my taxi and frantically wave him to pass the first car. He starts the motor and I jump in.

Just at that moment, M. Marville—how I remember his name in all my panic, I can't imagine, but I do—leisurely comes out of the hotel with his wife or whoever.

Before we can pass, the driver of the first car gets out and opens the back door and then the trunk.

I like slide down low in my seat and peek out the window to see if Regan has come out. He can't just be sitting there waiting for me to come out of the ladies' room all this time. Regan is not the waiting kind.

And where is Georges with the car?

There's nothing to do but wait for the Marville party to put their suitcases in the trunk and get into the car. But they're in no hurry.

Actually, maybe I'm building this up too much. What would really happen if Regan found me? Like could he force me to stay? This is my first time in Europe, and I don't know the language or the customs and even though Regan's French is far from fluent, he can be so forceful, even overwhelming. I know it's just panic taking me into this craziness, but what if he said I was stealing from him? He could make up anything.

Just as I'm working myself up to hysteria, the Marvilles close the doors on the first car and my guy turns on the motor. That's it. I sit up just in time to see Regan pushing open the hotel door.

I'm back like flat down on the backseat when we pass the Rolls waiting with Georges at the wheel.

How long before Georges tells Regan about the airport? He couldn't have bought the perfume business. And what would Regan do? Would he go to the airport to stop me? Could he?

For the twenty-five or so minutes it takes to get to the Nice airport, I'm *so* a wreck. My imagination is leaping off the charts. At best he would be fifteen minutes behind me. In the old days, before all this security, it would be enough time to jump on any plane, but now with all the checks, it like takes forever.

I try to control myself and think rationally. Regan would expect me to go to New York, probably on the flight we came on, the Delta direct. So I won't consider that at all. The best thing would be a flight to Paris or some major city where I can pick up a plane to New York.

The driver asks what terminal I want. Of course, I don't know. With hand motions I limit my words to "New York" and "Fast, fast!" It doesn't sink in until I bring on the tears. Now he gets it.

"*Air France à Geneva. Après New York,*" he says, and takes me to Terminal Two.

I pay him, jump out, and race into the terminal. The big sign with the departures says my plane leaves in twenty-five minutes.

With security today in the United States, it would not be possible.

Nothing to do but try. Of course, there's no line at the counter. I gear myself up for a long tearful story about why I so must be on that plane, but when I say first class to Geneva, the ticket agent just prints one out. It's probably a commuter flight, but the magic words are first-class.

Getting through security, I have to stop myself from turning my head constantly to make sure I'm not being followed, which, of course, probably makes me look like a terrorist except there's no way, even without my heels, I look like someone who's going to waste two-hundred-dollar jeans on a bomb.

Inside the plane, seated in the luxurious second row, I stuff my bag under the seat in front and, reaching some sort of calm, let out a huge sigh of relief. I was more frightened than I'd thought possible. The back of my T-shirt is damp with sweat and the heat from my head makes strands of hair stick to my neck. My makeup is probably running, and I'm traveling first-class in sneakers. But I got away. I'm safe. For now.

Soon I'll be in the arms of my sister, the safest place in the world, and exactly the reason why I wouldn't trade being a twin for anything. I have what everyone yearns for, another human being who will always be there when I need her and who keeps me from ever having to be alone.

But not anymore. Now Jessica was just like everyone else; the uniqueness of the twinship was gone. She and Elizabeth had been like one person divided in half, viscerally connected, but not anymore. Now they weren't even sisters.

It's true, she wasn't alone. She did have Todd and he loved her and he'd be there for her, but it would never be the same. He was another person, a separate human being, not a part of her.

She knew that she and Todd would have to deal with the Elizabeth problem in the future, but for now they felt like they were safe; they felt certain that Elizabeth would never come to Grandmother's dinner.

7

New York

The Wicked Teapot was a quiet bar in the early afternoon, but in the evening it metamorphosed into singles' hell. The street in front was jammed with smokers and drinkers and smoker-drinkers.

Elizabeth was not in the mood for this kind of scene. She'd just say hi to Liam and ask hey, could he maybe reserve a quiet table for her interview tomorrow? That sounded good.

She squeezed her way inside only to find it even more solidly packed than the sidewalk. Behind the bar were two bartenders, neither of whom was Liam. Maybe he was on a break.

"Is Liam working tonight?" She managed to get close enough to ask the young woman working the bar.

"He's through for the night. Got off a few minutes ago."

"Thanks," Elizabeth said, and turned to tunnel her way through the crowd toward the door.

"You might still catch him over there near the kitchen doors," the bartender called out over the crowd.

Elizabeth smiled a thank-you and shifted direction toward the kitchen where it was, thankfully, less crowded.

But Liam wasn't there. It was probably a dumb idea anyway. Elizabeth turned to go, then heard her name.

"Elizabeth!"

It was Liam, just coming through the swinging door. He looked even better than he had earlier. He was dressed in a perfectly fitted navy blazer with beige pants and a soft-looking beige-colored shirt. Not flashy, just cool. And very expensive-looking. Not at all like a bartender/out-of-work actor.

"Hi," Elizabeth said. "I just stopped by to reserve a quiet table for tomorrow afternoon. I'm going to interview Will. You know, the playwright."

"Sure, the guy from this afternoon. I'll take care of that."

"Hey, thanks. That's great." Elizabeth waved and turned to go. "See you tomorrow."

"Wait up!" Liam called out. "As long as you're here, can I buy you a drink?"

"This is a madhouse."

"I don't mean here," Liam said. "I know a little café a couple of blocks away that should be quieter. Okay?"

"Sure, maybe a cup of coffee."

On the walk over to the café, Liam told her a little about his life. The accent was real; he grew up in Dublin but had been living in the United States for six years. He had a degree in English lit from UCLA; his father was a surgeon on loan to Cedars-Sinai Medical Center in Los Angeles. His mother was a psychologist with a private practice.

Elizabeth told him about growing up in Sweet Valley just

ninety minutes outside of L.A. Turned out they were two California transplants with a lot in common.

Additionally, what she'd taken for romantic interest on his part wasn't really there. And that nonfeeling was mutual and very comfortable. They were having a conversation like friends, good friends, in fact. Strange, considering they had just met. But Elizabeth could tell when she had a friend, and she could tell when it was something else. Without any words, she could feel that something else, because it was physical, and it wasn't there with Liam. But the friendship was.

"Have you gotten any parts yet?" Elizabeth asked.

"One. Last winter I was in an Off-Off-Broadway piece called *Warfrats* at a loft in SoHo. Did you happen to cover it?"

"No. We only do Off Broadway."

"Good, 'cause I was naked for most of it, and it was damn cold in that loft. After that I got a job as a waiter here."

"How did it go?"

"First day I spilled the soup. Fred, the owner, figured the customers would be safer with me behind the bar. He's an ex-actor himself, a great guy, and good about giving me time off for auditions. Right now I'm up for a part in a revival of an Odets play at a café in the Village. I think I've got a pretty good shot. Still nothing my father can brag about so far."

"Will they come in for it?"

"Probably, but I owe them a visit now."

Elizabeth nearly jumped out of her seat.

"When?"

"When what?"

"The visit?"

"It's not set. I can go anytime. Why?"

"This is such a weird coincidence. I have to go back to Sweet Valley for my grandmother's birthday, and I would really love to bring someone."

"I think I saw that movie."

"Me, too. But I promise you it wouldn't be an acting job. No pretending you're anything but a friend. I just want the company so I don't have to do it alone. It's going to be hell either way, but I have to do it for my grandmother. So, how about it, Liam? But only if you happen to be going at the same time. Of course, you could let me tell them you're a New York actor, which would give me a little upgrade. But no romantic thing."

"When is the party?"

"Next Thursday."

"That's a possibility. Fred might give me a couple of days off if I said I'd be back by Saturday night."

"That would be perfect! I plan to be in for the party and out on the red eye that same night."

"Can't you get more time off?"

"It's a long story."

"Feel like telling me?"

It turned out she did.

They sat at the café for more than an hour, and at the end Elizabeth was feeling pretty good. She'd made two new New York friends in one day. Maybe with Will it was more like friends plus, but whatever, they were two people she actually liked.

It wasn't until she got home that the enormity of what she'd done hit.

First she tried telling herself that she'd invited Liam just for the company. That worked better before she did it, but after, it didn't feel so good. It felt like she was lying to herself, hiding behind a ridiculous excuse, which was an oxymoron, since how could you hide something from yourself when you're right there, listening?

Maybe she wasn't planning something exactly like Will's scene, but was there still some evil intent hidden there?

What if she was just moving up the inevitable? Jessica was never going to be faithful to anyone. It was her weakness. Always had been. There was no reason that should change. Elizabeth knew her sister better than anyone else did. Better than Todd, for sure.

Poor Todd. The guppy in the path of the shark. He didn't know it, but he was in for big trouble. He was definitely going to get hurt. But, of course, that wasn't her problem anymore.

If she could push away the ugly thoughts and just remember his sweetness, how he had always tried so hard to please her. Like that time when Jessica left Regan. Todd wasn't happy about having her stay with them, but he tried.

⌣

*I*t was the day Jessica was arriving. She'd left Regan that very morning, snuck out, and made a plane from Nice to Geneva, where she texted me just before she caught a flight to New York. From there she lucked into a JetBlue flight to L.A. With the time changes she would land at LAX just after five today and come directly to us.

I arrange to get off early, around three thirty, and dreading Todd's protests, I go home.

There I am, walking in the door, a door as neat and new and nondescript as any door in any development in Sweet Valley, a door that belies the grouchy, grumpy dissatisfaction of its tenant, who happens to be the man I live with. I'm armed with megatons of reasons why he has to be nice to my poor sister. I'm so busy with excuses for Jessica that I almost walk right into this huge oak-tag sign festooned with bows, curly, hanging crepe paper, and big red Magic Marker letters spelling out WELCOME HOME, JESSICA!

It's really ugly, like the handiwork of any cruelly untalented ten-year-old. Except this is a cruelly untalented twenty-seven-year-old man and, like I said, he's trying.

"I love it," I tell him. He's standing there with the most excited, delighted smile on his face, so I give him a huge hug and say how I love the artist.

It's a happy moment for both of us, and Todd practically hugs me off my feet.

"How did work go today?" I ask, throwing my papers down on the hall chair piled too high with dumped stuff ever to behave like a real chair.

"Who had time to write?" He gives me one of his irresistible smiles—not that I need anything more than the beautiful sign.

"Oh, God, I don't want to be around next week when your editor starts calling." Then I see the magnificent chocolate mousse cake on the kitchen table. With a good quarter of it missing.

"Cara?"

"Yeah. She wanted to leave some kind of pear tart, too, but I said you were allergic to pears."

"Good thinking,"

I hate when these things happen. Steven, Cara's husband, is my own brother and I love him, but he's such a shit. "I assume the double dessert means he's starting another affair. What is it with him that he keeps wandering off? And where is he going?"

Todd shrugs. Even if he did know, male camaraderie would keep him silent. "It's a pretty good cake," he says. "Want a piece?"

"No, thanks."

I've always looked up to Steven. And he has done great. He's just turning thirty, and he's up for junior partner in the most prestigious law firm in Sweet Valley. But he's a better lawyer than husband. As a husband he's an incurable wanderer. Even in school he was like that. There were always lots of girls. He'd go from one to another and never seemed to find what he was looking for. His wife, Cara Walker, the girl he ended up with after his first love, Tricia Martin, died of leukemia, keeps herself totally in the dark, baking. Obsessively. There's no one in the neighborhood who, hard as they try, can escape her endless desserts. Any new dalliance on Steven's part is sure to bring out a fresh festival of brilliant recipes. The latest gossip, compliments of Caroline Pearce, is that he's involved with Lila Fowler, Ken Matthews's wife.

I don't buy that; she's definitely not Steven's type. Who is, though, I haven't figured out yet.

Ken is our local celebrity, our own NFL star. I think he's the dearest guy, completely oblivious to his fame and good looks, and unfortunately, his roving wife. He had an injury earlier in the year and has been out for the season. The only good side of any of this mess was that there was sure to be a fabulous new chocolate mousse cake from Cara on everyone's dinner table.

I can't even have a bite without tasting her unhappiness.

"About tonight. I think Jessica will be too wiped out. I just don't think she's going to be up to going to Winston's. Okay with you?"

I hardly have to ask. Any excuse not to go to Winston's works for Todd.

We hardly ever see Winston anymore because Todd isn't crazy about his former best friend. In fact, very few people are. The money he made from a dot-com venture with Bruce Patman changed him radically. Now he has very few real friends, mostly hangers-on, a coterie of people who think they can get something out of him. But he makes them pay a high price—their dignity. Still, the ones who stay probably didn't have much of it to begin with.

Even before the money thing, Todd and Winston had some kind of falling-out. It happened in the spring of our senior year at Sweet Valley U. I never knew what it was about, but I know it didn't have anything to do with us.

Actually, it was a strange time for Todd and me that had nothing to do with Winston; it was the closest we'd ever come to breaking up. And it wasn't over a disagreement and nothing unusual had happened. We were doing the same things we always did, but suddenly our separate lives seemed to be eating into our together time. It wasn't only the physical separation; it was the emotional distance I was beginning to feel. I thought maybe the relationship was ending.

I was waiting for my heart to break, but strangely, it didn't. Todd must have sensed something, because I felt him watching me more intently than usual.

It took me a bit until I was ready to talk to him about it. But just before I did, there was a radical change, the distance between us suddenly closed, and it was as it had always been—we were together and possibly even closer. There was passion again. As for the Winston problem, I just figured Todd was beginning to know the real Winston, the man he would become. That would have been reason enough.

It was around that time that Bruce Patman and I were becoming really good friends. Close enough that I would have talked about this, but I never did. I was on the verge so many times, but for some reason, I held back. Even now I don't know why. Maybe because he and Todd were old friends, it seemed—I don't know—disloyal.

And then it solved itself. Now I have it all. Plus, the other most important person in my life is coming here this very day. I only wish it weren't so unhappy for Jessica. But, I tell myself, one of Jessica's best qualities is her ability to almost finger snap unhappiness away and move on. At least she could do that as a kid. Well, whatever happens, I'm here for her.

Here for her.

How could she have been so blind? Elizabeth thought. Well, not anymore.

Suppose she could find a way to satisfy her special need, pay Jessica back, and save the dumb guppy Todd, who really didn't deserve her kindness, from the shark's mouth? Even if the guppy was a shithead, it was normal to want to save the guppy. Additionally, it would tailor the revenge a bit closer to Elizabeth's sense of decency.

Maybe decency was pushing it too far. It was still a rotten thing to do, but why should she be the only loser? Okay, she still wouldn't be the Elizabeth everyone knew and loved, but maybe that girl was a woman now and finished being the patsy everyone took advantage of.

And after all, when it came to Jessica, she would be revealing only what was there to be revealed. And maybe saving both of them from a big mistake.

Taking it another step, it would give Todd a small taste of what she had suffered.

But would Liam do it?

Not if he knew what he was supposed to be doing. She had told him the whole story, but he still wouldn't think she could be so low and devious. And if he suspected some ulterior motive, Liam was not the kind of guy who would take part in some weird revenge scheme.

But he was an actor, and he might want to please a reporter and the reporter's friend, the playwright, especially if she put it to him the right way. Using some of her storytelling talent, she might be able to make it sound almost altruistic, like Save the Guppy.

Finally Elizabeth had to take half a Valium to shut down her brain activity, which was dancing all over the place. For the first time in months, she went to sleep not feeling so hopeless. Crazy, but not hopeless.

In the morning, the idea, even just thinking it, was repulsive. It was completely off the wall, underhanded and devious, something she would never want to be involved in. The more she thought about it, the more it sounded like fiction, not real life. It was comforting to know that she wasn't that kind of monster.

Taking Liam was a nice idea. He was planning to be out there sometime anyway. If it worked out that he could come with her, great, but it was nothing more than that.

She'd made up her mind; there was no way she would miss her grandmother's eightieth birthday.

Maybe all the thinking wasn't a waste of time. Maybe one day she would use the idea in a novel.

8

Sweet Valley

Jessica worked for MYFACEISGREEN, an environmental promotion company that helped introduce new, green beauty products for the popular cosmetics market. Though the company had started less than four years earlier, it already had an impressive client list of major companies like Revlon, Almay, and L'Oréal, who wanted to break into the green market.

MYFACEISGREEN had offices in Chicago and New York, but the home office, now fifty strong, was in Sweet Valley because its main financial backing had come from Richard Fowler, Lila's father. But if that contact helped Jessica get the job in the beginning, after two months, the CEO, Doug Spender, saw he had a genuine, runaway talent on his hands and acted accordingly by putting Jessica in charge of his biggest markets, Los Angeles and San Diego.

It was a tricky move that put her ahead of the owner's daughter, but Lila had so little interest in her father's company that she barely noticed Jessica's new role on the days she deigned to come in. Besides, it gave Lila someone fun to lunch with.

Since the planning and organizing was done in Sweet Valley, Jessica had to do a lot of traveling back and forth, mostly by car, to L.A. and San Diego. And it was only on those long, solitary trips that she was able to torture herself with her Elizabeth agony in peace.

Jessica had started working for MYFACEISGREEN right after she got back from France, and though she had been at the company only six months, she knew she was in the right place. Ironically, the only reason she had studied communications at SVU was because it looked like it wouldn't interfere too much with her busy social life. As luck would have it, it interfered like crazy; she loved it. She could socialize and advertise all at once by syncing her Twitter and Facebook accounts for both. She was a natural and seemed to know everything just by feel, even before she was taught.

Jessica had been put in charge of selecting and organizing debut cosmetics, which meant investigating the products and deciding how they would be marketed. Her first attempt was with a seaweed mask that was actually made of a sheet of raw seaweed and formed to fit the face when moistened. She debuted it in L.A., using models who dressed in gowns and funky plumes and pretended they were at a masked ball.

The *Los Angeles Times* came and liked it so much they used it for their lead story in the fashion section. Additionally, the product worked to some degree as a skin refreshment, leaving a bright, clean look to the skin. It was definitely hypoallergenic and about as green as you could get. Almay was very happy with the way she handled it.

After that, only Jessica could work on their products. Now she had a lifetime supply of unused seaweed masks and had discovered that by toasting them on top of the stove she could crisp them up enough to eat as a snack. Even Todd liked to nibble on them when he wrote at home. At least they were healthier than bacon bits, and besides, she felt too guilty to throw a gift out.

She had graduated to her own office with a window and became, for Jessica, a workaholic. That was her other protection from the Elizabeth agony, her work.

She actually loved it and was very comfortable with her colleagues. In fact, Jessica was a very different person at the office. Because she was known to be exemplary at her work, she was well respected and one of the first people to be consulted about new product promotions—not just by the junior staff, but often by people who had been in the business for years, especially Michael Wilson, a vice president who had been brought over from the Chicago office. He thought Jessica was brilliant, and even though he'd been in the business for twelve years, he was always interested in hearing her ideas.

No one here looked at her as if she were still high school Jessica, half a twin—and not the best half, either, ex-cheerleader and, it has to be said, a somewhat shallow person. But if they did they would be wrong. Jessica was every bit as smart as Elizabeth, but had a totally different style. Hers was a fabulous style, adorable, lively, and very underestimated.

Most of the people in the office were new to Sweet Valley

and had no idea about her background. She was not the lesser of the twins, because hardly anyone knew she had a twin. It was the first time in her life she was being taken seriously as her own person. Maybe it mattered that Elizabeth wasn't around. There could be no comparisons.

Of course, Todd took their love seriously, but even with him she had never really completely shaken the earlier high school image, which she knew sometimes made him nervous. Some of it was still true, but not when it came to her work. There she was anything but shallow.

And Michael Wilson, the vice president, knew that and valued her. If Jessica could create the perfect man, Michael would come pretty close. He was not pretty-boy handsome, not nearly as handsome as Todd. He was about five-ten, sandy-haired, and boyishly slim. Boyish was the charm of his appearance. Quick to smile and warm and without pretention, Michael was the sort of person everyone liked. Additionally, it was obvious to anyone with any perception that he was more than a little interested in Jessica.

The few times that Lila showed up at the office, she filled Michael in on her best friend's background, especially the Todd part. So, he held his interest in check, never overstepping.

And he never mentioned knowing anything to Jessica, keeping a very clean, professional distance from her. Their relationship was friendly but all about work.

This last week he had been involved in a project for promoting a new face bronzer made entirely of organic flower stamens. Once applied it lasted for days, a terrific advantage until you wanted to take it off. Then it was more like a stain than a surface coloring. How to get around that? How to make that seem like a plus? Only one person could possibly do that.

"Have you seen Flower Pure yet?" Michael caught Jessica just before six as she was leaving the office.

"Actually, no. I heard about it, though. Sounds pretty good."

"It is, until you want to take it off."

"Why would you want to take it off?"

"A question I never asked. You're brilliant."

Jessica had to smile. She was scoring all the time just being natural. Not trying too hard or pretending to know something she didn't know. The truth was, she always seemed to really know.

She could see that Michael was delighted. She'd done it again.

"I've been struggling with the thing for days. And just like that you solve it. You're incredible. Thank you," he said, and he hugged her.

It was a warm hug of gratitude.

It was nice for Jessica to be so appreciated.

For Michael it was a little too nice, but he controlled himself.

"Let me buy you a glass of champagne," he said. "We can go right next door." Controlled, but not completely. "You don't know, but you made my day. Now I can go home and do nothing without guilt. The first time in a week."

Jessica couldn't help smiling back. He was so cute. Michael was a very different kind of guy for Jessica, who always seemed to have the jocks and the bad boys. Todd was a nice combination of jock and real person. She was lucky.

Jessica was feeling very good and didn't want it to end too quickly. A glass of champagne and more talk about how fabulous she was was appealing. Except Todd was expecting her home by six thirty to have a bite and maybe catch a movie.

But having a glass of champagne with an appreciative vice president was tempting, a great ending to the day.

"Maybe a quick glass would be all right. Let me text my friend and see what's up."

She could have said boyfriend, but she didn't. Jessica took out her iPhone and tapped in her text to Todd.

HEY, STUCK AT MEETING. C U AROUND 7.

That seemed like the easier way. Not going into a big thing about Michael's project and the champagne. TMI. She'd tell him when she got home.

Who was she kidding? This was not full disclosure. And what was she really going to tell Todd when she got home? This kind of thinking was pure, familiar Jessica Wakefield, but now it came with a tinge of discomfort.

Michael was stunned at his good fortune, so rather than chance a mind change, he grabbed his attaché case from the chair and put out an after-you arm as Jessica took her purse and stepped through the doorway of her office.

The place next door was a popular bar, its few outside tables jammed with after-work young people catching the late afternoon sun. All of them seemed to be BBMing on their BlackBerrys and texting on their iPhones, even the ones sitting together at the same table. That's where all the action was. Jessica moved toward the one empty table, but Michael took her arm and gently directed her into the darker bar area, toward a table in the back.

"It's quieter here," he said, pulling out a chair for her.

She sat down. This was way weird, Jessica thought, like being on a date. It had been more than a while since anything like this had happened.

Michael was cute. Better than cute. He was smart, nice, successful, and they had so much in common. Best of all, their friendship was totally uncomplicated.

As far as she knew he didn't belong to anyone else. He had never been married, had no children. According to Cecilia Brown, who worked in marketing, Michael had a nice house, some family money, and a law degree. Plus, he drove a silver BMW. Definitely Jessica Wakefield material.

There must be something pushing her, she thought. Why would she have lied to Todd? Should she trust her instincts? Instincts know in a flash what takes the mind so much longer to figure out.

Listening to this instinct, pure and simple, could change her life completely. No one would despise her for this choice. It wouldn't even be much gossip; it would be so old Jessica that hardly anyone would notice.

So many things in her life would be different. Jessica knew she was saving the best for last. And she savored it.

Then she had to admit it: Without Todd she could have Elizabeth back. She could be rejoined with her other half, complete again. She and her twin could be sisters who could talk and laugh and hold each other. She wanted Elizabeth so desperately.

It wouldn't be immediate; it would take some time, but not that much. She could go to Elizabeth and beg her forgiveness and there would be no Todd to forever keep her crime alive. And Elizabeth wouldn't want him back, either.

All she had to do was give up Todd.

"Brut?"

"That's not fair." Her guilty thoughts interrupted, she was momentarily offended, until she realized it was not an accusation. Then, doubling back, she smiled as if she knew all along it was a joke. "Brut, yes, that's me."

"No way." Now Michael took up the joke and was smiling.

Good teeth. Beautiful teeth. Very white, but not that artificial paint white they do in those storefront shops. His teeth were slightly transparent, just right, and perfectly even. Also, there were no show-off dimples or chin clefts. His was a look for the long term.

The waiter brought two glasses of icy champagne.

Michael toasted her. "Thanks for your help."

"You're very welcome."

They drank.

Michael took a deep breath and then said, "Actually, I've been waiting a long time for this."

But Jessica's mind was far away from Michael's words. Yes, she thought, Elizabeth would be hers again, loving and joined together the way they were meant to be. All she would have to do is give up Todd.

Instincts could be good and, often, useful; they could even save your life. And clear thinking could be wise, but nothing can stand up to the power of that uncontrollable tornado that sweeps out everything in its path. Nothing matched the power of love.

That's what was in Jessica's heart and head. If she hadn't

known it before, she knew it now beyond any doubt, and all she was capable of doing was taking another sip of her champagne, standing up, thanking Michael, and telling him that anytime he needed her ideas, they were his.

But, she thought, that was all. The rest belonged to Todd.

They said good-bye and Michael thanked her again for her help. Knowing he had lost, he just sat there and finished his champagne and what was left in Jessica's glass.

Jessica almost fled to her car, as if speed could erase the misstep. Even calling it a misstep was a kindness she knew she didn't deserve.

By the time she got into her car, the enormity of what had just happened and the decision she'd made brought tears to her eyes.

She was losing Elizabeth again, this time consciously giving her away, and it was very different from what had happened eight months earlier. Then, she had no control. This time, in total control, she had chosen Todd.

Now she fully understood what she had done that horrendous time eight months ago when she came back to Sweet Valley and destroyed her sister's life. Never in a million years did she intend to do such a thing to her beloved Elizabeth, but that's what she had done.

Now she knew why.

God knows she didn't mean to do it, she didn't want to, but that's what happened.

When Elizabeth picked her up at the airport Jessica should have known that it was a mistake coming to Sweet Valley. Even though she so desperately needed to see her sister, it was selfish and cruel.

But she felt she had no choice. Her parents were away on a cruise and, not wanting to spoil their vacation, she couldn't tell them yet about the breakup. They wouldn't be back for two more weeks. And besides, she needed Elizabeth desperately, needed her love, her warmth, and her total understanding. When Elizabeth cared about someone, especially her little sister, she'd step in and take care of everything. You could put yourself completely in her hands and not give it another worry. Well, at least Jessica could.

Additionally, and perhaps most important, Jessica was in the habit of being Jessica Wakefield. Especially when it came to her sister.

$\smile$

The drive home is filled with Elizabeth's excited news about all the wonderful things that are happening. Her work at the paper is finally paying off. No longer is she covering garden parties and unimportant social events. Now she's getting political assignments and last week, even a bold midday robbery of a jewelry store at the mall. That was a front-page story with her byline. They still haven't caught the thieves, so she's still on the story and filled with a million theories.

By the time we pull into the driveway, I'm feeling so guilty, it's like choking me, and I can hardly speak. Elizabeth has taken over the entire conversation, spilling out the happy bombshell about her plans with Todd. Yes, they're finally ready to set a date.

Elizabeth stops the car and with the joy of sharing her thrilling secret lighting her smile, turns to me, waiting for my response. I manage a camera smile in return.

"Maybe even as soon as this fall," says Elizabeth. "What do you think, maid of honor?"

And with only a nanosecond's hesitation, only the time it takes for me to swallow the news, I like lean over and hug my sister.

"I think it's wonderful, and I *so* love you and I'm really happy for you. For Todd, too. I guess it always had to be, didn't it?"

"For a while I wasn't sure. There was something . . . I don't know what it was, some shadow of something that stopped me. Maybe I was just scared, but whatever it was, it's past and now I know it's right."

"Have you told Mom and Dad?"

Elizabeth takes my hand. "Of course not. No one could know before you."

There is nothing left for us to do but cry. Which we do. Hers the happy tears, and mine? Who knows? All tears look the same.

With no luggage beyond my overstuffed purse, I have nothing to delay my entrance, so arm in arm we walk to the front door. It's not locked, and Elizabeth throws it open wide with a proud *"Ta-da!"*

And there it is, the big WELCOME HOME, JESSICA sign. It actually gives me the first true smile of the day.

"I love it! But your art talent is definitely failing. Actually, it sucks."

"I didn't do it. Todd did."

Before I can comment on that surprising news, Todd himself appears.

I just stand there, hot, flushed, and empty of words, stunned at the intensity of my own response.

Then, pushing my Jessica the Adorable button, I smile and shriek, "I love it!" and rush in to hug my soon to be brother-in-law.

I can feel his slight withdrawal, but it doesn't stop me from squeezing my arms around him. Within an instant, he responds and returns the embrace. For a moment, the feel of our bodies touching hits both of us. Like an electric shock, it spins us back so we're almost jumping away from each other.

I'm sure no one watching would know anything unusual happened. Certainly no one who didn't want to see anything unusual happening. Like Elizabeth. So the welcoming goes well.

That night and the next day, Elizabeth is like clucking around the two of us, making sure her chicks are comfortable, encouraging us to talk and working hard to squeeze some smiles out of us with old-time high school stories. The awfulness of Winston is her best subject and one that Todd is most likely to join her in. She's so busy arranging things that she doesn't notice the thinly disguised wariness and unease with which we treat each other. Nor does she notice—not consciously, anyway—the fact that he and I are rarely in the same room together. And when we are, we barely look at each other.

That's the way it had continued for that entire week: Jessica Wakefield, living in the same house as Todd Wilkins, who just happened to be writing at home, all day, every day, for the next ten days. They had given him an extension on his deadline for the second and third piece. Of course, Jessica wasn't working, so she was right there, too. Elizabeth kept talking about what a perfect trio they would make, what fun they could have, the three of them together, if only she could have been there, but she wasn't. She had to work. All day, every day.

That's how Jessica destroyed her sister's life.

Perhaps, if Elizabeth had looked more closely or been less Elizabeth . . . But of course, that was impossible. Though she was always very observant, when it came to her sister, her acute observation was blinded by an unconditional love that no one should have after the age of five.

Besides, on the surface the Jessica-Todd relationship didn't look any different than it had for years.

*I*t's not that I don't know that there's tension between Todd and Jessica, but they've always had their little problems, even in high school. Though on the surface this last week, they seem like old friends. Sometimes, anyway. And, after a couple of glasses of wine and a nice dinner, pretty comfortable with each other. But there's an undercurrent that keeps me a little uneasy.

Neither of them thinks I know what it's about, but I do. Though it makes me unhappy, there's nothing I can do about it.

It's possessiveness. On both sides. They each feel they own a piece of the same person—me.

No matter how they feel about each other, there's no choice. Jessica needs me, and that's it. Todd will have to accept that he's involved in an unusual situation. We're twins and always will be, with all the unique baggage that carries.

If only I could talk to a friend about it. But there's no way. It would be a betrayal. I have never betrayed my sister and, no matter what her faults, she would never betray me.

I wish I could be home with Jessica, that all three of us could be together. Maybe then they would get over whatever animosity they have for each other. After all, they're going to be related soon enough. Very soon. Probably this fall.

9

Sweet Valley

Todd was awake and out of bed before seven the next morning. Even though the sky was overcast and the report was for rain, he grabbed his sneakers, shorts, and a T-shirt, dressed in the hallway outside the bedroom, and slipped quietly out of the house, careful not to wake Jessica. Not that she would have wanted to run on this kind of a morning—it was hard enough to get her out on a sunny day—but he didn't want to take the chance. He needed to be by himself.

As it turned out, though, he wasn't going to be. Just as he got to the end of the driveway, he saw Ken Matthews turning the corner onto his street and waving. There was no way Todd could pretend he hadn't seen him.

There was nothing to do but wait up for him.

Todd had kept up a fairly good friendship with Ken; they had the sports stuff in common—Todd the writer and Ken the player. But Todd and Jessica hadn't seen much of the Matthews in these last eight months, not only because of their impending divorce, but because neither he nor Jessica was feeling very social in these last months. But Todd still maintained a separate relationship with Ken. Not close enough for him to talk about his elephant in the room, but better than just bullshit guy talk. Besides, Ken had his own elephant.

Ken caught up with Todd, and they started running. Silently, through the soft, early-morning haze, past the neat lawns and newly planted trees that would need another forty years before they looked as if they belonged.

After about half a mile they left their development and hit empty space, vacant farmland that would probably be more houses in another year or so. Ken started talking.

"What's happening, man?" he asked, not even breathing hard.

Todd was. "Not much," he huffed. "How about you?"

They were moving at a medium-fast jog, and Todd felt it. He hadn't been doing much running lately since much of his time was spent with Jessica, who wasn't terribly interested in sports, either watching or playing. And he certainly wasn't playing basketball. The team from Napkin, the local restaurant, hadn't asked him, so he was a little out of shape. It was better when he let Ken do the talking.

"Status quo," Ken said. "Not too exciting. A little weird, I guess, you saw the other night. Not your usual separation, but I'm doing what I want until Lila tells me different."

"You two look pretty good together. Are you going to work it out?"

Thanks to Caroline Pearce, everyone knew they were seeing lawyers and working on a divorce, but also that Ken was still hanging around the house more than often. That was also a Caroline tidbit.

Obviously, Ken was conflicted, and Lila must have had some of the same hesitancies because she let him stay. And Lila wasn't one to do favors, so maybe it wasn't quite over.

"I don't know," Ken said. "Even though she's been my wife for almost two years, Lila's unpredictable."

"What about you?"

"Who knows? Sometimes I think I'm still in high school, chasing the cheerleader. Sick, huh? I'm almost thirty, so why am I still playing that game? On the other hand, it's like I'm still on the varsity team. Okay, it's NFL, but the life is not a hell of a lot different. Everything is still about winning and losing."

Todd didn't say anything. It was too close; Lila and Jessica had been best friends since grade school. He always thought they were too much alike. Now he hoped he was wrong, but there were undeniable similarities, enough of them to make him a little nervous.

Was this just high school for him, too? That whirlwind of sexual obsession and heart-ripping passion that charged in and knocked you out of reality? Sometimes it was worse, ripping up everything around you leaving nothing but destruction and broken lives.

Just because you admit it doesn't absolve you, he told himself, then gave himself a little leeway. It helped to know he was aware.

"Of course, if you want a better scoop," Ken was saying, "you could always ask Caroline. By the way, Jessica was beautiful the other night, the way she chewed her out. Of course, it doesn't really make any difference. Nothing stops Caroline. Jessica gave it to Lila, too. And she wasn't all wrong."

He had to admit Jessica was good that night. She surprised him with her strength. It was almost like what Elizabeth would have done. Bad job, comparing them.

Stay light.

"Jessica asked me if I thought Caroline would come to the wedding."

"Are you kidding?" Ken laughed. "She wouldn't miss it for the world."

Todd stopped and, leaning over, he put his hands on his knees and took some deep breaths. Ken waited on the side and watched him. Between breaths, Todd said, "Desk job. Went from a player to a watcher."

"Miss it?"

"Yeah, but I miss a lot of things."

"Can't tell by looking at you."

That came in handy, Todd's laidback demeanor. He was always hard to read. He'd never needed that talent more than he did when Jessica first came back from France and was staying with Elizabeth and him.

My head is pounding from Jessica's endless why-I'm-leaving-Regan stories. Turns out he's a monster, or she thinks he is, anyway. Of course Elizabeth, the big, protective sister, goes with anything she says.

Just hearing his name bugs me. I don't know if I buy all the monster stories, but no matter, I don't like him. Right from the get-go I thought he sucked. He was arrogant, too full of himself, and looked like a dumb mistake that only Jessica could make.

Yeah, I'm angry, and I don't even know why. The last thing I want is to find out.

The combination of my deadline for the second of a three-part series, which, of course, passed last week, and the guest is getting to me.

Ah, the guest. How do I avoid her? Not easy in this small house, but lucky for me she's been out mostly, busy running around, seeing all her old friends.

It's ten thirty in the morning and I'm closing in on my computer. Physically getting to it, I mean, but I'm not there yet; I'm still reading the newspaper at the kitchen table. And Jessica is still asleep in the guest bedroom just down the hall from my office.

A couple of minutes ago I heard sounds, moving-around sounds, closet doors opening, footsteps, and general waking sounds coming from Jessica's bedroom. She's been staying here for more than a week, and it's still no easier. Hey, I'm totally over her, but she'll always make me uncomfortable.

That almost stopped me from marrying Elizabeth. Not that I don't love her, because I do. Who could not love Elizabeth? But with her as my wife, it's a package deal; Jessica will always be around someplace.

I liked it better when she was married and off in France.

Maybe one day this whole thing will fall into perspective—all about being young and dumb combined with too much to drink—and it'll fade into a vague memory, always unpleasant but not torturous.

Or am I letting myself off the hook too easily?

Maybe it's really not that important. When I'm forty and look back, is it going to look like a mistake that didn't have legs, that just went away, or a life-altering event?

It doesn't look like it was that important to Jessica. It was probably just another nothing fling that, no doubt, she regrets. After all, it was her sister. But she's probably found a way to rationalize it so it comes out looking like an alcohol-based indiscretion.

Wouldn't she be stunned if she knew all the time I spend agonizing over that month.

Like this morning. This morning was another one of those tremendous times in bed with Elizabeth that got spoiled when Elizabeth mentioned her name.

I can't let myself get caught in this shit, so instead I grab my jacket and head out the kitchen door to my car. I look like a thief escaping from a crime the way I run down the driveway. Head down and shoulders hunched, I fling myself into the front seat, turn the key, ram the car into first, and speed off. To safety.

I would dearly love to stay away all day, but I've got this serious deadline I'm already late for, so I just pick up a coffee at the Coffee Bean and head back.

My first piece of the three-part series for the *Sweet Valley News* comes out tomorrow. I could work at the newspaper office, but then they would see that I was just starting the second piece. That would really put them on my back. I suffer from deadlineitis. The minute I get the assignment—it could be three weeks in advance—I start suffering and planning excuses for being late.

Actually, having Jessica in the house should be good discipline. It should keep me locked away in my office, where I have no choice but to work. Or YouTube some old game or watch porn. Wouldn't be the first time.

When I pull up the driveway, I can see Jessica in the kitchen reading a magazine. There's no way to avoid her. She has to have seen the car, so

I have no choice but to come in the back way through the kitchen; otherwise it's too obvious that I'm avoiding her. Only strangers use the front door.

Since Jessica is Jessica, totally involved in her own feelings, I figure she probably isn't even aware of my angst. After all, the whole thing happened more than five years ago and was so quick, only a month. I was probably one of a lot of guys who fell for Jessica over the years. It was almost a natural rite of passage. That's all. Kids' stuff.

But I can't fool my own responses, and even thinking about that time sends a quick, disgusted shudder shooting through my body. How could I do that? I still don't know. I quickly shake my head like that could wipe out the thoughts.

Instead, I force myself to think about this morning, about making love to Elizabeth, about the deep, satisfying warmth of that love, of her soft, pliant, trusting body in my arms. Mistake. That only makes the guilt all the worse.

As it happens, I was wrong. Jessica didn't see me. In fact, she's so involved in her magazine that she doesn't even hear me coming until I open the door, and then she jumps and lets out a little yelp.

"Hey, sorry. I didn't mean to scare you." I am really sorry, but still it was kind of funny the way she jumped. I give a little laugh.

She does, too, and it's the first comfortable, natural response either of us has had since she arrived last week. I'm still smiling because it really was a funny sight and because, despite myself, I like the comfort.

But our smiles dissipate, and there's a sharp drop into silence. The chasm between us, deep and dark, reopens.

"I have to work," I say, and it comes out stronger than I meant, like I'm blaming her for keeping me. Without waiting for a response, I walk out of the room toward my office.

"Yeah, right. Like I'm stopping you," she says, almost under her breath.

But I hear and, turning to look back, say, "You don't *anything* me."

I don't know why she makes me so angry, but she does.

Maybe I'm the one who doesn't belong here.

⌒

Ken was sensitive enough not to ask Todd any questions about how it was going with Elizabeth. Like, was there going to be a rapprochement between the sisters? Was Elizabeth coming in for the wedding? All the things he'd have to wait for Caroline to tell everyone.

They managed to have a good conversation over the next hour, a half hour down to town and a half hour back, without anything too personal. Only guys can do that.

When they hit downtown Sweet Valley it was closed up tight. The main street was almost empty except for some shopkeepers hosing down the front of their shops. Without the girls in UGGs and the guys in jeans, it could be right out of an old MGM movie of a small mid-twentieth-century town in the Midwest, where everything was clean and safe. And happy.

Actually, Sweet Valley still retained a lot of those qualities. It was probably one of the reasons Jessica didn't want to leave. She wanted this life for herself and for her children.

People thought she would be the first one to escape to the big city, L.A. or New York. And she did, with Regan, but truth be told, she hadn't liked it. She missed Sweet Valley and all the people, even the ones she didn't like so much.

Maybe Todd fell in there someplace. Those couple of weeks when she first came back from France and was living in the same house with Todd were excruciating. Sometimes explosive, like the day they were alone in the house, both desperately trying to avoid each other. She had to wait for him to leave the house before she could safely sit in the kitchen and read instead of being trapped in her bedroom.

But then he came back unexpectedly. And he was so nasty he practically accused her of standing in the way of his work. She'd shot right back with the same bite.

⁓

Yeah, right. Like I'm stopping you," I say, almost under my breath. But he hears me and turns around and says with a really nasty look on his face, "You don't *anything* me."

How dare he say that to me. You don't *anything* me!

I'm sitting there, in the kitchen, fuming until I can't sit anymore. I tear down the hallway to his office. The door is closed, but I'm way too angry to knock—that feels too supplicant—so I go straight to my bedroom, grab my purse, and storm out the front door, where I practically run into Caroline Pearce. In fact, she's blocking my way with her big, ugly body.

"Wow! Lovers' quarrel?" Caroline says.

"What's that supposed to mean?"

"Sorry." But, of course, no one could be less sorry. "I thought you were Elizabeth," Caroline says, running her hand through the new growth of red hair that's just beginning to grow back after her chemotherapy.

"You're sick," I say. Then it hits me: She really is. But I'm still annoyed at her. I say, "You know what I meant."

I suppose anyone else might have spent a little more time like trying to rectify that unkind error, but unfortunately for Caroline, she hit the wrong sister.

"Elizabeth's not home?" Caroline asks. "How about Todd?"

I don't even answer. Or look back. I just race over to my rented Mustang convertible. Hey, I still have the credit cards. Knowing Regan, probably not for long.

No question that he hates me. Todd, I mean. Not in front of Elizabeth, but if she isn't watching, it's like loathing. Like it was all my fault and he wasn't part of it.

It's not true. It was both of us. Crazy. Horrible.

Until he didn't.

Being far away helped, but it wasn't a cure, only a palliative. I'm too impatient for palliatives.

I have to get out of here.

I spent the last week seeing everyone I wanted to see and lots I didn't want to see. I even spent time with like Winston, who expected me to fall head over heels for him. Well, over my heels anyway. But I've *so* had it with rich men. Besides, he'll always be the class clown to me—except now he's become a decidedly unfunny clown, egotistical and arrogant. A real prick.

No place to go, nothing to do, just sit around and wait for Regan to call and then not answer the phone. Strangely enough, he hasn't called, which is way creepier than if he did. The silence is unnerving. How long before he decides to come out here? Except that I don't think his pride and vanity will let him. No, Regan is definitely not the sort of man to chase a woman.

Besides, he's probably still stunned that I would leave him—wonderful, rich, gorgeous him. On the other hand, he isn't a man used to losing.

That last thought like unnerves me. The power that originally attracted me to him, redirected, could be very scary.

Right now, there's no good place for me. But the best of the no-good places is here, with Elizabeth. At least it's best for me.

And there I go again, selfish Jessica, always wrapping the world around myself.

What can I do? Twenty-seven is too late to change. Besides, I have some good qualities. My best one is that I love Elizabeth. I would give up my life for my sister. I almost did. One time when we were in high school, this lunatic madman came at her with a sledgehammer. I jumped in between them, and I didn't even have a weapon. All I had was crazy fury and determination to save my sister's life.

And later, afterward, I knew I really would have sacrificed my life for my sister, and that gave me way the best feeling about myself I have ever had.

So how could I ever explain the Todd thing to her?

I drive the two blocks over to Lila Fowler's house. Even though Lila is my longtime best friend, we actually haven't seen much of each other since I left Sweet Valley, but like old friends, five minutes together and we're back in high school.

But Lila isn't home. The housekeeper says she's at the hairdresser. A place called Dario's at the new mall between the Gap and Starbucks, not the first Starbucks, the third one.

I have a little trouble finding the right place since there's a Starbucks next to almost everything now. I find the hairdresser, but Lila isn't there and not expected. No doubt she's out screwing someone. According to Caroline probably my own brother, Steven, the shit. Not that I can afford to take such a disapproving position on infidelity, but it's different for me; I'm in control. Steven's the kind who falls in love. Men are no good at keeping cheating in its place. And thanks to Caroline, everyone knows everything. Except my pathetic sister-in-law, Cara Walker Wakefield. At least *she* would be home. Baking probably. Baking certainly.

They say the wife is the last to know. But like who's going to tell her? What a momentous, Godlike thing to take on, bringing news that could demolish someone's life. Who has the right to do that? What if she still loves him? Of course, I always think I would want to know.

Would Elizabeth want to know?

No way.

So everyone knows about Steven's infidelities and no one tells Cara.

I can't go back to the house and spend the entire afternoon avoiding Todd. That's totally depressing. Instead, I drive downtown to see if I can find anyone to mess with.

Downtown Sweet Valley hasn't changed that much since my high school days. The big changes happened before, in the late eighties. It had been years since the little shops were driven out by the malls and supermarkets, and I can hardly remember what Sweet Valley looked like back then. Which is depressing because I'd like to go back in time. Life was wonderful and simple when I was queen of the prom, when all that seemed to matter was how cute you were? And I was very cute. Just thinking about those days that are so gone so depresses me. Everything depresses me today. Especially my own life. The only cure is a drive out to the beach.

They say Sweet Valley is only fifteen minutes to the shore, but that's on those rare days when for some inexplicable reason, there's no traffic. Fortunately, today is one of the good days.

It is, in fact, a gorgeous, sunny day. Well, it is Southern California, but still it's especially clear today. And it's especially nice to be out of contact. I left my cell phone at the house. It's probably the first time in months that I have been totally unreachable, completely free. Textless. Even Regan can't find me. No one can find me. But then, who would want to find me?

That thought almost wipes out the sunshine and puts me back into the funk.

I make it to the beach in less than twenty minutes, and it looks almost empty. Lots of parking.

A nice walk along the beach will cure everything, right? Not my problems. But it's nice to take off my shoes and toe kick the sand down to the water's edge. But not in the water. It's always too cold in California. Like you got all those miles of gorgeous beaches and you didn't really want to go in. Even in the summertime.

I'm not three minutes into my cure when I see a familiar figure about a hundred feet away. It's a body I would know anywhere, even from the back: broad shoulders, neat waist, good legs. So many men have spindly legs, but not him. And they're in great shape and not too hairy. In fact, he's an absolute hunk, even if he is my brother.

Maybe he's just the right person to cheer me up today. Oh, God, no. He's with Lila. Not that I can see her; Steven's body is blocking her, but I see the way his hands are resting on her shoulders, then drop down, caressing her arms. Of course it's Lila. Thanks to Caroline, it isn't like it's really a secret. Besides, of all people they can trust, I'm the one: his sister and Lila's best friend.

I so need the company. I start walking down the beach toward them, but neither of them sees me. When I'm about twenty feet away, they turn.

It is Steven, but it isn't Lila.

I'm stunned. It can't be! It's not possible! Not Steven!

I read his face. He's as stunned as I am. And then there's a flash of disappointment. I'm not Elizabeth.

No one moves. Not me, not Steven, and not Aaron Dallas. In fact, Steven's hand is still on Aaron's arm.

Now, as if he's touched a hot stove, Steven jerks away and drops his hand to his side. He stares at me.

Aaron's expression is harder to figure. There's like shock, mixed with belligerency. Like, so what are you going to do about it?

A million thoughts shoot through my mind, all the way from Steven's gay? to Maybe it's not Steven. Only the first is right.

Before I can say anything, Steven says, "Now you know."

My mouth is open but no words are coming out.

"So what are you going to do?" Steven asks.

"Nothing, I mean . . . nothing . . ." I say, finally finding my voice. But it isn't even really mine; it's a squeaky sound about two octaves higher than my real voice.

"Yeah, I believe that," says Aaron. He turns and walks back to their towels. I never liked him, and I really don't now. I remember him from high school—sort of slight build, cocaptain of the soccer team and I used to think, a nice guy. Until his parents divorced. Then he just lost it. Now I think maybe it had more to do with his sexuality than the divorce.

He still looks very young, like a kid, except for his eyes. Like too much experience. And maybe too much of it bad.

"How come you didn't tell me? What about Cara? Are you going to tell her?" I ask.

"Look, I don't want to talk about this now. And I don't want you to, either." Steven's agony is all over his body, from his hunched shoulders to his twisted mouth; it's obvious that he's in great pain. "Why couldn't you have been Elizabeth?" he says.

"Wow, that really sucks. You think Elizabeth wouldn't be as shocked? You could have told us. I mean, we're your sisters . . . unless, unless you already told Elizabeth. You did, didn't you?"

"No one knows."

"I don't believe you."

"It's true, Jess. No one knows."

"Not Cara?"

"I'm just finding out myself."

The way Steven says that touches me. He's my brother and I love him, even though we don't always get along. He's always very partial to Elizabeth, but I'm the one he should be confiding in now. I'm the one who really understands that world. Like I lived with this gay guy for practically my whole sophomore year and we got on great. We were really close. Elizabeth barely knew Neil.

"Hey, it's okay, Steven. Don't worry. I'm not going to say anything. I wouldn't. You're my brother and I love you."

"Thanks, Jess."

"What about Elizabeth? Should I say something?"

"I'll do it."

Then I nod slightly toward Aaron, who's sitting on the towel now purposely not looking in our direction. I lower my voice.

"I know he was a great soccer player, but I never thought he was that cute, even in high school. I mean, you know he's got one brown eye and one blue eye and he's never—"

"Jessica!" Steven says, cutting me off.

I'm not going to stand here and have this kind of argument in front of Aaron. "Look, so I'll see you later. Right?"

"Later."

I turn and start to walk away, then I turn back again and give a sort of wave to Aaron, who's like deliberately not looking in my direction.

I keep walking.

⟨⟩

Steven just stood there, rigid, his toes biting into the sand, watching the wrong sister walk away down the beach, probably taking his life—at least the one he'd had up till now—with her.

The upheaval of the last two months had been the most exciting, terrifying, unhappy, and happy time in his life.

In that time he had tried to put as much of his life up to scrutiny as objectively as possible. Things like the ease and pleasure he'd always felt hanging out with other guys. It was simple to take the bite out of that by telling himself that it was only for the feeling of friendship and camaraderie without the pressure a girl would bring.

He'd had best friends growing up, guys he was really close to, and a couple of them he could honestly say he loved, but not like the love he'd felt for Tricia Martin. And if he got aroused in the showers at the gym, well, so did other guys. He had worried sometimes about his sexuality, but then he'd read that around puberty, and even into their teens, a lot of guys worried. And when Tricia came along, he was able to put that worry away. And it stayed away even into his relationship with Cara.

Then, two months ago, he ran into Aaron Dallas. He hadn't seen him in almost ten years.

After graduating from Sweet Valley, Aaron had gone to Stanford to study architecture and had stayed in San Francisco until recently.

He remembered always liking Aaron, but Steven's being a year ahead made a big difference, so they were never close friends. He would run into him at school. In fact, sometimes maybe even go out of his way to see him and say hello, maybe even hang out a little. He liked him that much. There was just something about his personality that appealed to Steven. Additionally, he had a terrific sense of humor and could crack everybody up. His looks were okay, nothing special, but he did have a good body from playing soccer, and Steven could see why girls liked him. And he looked like he liked them, too.

And that's the way he remembered Aaron until two months ago when he ran into him outside a Starbucks in the mall. At first he was shocked to see him in Sweet Valley after all this time, and then delighted. Actually, it was exciting, and Aaron seemed to feel the same way. Like two old friends meeting up again after too many years.

They'd gone into a bar and hung out over a couple of beers for almost three hours. He couldn't even say what they talked about beyond a lot of reminiscing and catching up on what they were doing now. Aaron was an architect and he'd come back to work for his uncle, who had a very successful architecture firm about a half hour outside of Sweet Valley. In fact, Steven's firm had done some business with them recently.

They could have gone on talking for even longer, but Steven

had a meeting back at the office and he was already fifteen minutes late. They made plans to meet again the following Tuesday.

The office meeting had already started by the time Steven
arrived. It went on for at least an hour and Steven contributed
nothing; his mind was still in that bar with Aaron.

In the days that followed he found that he couldn't wait to
see Aaron again, and on some pretext about having to meet a client the next Tuesday, he was able to move their appointment up
to Friday of that very week. At that point he had no idea that
Aaron was gay, at least not consciously so, because Aaron hadn't
mentioned more than that he wasn't married.

The next time they met, Aaron told him. Steven was uncomfortable with the information, but he was able to rationalize
it: So what, he can't have a gay friend? Hell, it's the twenty-first
century, he can have any kind of friend he wants.

And they arranged to meet again.

At home with Cara, he only mentioned running into Aaron
that first time. He felt a little guilty not telling her more. He could
have; after all, Aaron was just an old friend. And she remembered
him. But he didn't tell her. And he didn't tell her Aaron was gay.

The third time they met was different.

*The meeting is at five at the same bar as last time. I can barely wait
in my office. I keep watching the clock, willing it to drag itself
past two and then three and finally at ten after four I shove whatever's on
my desk into the drawer, tell my secretary I have an appointment and*

won't be back today. There must be something weird about my expression because he gives me a questioning look, waiting for more explanation since he doesn't have any appointment in his book. I don't even try, I just say, "See you tomorrow," and leave.

I'm fifty minutes early and he's ten minutes late. The anticipation is surprising me. It's ridiculous, but I can't wait to see the guy. Every time the door opens, I get a kind of rush of excitement. No matter how I rationalize I know it's beyond what you're supposed to feel for a new friend. But that's the way it is.

And then, at ten after five, he arrives. And he looks good, sort of casual elegant, khaki jacket, beige T-shirt and chinos, like you would see in some men's magazine. Right away, I feel stodgy in my charcoal lawyer suit and, of all the square things, a red tie.

Stodgy and very straight. Okay, so I'm worrying for nothing.

"Sorry," he says, sliding onto the next stool. "At the last minute a client called."

"The one with the lake house?"

"You remembered."

"Of course, it sounded great."

"Would you like to see the plans? I brought them." He opens his attaché case and takes out some folded papers.

"Absolutely."

He unfolds them and we lean in together, our heads almost touching. Close enough so that the plans fuzz into a haze and all I'm aware of is his face next to mine. There's a light aroma of aftershave, more than just left over from the morning. He put it on for me.

I force myself to pull back.

Aaron turns to me, his look a cross between confused and hurt.

"Sorry," I say, "I just need better light."

But I can see he knows that's not the problem. He folds his plans and slips them back in the case.

"Enough beer," I say. "Let's have a drink."

"I'm okay," he says, but I can tell he's uncomfortable.

I have a martini and he has another beer. Mostly we're just staring at the mirror behind the bar, pretending to be relaxed. And we don't say a lot.

Even though we're quiet, I like being with this guy. And I don't want it to end.

I don't want to go home. Not to my house, anyway.

I'm done for.

Just using that expression in my head almost makes me smile. Like dialogue from an old movie. But it's the truth. I'm at the edge of a line. I don't know what's on the other side, but I want to cross it. And it's not the martini.

I can't ever remember wanting something, someone, so much. Not even Tricia.

Aaron must feel what's happening. He looks at me and says, "Let's go."

He pays the tab and we leave. Even the fifteen-minute drive to his house feels too long. Too dangerous. If whatever urge I feel now deserts me, how will I get out of this? It's all too crazy. Too fast. Not fast enough.

I watch the familiar streets of Sweet Valley, the town that holds my whole life, pass by and disappear behind me.

What's happening to me? The only life I know just got swooped out from under me and I'm letting it go. Is it just for the sex or for a truth I've never allowed?

I'm going to land on foreign territory where I don't even know how anything works. I'm a lawyer; I need to know the rules.

Damn it! I'm touching thirty and I'm married. Do I just throw it all away? Or maybe I can hang on to it? Cara loves me. Just thinking her name now is too painful; the guilt is almost crippling. I can't do that now. Right now, it's my own survival.

But if, somehow, even if I was able to keep the life I have now, do I really want it?

Aaron is at the wheel. The air conditioner is on full blast and I'm sweating. Sweating enough so that the drops run down the sides of my face.

They're not tears, but they could be.

I walk down the beach toward my car, it's like I'm no longer depressed and actually not even thinking about myself.

I'm thinking about Steven and how I can help him. I'm the only one who knows and he so needs me now. I'm not going to tell Elizabeth. Not because Steven asked me not to, but because I like being the only one who knows. It's always been Elizabeth, and when it comes to Steven like I always feel shut out. Even though I love my brother as much as Elizabeth does, he never confides in me. But this time I'm the confidant, the close one, the intimate. I feel like I love him more than I ever did. And because I'm the only one who knows, he so needs me now.

My heart goes out to him. Imagine having such a secret and not being able to live your life the way you want to. That's really wrong. If he's gay, and he must be, like he should come out. You only have one life, right?

That's when I know what I have to do. For Steven and for Cara.

But it has to be done with kindness and love. It's hard news, and it takes a lot of courage to tackle it.

Poor Cara. She was a math whiz in college, even got accepted to a graduate program at MIT. Everyone thought she would be a professor at least, but she gave it all up when Steven decided to go to law school in L.A. She stayed with him and, as far as I know, she never even talked about what could have been. In fact, she talks very little. At one time Cara was very personable, but over the years she seems to have lost all her confidence.

Okay, I'm not like Elizabeth, who really loves Cara. I never had much patience with weakness. Even before, when I thought it was Lila and Steven, I felt Cara should know the truth. It's wrong that everyone else knows and not the person herself. If people think they're being kind, they're wrong. They're just making a fool of her.

If it were Regan, now, I would damn well want to know. And I would hate anyone, especially a friend or a relative, who knew and didn't tell me.

It's different with Todd and me. No one knows about us, so they can't be talking. Plus, it was so long ago and so over.

It's weird, but I actually feel something like love for Cara now. And I know that whatever I do will be with love. I'll do it the way Elizabeth would.

I'm going to help them. Maybe, in some strange way, I don't know how, it will help me.

Obviously, Steven doesn't have the courage. Well, the selfish twin is about to do something caring and entirely unselfish. It's pretty much going to be kill the messenger, but I have to do it.

Cara might be grateful in the long run, and Steven, too, but right now not. Still, it's the only way to free my brother. And I do love him dearly.

Elizabeth would make this sacrifice.

Before I lose my courage, I drive straight to the Heights, but not to Elizabeth's house. Instead, I turn right onto the next street and park in front of Steven's house, which is very much like every other house in the Heights. It's like they made up the word *modest* just to describe these houses with their neat little squares of grass in the front. They're just like the little box houses I used to draw as a kid. I never want to live here.

The minute I get out of the car, I can smell the heavenly odor of caramelized something. Lately everything Cara bakes seems to be caramelized. There's no going into a kitchen without caramelizing. Whatever this is, its fabulous aroma is wafting through the open windows. Of course, it doesn't take a psychiatrist to know that her constant baking is like only a compensation for her marriage problems, but as compensations go, it's a pretty useful one. Luckily for everyone around, she's talented. The amazing thing is that the aggravation must counterbalance the extra calories, because Cara stays perfectly slim. In fact, she looks almost exactly like she did in high school. Stick-straight dark brown hair that she wears in the same style, cut just below the ears. A little makeup around the eyes would highlight the deep brown. I suggested it once, but she never did it.

For a split second, when Cara opens the door, her face lights up. Then she realizes I'm not Elizabeth.

"Hi, Jess. Come on in." Cara never has any trouble telling us apart. For her we're night and day. And I'm like not day.

"Hey. Steven's not home, right?"

"No. He had a meeting with some clients."

"On Saturday?"

"Yes, they were from L.A. and only in for the day. Was there anything special you wanted him for, 'cause he didn't think he'd be home until at least five."

"That's okay. I really came to see you."

For an instant, Cara looks puzzled. I don't normally visit her. I can see that she's thinking, Can't be good.

"Would you like a piece of pear tart? It's still warm."

"Sure." I pick up on a slight waver in her voice. Maybe she knows more than she lets on. If she does know, she probably needs a confidant. Why does it always have to be Elizabeth?

Well, not this time.

I pull out a kitchen chair and sit down in front of the triangle of tart Cara has cut for me. I put my fork into the crispy crust, which flakes off almost on contact. One taste of the juicy pear under the thin, transparent, caramelized shell and I can almost forgive Cara her weakness. Like everything Cara bakes, it's divine. Knowing the truth could kill the baking. It's a risk, but I feel it's my duty.

I soften my voice just a touch to capture a little intimacy, and in my kindest sister-in-law voice, shades of Elizabeth, I say, "Looks to me like Steven works a lot on the weekends lately, huh?"

"Yes, well, he's trying very hard to make partner, and I guess that's what they expect, you know, to be on call all the time. It's okay, really, 'cause if he wasn't doing that today, he'd probably be playing golf."

"Since when does Steven play golf?"

"Actually, it's only been a couple of months, but he loves it. Can't get enough." Something about the look on my face must make Cara uneasy and she tries to like change the subject.

"Would you like another piece? It's a new recipe I'm trying. What do you think of it?"

"It's okay with you that he's away so much on the weekends?" I don't let it go, but I do take another piece of tart.

Cara slices the tart with more force than it needs. A sliver jumps up and lands on my lap.

"I wouldn't like it," I say. It's like she sent that piece flying on purpose. I struggle to keep my tone comforting and still flick the piece of crust onto the floor.

And she may have. I know she's not crazy about me, but my decision is right. And someday they'll thank me, but right now Cara doesn't look like she would thank me for anything.

"Cara, you know how much I care for you. . . ."

And I can see by Cara's expression that she's steeling herself.

With the mouthwatering aroma of caramel still hanging in the air, I begin my mission. I feel my words cutting into the sweetness and turning the kitchen sour, then rancid with the bitterness of unasked-for truth, but a hero doesn't stop just because it's uncomfortable.

10

New York

For the first time since she'd started covering Will's play, Elizabeth didn't hide in the back of the theater. She chose a seat a couple of rows discreetly back from the power group but not out of sight.

The houselights were on, and she could see Ross, the director, talking to one of the actors. The producers were in their usual seats. The only one missing was the playwright. Elizabeth was worried for Will. He was her friend now, and she didn't want to see him crushed by Ross, who kept turning toward the back of the theater, obviously looking for his victim.

Will arrived and strode down the aisle. Didn't walk. Strode, head held high, looking every bit the conqueror. Elizabeth held her breath for him.

It was going to be even more horrendous than she'd thought. Like big bullmoose charging with their antlers.

But it wasn't. Everyone turned to greet Will, even Ross, with smiles. And as he passed Elizabeth, he gave her a small wave. She couldn't imagine what had happened to change everything so radically.

Had she been more experienced in the theater, she'd have known that arguments rarely lasted more than one *Fuck you!* Shakespeare was right; the play's the thing and everything else gets either eaten or put aside. No grudges. Unless the show flops. Then it's out-and-out hate forever. Or until you have to work with the same people again.

Bala, all Texas charm, had educated Will that very morning. He even had a pad with him to take notes.

The rehearsal went smoothly, and Luke Billen, the actor playing Samuel Johnson, read his line exactly as Will had wanted.

At twelve thirty they broke for lunch and Elizabeth and Will went across the street to the Wicked Teapot for their interview.

"I'm not going to ask you what magical thing happened to make everything perfect today," said Elizabeth once they had settled at a quiet table in the back. Liam wasn't there, but he had arranged the reservation. "But what happened?"

"I had breakfast with Bala this morning and we talked about Ross. He's very enthusiastic about the show. And he's good. She explained the purpose of the arrangement. There's no way he gets things done if he's not in total control. It makes sense, and for the most part we agree. If we don't, I give him a note. Obviously he talked to Luke because Luke read the line perfectly today."

"You mean there aren't going to be any of those famous *Fuck yous*?"

"Are you kidding? Even in summer stock in Chicago we had them. Just be patient. I guarantee it won't take long."

They ordered lunch. Elizabeth was feeling happy. Well, maybe that word was a little strong, but maybe not. It had been so long since she'd felt plain, uncomplicated happiness that she had forgotten what it was like. This Will guy had definite possibilities.

"I was thinking about your little scene," she said, when their sandwiches came. "You know the one where I bring Liam to my grandmother's party."

"It's yours. You can use it in your next novel."

"How about next week?"

"I hope you're kidding."

Suddenly, Elizabeth felt uncomfortable. She had to explain that it wasn't like it sounded.

"You're bringing Liam to your grandmother's party to seduce your sister, right?" said Will.

"No. I'm bringing him because I don't want to go alone and Liam happens to come from L.A. and he's planning to visit his parents."

"And . . ."

"I suggested he come with me as my friend. Since he was going there anyway. Or almost there. Sweet Valley is only a little more than an hour away."

Will shook his head. "Bad idea."

"The way you put it, it's a bad idea, but that's not the way I meant it."

"Whatever you meant, you're testing your sister and setting her up to fail. You know her better than anyone. You know she will fail. You're using your twin knowledge for evil. It's more than dishonorable. It's sleazy. It really sucks."

"Hey! Wait up! I told you it's not like that at all. I just don't want to go alone! And I have no one else to ask. Not being alone, that's all it's about." And at that moment, that was what it was about, feeling sorry for herself and needing someone to understand that. "How about a little understanding for me?"

"Hey, Elizabeth, I do understand. That's the problem. You may be fooling yourself, but you're not fooling me. This is your revenge, your way of getting between them. And it's cruel. Big-time."

"And you're the expert on cruel, aren't you? I suppose Wendy would attest to that, you walking out like that and not giving any decent reason," Elizabeth said, stuffing her notebook into her purse.

"You don't have to be an expert to see this one," Will said. "It's horrendous!"

Elizabeth stood, shoved her chair out, grabbed her purse and, leaning into his face, said more in a hiss than a whisper, "Fuck you!"

Then, standing up straight, and with a smile of fury, she announced, "You were right; it didn't take that long!"

With that she stormed out of the bar.

She wasn't home ten minutes when her cell rang. She was still fuming from her encounter with Will and wasn't going to answer it until she saw it was her best friend, probably the only other person she would want to talk to.

Maybe she wouldn't tell him the whole story, but just hearing his voice would calm her enough.

"Bruce," she said, putting the phone to her ear. And smiling. He could do that for her.

"You got me. I sent you a text about an hour ago."

"I had it turned off. We were in rehearsal."

"How's it going?"

"Good. I think. You get too close when you see the same scenes over and over again. And out of context, too. I can't tell anymore. Though the feeling seems to be up."

"Are you coming for your grandmother's dinner?"

"How did you know?"

"Your mom called to invite me. I'm your surprise date."

"Oh, no."

"Am I that bad?"

"She should have said something. I invited someone already."

"Who?" There was no fun in his voice.

"Oh, just someone I know."

There was a long pause, and then Bruce said, "Someone you're dating?"

"No, not really." This was a conversation Elizabeth really didn't want to have.

But Bruce was not going to let it go. He was sounding unusually proprietary, even a little sharp. "What do you mean, 'not really'? Is this some guy you've been seeing?"

"It's a long story." Elizabeth was more than reluctant. She was desperate for a way out.

He didn't give it to her. "I got time."

"But I don't. Sorry, but I'm already late." It was rare that she and Bruce had this kind of conversation. They were close, but this was over the line. This was strange and not something Elizabeth could handle now.

"Sure," he said. "Whatever. Talk to you later."

And he hung up.

Bruce had never hung up on Elizabeth before. She didn't know what to do. If she called him back they would have to talk about what was really happening. Liam. She couldn't do that. Embarrassment? Discomfort? Awkwardness? All those paling by comparison to the real one, shame.

On the other end of the line, the guy who hung up was beside himself. He was sitting in his house on the outskirts of Sweet Valley. Not a Heights split-level, or anything like that, but an architecturally bold interpretation of a Richard Meier design set on two acres of wooded land about twenty minutes outside Sweet Valley.

Bruce Patman was unusual, rich with taste. But right now it all looked like shit to him. The most important thing in his life, his friendship with Elizabeth Wakefield, was threatened.

Friendship was a totally inadequate description he was stuck with, had been for too many years now. It worked for Elizabeth, who had always been so blindly in love with Todd she never noticed anyone else.

Why fight a losing battle? he'd asked himself so many times over the last few years. Never with a good answer. The only answer that seemed to make any sense was that maybe he didn't have a choice.

But now? Now things were different. Todd was out of her life. And he was still stuck being Number One Friend.

He'd missed his chance.

In high school he was usually paired with Jessica. They seemed like the same type. And in those years he was completely solipsistic, spoiled by the attention that everyone, especially girls, gave him. By high school standards, he had it all: the best car, the best house, and he was no dummy, he knew he was pretty good-looking, too.

Girls were just conquests to him, until Regina Morrow. It was different with her. He fell in love for the first time. But he wasn't ready for that kind of exclusive love, and he screwed up. He hadn't lost the habit of other girls, and she found out. He never got a second chance. She went to that party with the drugs, tried some cocaine, and it killed her. After that he was even worse. Nobody meant anything to him.

His parents wanted him to go east to school. His mother had graduated from Brown and Bruce was smart enough to have gotten in. All he had to do was concentrate a little more on his schoolwork, but it didn't fit into his schedule. In the end, he didn't even apply. Sweet Valley University was good enough for him. He knew he could coast right through still safely being Bruce Patman.

And that's just what he did until his last year in college, and the car accident. His mother was killed instantly, but his father survived for six days in a coma, and then there was no choice but to follow his living will and take him off life support.

It was in those endless hours in the chill of the hospital waiting room, waiting for the miracle that didn't come, that Bruce's life changed. He let the change in. It was almost overnight. When he came out of the grieving, he knew he was different. Those same people he had known all his life, those people he had locked into the most superficial categories, mostly by appearance alone, suddenly became people of kindness and caring. He looked at them in amazement, having never really seen who they were before. They came to the hospital to sit with him for hours. Especially one.

$$\smile$$

It's almost a hundred degrees outside, and I'm freezing here in the waiting room. I haven't worn socks in years, but I learned the first day that after about two hours at hospital temperature, your feet freeze. It's not my look, but I wear them.

It's not even nine in the morning and the hospital is quiet. The waiting room is empty. I bring the *L.A. Times* and a couple of books with me. I bring them every day, but I don't read them. I don't even look at the paper.

I just wait.

He's still in a coma. Some of the time I sit in his room, but when they do some of their procedures they ask me to wait out here.

"Bruce? Hi."

I don't even hear her come in. It's one of the Wakefield twins. Of course, it's Elizabeth. I can't picture Jessica waiting around a hospital. But actually, I've always seen a physical difference. There's a calmness and gentleness about Elizabeth that's right there in her face. Mostly in her eyes.

"Hey." I smile a kind of welcome.

She hands me a coffee. "I have milk and sugar if you like."

"Thanks, but I take it black."

"How is he doing? Any change?"

I shake my head.

She sits down next to me on the plastic couch and we drink our coffee. Every once in a while she smiles at me. After we finish our coffee, she takes the empty containers and puts them in the wastebasket. Then she comes back and sits with me.

We don't even talk and it feels comfortable.

At some point the doctor comes in and tells me the same thing he told me yesterday: They don't know. He's not responding. All we can do is wait.

Then the doctor leaves and I feel Elizabeth take my hand. Hers feels surprisingly strong for such a small, soft hand. The hospital goes on as usual, nurses and staff passing back and forth. I sit there with Elizabeth. I don't know what we are saying or even if we talk at all, but I feel a deep comfort. When she leaves, I'm adrift.

She comes every day, and I wait for her. But it's a different wait. When I see her coming from the elevator my heart starts to speed up and I feel my breath coming in shallow gasps. Like a heart attack, the love kind.

I wait for him and I wait for her.

Then it's over. We get through the funeral and then on with our lives.

I'm better now, able to control the physical symptoms, but the ache for her is still there, the longing and the love. It's more than five years now. It has only grown stronger.

Around the same time Bruce was falling in love with Elizabeth, and she was loving Todd, something was happening with Todd. Bruce knew the something wasn't Elizabeth.

He didn't know it was Jessica. Not then.

But he knew something was up, because at the time, he and Todd and Winston were fairly close. It wasn't difficult to recognize the signs in Todd. All he had to do was think of himself with Elizabeth. He and Todd were in a lot of the same classes and spent time together, but it was very superficial. Neither was really there, at least not emotionally. Both were caught in a secret passion, a passion that totally consumed them.

Then one afternoon, taking a shortcut back from the Porsche garage, he stopped at a crummy diner outside of Sweet Valley and accidentally walked in on Todd and Jessica. One look and Bruce knew Todd's secret. He could see it from the doorway and was nice enough not to go in.

More than five years had passed, but Bruce remembered how he struggled with the secret, the one that could have given him a distinct advantage but would hurt the woman he loved.

⌒

Hurt is an understatement, destroy is probably closer. So far, I've resisted, sparing Elizabeth.

I even try to talk Elizabeth out of having Jessica stay with her when she comes back from France, but since I can't tell her the truth, my arguments are too weak to keep her from helping her sister. Just like in high school, Elizabeth would probably never believe anything against Jessica anyway. Without the truth there is no other way I can keep her from helping her twin.

But I know I have to tell her before it's too late, before she and Todd set a date. It's a long shot, but if I don't go for it right now, there might never be another chance. But telling her isn't enough. I have to find a way to show her.

I'm a guy who pretty much always gets what he wants. And I've never wanted anything the way I want Elizabeth. I'm not going to break that winning streak, no matter what I have to do.

Hey, the old Bruce wouldn't have let it happen. Maybe that's what I have to do: Call on the old Bruce, the no-limits guy, the Bruce who doesn't lose.

It's been a long time, but when you want something badly enough, the way I want Elizabeth, you can't always play by the books. All's fair and all that sort of thing.

I haven't been thinking like the old Bruce for a long time now. It's strange how powerful it feels. And how easily it comes. Maybe it wasn't so smart to change. After all, I'm not an asshole like Winston. Or am I?

What can I do? Trick her? Find some underhanded way to steal her from Todd? The guy she loves isn't worthy of her; he betrayed her with her own sister. It's so easy. I don't even have to lie. I could even do it so that she doesn't know where it came from.

No good. How can I even think of playing those despicable games with the woman I love? Either I win her fair and square or I lose her forever.

Forget it. I can't lose her.

Then she gives me the opportunity.

It's late afternoon, about six thirty, and I'm browsing through Facebook pictures when the phone rings.

"Hey, Bruce."

Her voice is enough to make me tremble. Lucky no one can see.

"Hi, Lizzie, what's up?"

"You're amazing. You're one of the few people outside of my parents who can always tell us apart on the phone. You can, can't you?"

"Absolutely. What's up?" I struggle to keep the happiness out of my voice. Whatever she wants, I'm ready to do.

"I'm living with a house of deadbeats. He's working or not working on whatever in his office. And my sister is sulking in her room. Probably a Regan thing. I have to get out of here. I need action, best friend. How about a pizza or a drink or anything that's not here?"

"I'll pick you up in twenty minutes. How's that?"

"Perfect," she says. "I'll be outside."

She's waiting at the end of her driveway when I pull up. First sight of her is always overwhelming. She's in a haze like a painting. Exquisite. A Monet. Sometimes I'm so hopeless about her, it makes me laugh at myself. Imagine when technology finds a way to read your mind. No one will ever be able to leave the house.

I'm in my black Porsche convertible, the last vestige of the old Bruce that I can't give up. And what a great vestige it is: sleek and shiny outside with a polished wooden dashboard and soft beige suede upholstery, beautiful enough to be living room furniture.

Years ago Elizabeth would make fun of this extravagance and consider it pretentious and irritating. Now she sees it as the ordinary car craze of a best friend. A guy who's always there for her, so now she humors me.

"Wanna lift, girlie?" I lean over and give her an exaggerated wink and leer as I shove open the passenger door.

"Desperately. Get me away from that house of misery." Elizabeth smiles, sliding into the front seat close enough to give me a kiss on the cheek. "Save me."

"What's happening?" I try to listen, but I'm still hooked on the smile.

"He's in the throes of a deadline, and she's just in the throes, and I'm not about to waste a gorgeous evening finding out why."

"Pizza?"

"And a dirty martini."

"You're on." I gun the motor and we shoot off in a roar just like the old Bruce. I like that it makes her laugh.

"So, what are you working on?" I ask, not at all like the old Bruce, who never would have been interested in Elizabeth or her work. She tells me about her assignment, a neighborhood up in arms about the construction of a new house taller than all the others. And how acrimonious it has become—even to the point of a mysterious sabotage of the construction site.

"I think there's a good story there, but nobody wants to talk to me," she says.

"Is that Louella Gatwick's house?"

"No. It's her niece, Ella. Do you know her?"

"I don't know Ella too well, but Louella's practically an aunt to me."

The only spot free is in front of the restaurant. I'm only half blocking the steps.

Elizabeth smiles the fabulous smile.

"What?"

"Not possible to change everything, especially when it comes to guys and their cars."

"Hey, you want me to call Louella? Maybe she can put in a word."

"I love you!"

If only.

She's thrilled, and she gives me a huge hug that catches me off guard. We bump noses and, I don't know, maybe too much shows on my face. Enough that she's momentarily taken aback and pulls away.

"Sorry, I got carried away," she says. "Did I hurt you?"

For a second I don't answer. Can't. She looks confused and then I recover.

"No. Hey, I love your enthusiasm. I'll call Louella first thing tomorrow."

We go into the restaurant, the same old place we've been going to for years, now called Napkin to keep up with the current fad of meaningless one-word names, but we always refer to it simply as Pizza. Though it's been renamed a half-dozen times, it's never been refurbished or even repainted. It's still one up from a dive, but it's loved by all Sweet Valleyites of a certain age. It was the special place where we all hung in high school.

No matter what time of day it is, the restaurant is always dark, giving it a slightly sexy, secret feel. Fortunate, too, because on the rare times when a little sunlight does slip in, you can't miss the tacky, none-too-clean look of the decorations—if you can call the yellowing artificial flowers on the tables, probably the same ones from my school days, and a string of equally grim lights circling the ceiling of the room, decoration.

Pizza, or Napkin, or whatever, has long since fallen out of favor with the current high school kids but is still a sentimental favorite of our guys. I've been with Elizabeth, sometimes with Todd, and dozens of other times, alone or with other friends, but it's different tonight. She doesn't know why, but I do.

As soon as we sit at our usual table and give our usual order, she goes right at me. "Something's wrong. What is it?"

We're old, good friends, the kind that don't have to work up to a big question; we just ask. And we're good enough friends so that if one doesn't want to answer, that's it. Topic dropped.

I'm not ready to answer.

The waitress brings Elizabeth her dirty martini and me a Bud, and we move on.

We spend a lot of time talking about Elizabeth's job. I give her some ideas about stories, but there's something different, and I think she feels it, too. I'm not good at hiding. Not something as big as this.

The pizzas come just as Robin Wilson, an old Sweet Valley High friend, walks in with Dan Kane, a lawyer I know from Steven Wakefield's office. He's slim but he's got that hidden threat of an incipient eater with the rounded cheeks and the beginnings of a small softness around his middle. He's a good guy.

Elizabeth tells me she remembers meeting him when she first went to work at the newspaper. She was covering a cocktail party to raise funds for some benefit, maybe saving greyhounds or something like that. She remembers Dan was more interested in the hors d'oeuvres than the dogs, or whatever the charity was.

They come over to the table and Robin starts to introduce Dan to Elizabeth when he stops her. "I know you," he says. "From where?"

"Greyhounds?"

"Right. The little shrimp hors d'oeuvres that had the crunchy stuff around them?"

Obviously the perfect date for Robin, who is deep into the catering business. A courageous choice for someone who fought her weight in high school.

Robin is a good friend and normally we would ask her to join us. Elizabeth is about to do just that, but she reads my face and doesn't say anything. Robin reads the silence and says, "Don't let the pizzas get cold. We'll be over at the bar. Catch you later."

As soon as they leave Elizabeth says, "Don't tell me nothing is wrong, because I can feel it." She is almost accusatory.

"I'm not ready to talk about it. Let's talk about you. What's happening with you and Todd?"

"Funny you ask now, because I think something is."

"Does it have to do with Jessica?"

"You mean because they don't get along so well? Actually, that's disturbing, but that's not it. It's about us."

Before I can contain it, the smallest, most fragile flicker of surprise leaks through. "You mean you and me?"

I can't believe I said that.

Elizabeth takes it as a joke. "Come on, I'm being serious. I mean Todd and me. I think we're ready."

"How come now?"

"It's only been forever. Don't you think it's time?"

"I don't know."

Suddenly Elizabeth picks up that we aren't talking about the same thing. "Okay, now tell me. What's really up? Something is wrong, I know it. Did I do something? It's been weird since you picked me up. I can feel it."

"Let's eat."

"Okay, if you don't want to . . ." Elizabeth says, sliding a piece of pizza onto my plate.

"Actually"—I push the plate away—"I'm not so hungry."

"This is girl trouble. I can recognize the signs. You have to tell me. Who is it?"

Elizabeth's certain she's hit it. She picks up a droopy slice of pizza and is about to take a bite when she changes her mind and puts it back on her plate.

"No, not a girl."

I don't say anything. Which feels more hostile than I want. She senses it, and for the first time since our friendship started, we're both a little uncomfortable.

"This isn't about Todd and me. This is about you. I'm your best friend; you have to tell me. I know I can help."

"Maybe I can help *you*."

I can see that's not the answer she was expecting. "I don't think I need help." Her response is defensive, with a touch of antagonism.

"Maybe not," I say. "I'll let you judge."

"Wow, I don't like this. What's going on, Bruce?"

Whatever arguments I have with myself have been decided, and there's no stopping me now. The only choice I have is how to do it.

Ultimately, the question is Am I doing it for her or for myself? If I'm doing it for myself I'll leave her no way out of the bitterness against the two people closest to her. She'll be shattered. But, of course, I'll be there to pick up the pieces.

Or I could tell her in a way that leaves room for forgiveness. It did happen a long time ago when we were all different people. I certainly was, and I could use that defense for Jessica and Todd as well.

Whichever I choose, silence is no longer a possibility.

"Maybe this isn't the place," I say. Maybe I'm losing some of my courage.

"Yes, it is." That line of steel inside Elizabeth always surprises me.

"Okay, then," I start, still not knowing which choice I'm making. But I don't get beyond those first two words before Ken Matthews bursts into the restaurant with enough force to send the door flying open and slamming behind him. It's such an urgent, noisy entrance that everyone turns. Ken looks around, sees us, and comes over in a half run.

"What happened?" Elizabeth jumps up from the table, instantly panicked. "Jessica!"

"No," Ken says. "No, it's Winston."

"Oh, no!" says Elizabeth, grabbing my arm for support. "An accident?"

"Is he okay?" I ask, covering Elizabeth's hand with mine and pulling her closer.

"No," says Ken.

"Oh, my God. He's in the hospital?"

"Winston is dead."

11
Sweet Valley

"I think your grandmother's marvelous." Aaron Dallas was making a mixed chopped salad, Steven's favorite, with iceberg lettuce, tomatoes, Vidalia onions, red peppers, and cucumber. "Turn around so I can put the anchovies in."

They were in temporary quarters, Aaron's one-bedroom apartment in downtown Sweet Valley. Steven had given Cara the house in the divorce.

Steven Wakefield was contentedly watching his partner of six months make dinner. It was crazy how much he loved him. Jessica was right, he wasn't the best-looking and he did have one blue eye and one brown one, but he had everything else—he was smart, funny, and he had a heart. And he wasn't a pushover. En plus about the sexiest man he'd ever seen. But, of course, Steven hadn't really been looking at men in any kind of sexual way, or if he had been, he didn't know it. Not until he met Aaron. Actually, remet him. They'd been in school together, but they were both very different people then. Neither of them understood how different they were.

"Light on the anchovies. You know I hate them. They have hair," Steven said. "So, go on. What about my marvelous grandmother?"

"You wouldn't even know they were there unless you saw me put them in. I make them into paste. It's just to flavor the dressing. How could you be married to Cara and still be so unadventurous about food? Worse than straight."

"Yeah, right. So back to my grandmother?"

"Nothing."

"Oh, beautiful. Is this going to be a Jessica thing?"

"Okay, I'm not saying I'm not going to the birthday dinner. I just want to make sure I'm not sitting next to my faux sister-in-law."

"Done."

"And I'm not crazy about him, either."

"Hey, I'll do my best, but it's a small dinner party. What are we? Counting Elizabeth—and I can't imagine she's really coming—eight or nine at the most. Even if you don't sit next to Todd or Jessica, they're not going to be very far away."

"He's hard to look at."

"Not really." Steven smiled.

"You think he's good-looking?"

"Right. Hey, I'm in love, not dead." Steven gave Aaron an affectionate guy tap on the shoulder. "What are you doing?"

"For that I'm throwing in another anchovy. A real hairy one."

Sometimes Steven was struck by how heterosexual his homosexuality was. He could have done this little riff with Cara easily. If he had loved her. But he didn't. Maybe hadn't ever. He had been doing what he was supposed to be doing. It was getting-married time.

Steven had been thinking about that day at the beach for the last eight months. What if Jessica hadn't found them? Would he have had the courage to declare himself?

Sometimes, way in the back of his mind, where he could almost hide it from himself, the other thought crept in. What would have happened if Jessica hadn't forced his hand?

In the better part of his mind, he believed he would have told Cara. It was just a matter of time.

"Maybe I'm not a whole lot different from Todd," Steven said.

"Yes, you are."

"How's that?"

"He's much better-looking."

But Steven knew he had betrayed Cara just as Todd had betrayed Elizabeth. The things you do for love. As if just admitting it could be an excuse. He remembered that horrendous day on the beach when Jessica found Aaron and him together. His first thought was Let it be Elizabeth. He knew he was never really fair with Jessica. She loved him, and in his brotherly fashion he loved her, but she was hard to take. If she weren't his sister, they would never be friends. Maybe it was the comparison with Elizabeth, who was so extraordinary. He guessed that was unfair. Still, what possessed her to tell Cara? He had exploded. As soon as he found out he went directly to Elizabeth's. He was raging.

I'm too furious to ring the bell, and I know they never lock the door, so I just throw it open and shout,

"Jessica! Where the hell are you! Get out here!"

I don't even wait for a response. I head right down the hall to her bedroom and shove the door open so hard it bounces off the wall. At the top of my lungs I shout, "How could you fuckin' do that to me!"

I think I would have leaped at her except I feel Todd holding me back. I didn't even see him come in the room. Now I'm straining to break his hold.

"Please Steven, I . . ." Jessica moves as far back as she can against the wall.

"Don't 'Please Steven' me. You're just a bitch. You know what you've done to Cara?"

"Me?" Jessica says, pulling up enough courage to defend herself. "How about you?"

"You promised you wouldn't say anything. I told you I was going to deal with it."

"Yeah, right. How long have you been waiting to 'deal with it'?"

"None of your goddamn business." I shake out of Todd's grip.

Todd, the extra person, just stands there, silently. I can see he doesn't know whether to stay or leave. Not trusting my restraint enough to leave, he settles for a compromise and moves into the doorway, technically out of the room.

Our shouts and accusations continue, and Jessica finds strength in her own righteousness, snapping at me, "Years?"

"Two months, if it means anything to you. And why it should I don't know. You have no right to destroy someone's life like you did this afternoon."

"You may not believe this, but I wanted to help you. Both of you."

"Yeah, like you've ever wanted to help anyone in your life but yourself. I always knew you were selfish, but I didn't know you were vicious." I push past Todd, on my way out of the room.

Then I stop and turn back.

"You're not my sister anymore. You're out of my life."

And I'm gone.

It's quiet behind me until Jessica lets out a terrible moan that goes right through my body. Then I hear the sobbing. But it's too late. I'm out and never coming back.

⌒

"Don't worry," Aaron said, pulling Steven back to the present. "It's your grandmother's birthday and I'm not going to make it difficult. I really do like her."

"Thanks."

The happy couple sat down to dinner. Steven made a quick search for the errant anchovy and, finding none, smiled, picked up his fork, and dug in.

Incredible how quickly they had metamorphosed to be like any good marriage.

Meanwhile, at Jessica and Todd's house, only minutes away, a similar situation was taking place.

Dinner.

Only instead of salad, it was Chinese takeout.

Jessica was not quite up to cooking. Alice had bought her a couple of basic cookbooks, but she hadn't yet gotten around to opening them. And Todd would never be up to cooking. The little bit of bartending and kitchen work he did when he briefly dropped out of school was enough for him. Lots of guys were into cooking, but as graceful as he had been on the basketball court, he was clumsy in the kitchen. On the rare times he did cook he left behind a festival of crumbs and drips and cabinets hanging wide open, waiting to whack the next person who walked in. The fact that he really did like takeout made Jessica's life home cooking–free.

It should have been a nice night at home, but Todd couldn't shake the uncomfortable feeling left over from his run with Ken this morning. How were they ever going to move on when everything around them stayed the same? That was the conundrum. The very beauty of small-town life was that you could count on things not changing—good things like security, warmth and friendliness and happy memories that would always be there every place you looked, and there were no unfamiliar roads to get lost on.

Maybe you sacrificed adventure and the excitement of the new, but even in familiar territory, there would be new. He and Jessica would be new; they'd be newly married then new parents, lots of new things in their lives.

Of course, nothing is perfect, but the good of Sweet Valley life far outweighed the bad, and Freud said the mind represses bad memories. Todd was counting on that.

All this was going on in Todd's mind, and Jessica could almost read it. It was easy, because it was always the same.

Maybe she was wrong to insist they stay. It had cost them so much already. Elizabeth was the greatest loss for both of them, and Jessica's relationship with Steven had been badly damaged.

She'd tried to help, to do what she thought Elizabeth would have done, but she could see now that telling Cara had been a mistake. Jessica would never be Elizabeth. And Steven was out-of-his-mind furious with her. He didn't understand that she was only trying to help him. She loved him. She wanted to free him.

She remembered how he shouted at her, calling her a selfish bitch, telling her she was out of his life forever, and storming out of the house.

⸻

I stand there, stunned; I can't move. He's so wrong. He doesn't understand. I bury my face in my hands and the tears come and I hear myself sobbing. My whole body is shaking. What have I done?

When I look up, Todd is there. He's standing in the doorway watching me. I think he's going to leave, but he doesn't. Instead he comes toward me. I feel his arms around me. And I fall into him.

"It'll be okay. Whatever it is, he didn't mean it. Please, stop crying."

I can't. And it isn't what Steven said, it isn't what anyone said, it's the feel of Todd's arms around me, the length of his body pressed against me. All the longings of five years are answered. And I know from the strength of his arms locking around me and the heat of his body against mine that he's lost, too.

All my good sense and fairness and even honor, 'cause I have honor, are way out of reach. All I feel is passion, that same wild passion that I felt five years ago. It's all back. I'm out of control. And so is he. And we kiss and it's so deep and I need it so badly. . . .

But I can't! I lean my face away from him. I'm still in his arms.

"Oh, my God!" It's not my scream. It's Elizabeth's. She's standing in the doorway.

Todd and I look at each other in horror, too shocked to let go.

"Oh, no! This is a nightmare!" Elizabeth puts her hands to her face and sobs.

Now we turn and I see Bruce standing behind her, just watching.

I don't know what to do, and then I do what I have to do: I rush over to my sister.

"Lizzie, Lizzie, this is so terrible. I can't believe it's happening!"

Elizabeth takes her hands from her face, all shiny with tears, and stands there shaking her head, whispering over and over again, "No, no."

I turn to Todd, hoping for help, but he's still frozen to the spot, watching my sister's agony.

"What can I do? What can I say?" I put my arms out, but I can't bring myself to touch her.

"There's nothing to be said, is there?"

"No," I say. "Nothing."

"Ken found us at Pizza and told us."

I don't hear her right.

Behind me I feel Todd move and then come over to Elizabeth.

"Ken?" he says.

I don't know what they're talking about.

"The housekeeper found Winston and went running over to Ken's house. She's the one who called the police."

"Winston?" It's something with Winston. It's not us. I don't dare look at Todd. Or Bruce.

"Can you believe it? He's dead. Winston is dead!"

A minute ago I'd lost everything, and now I have a reprieve. Winston's death. Death trumps betrayal. How disgusting am I?

"I still can't believe it," I say.

Yes, I'm fast on my feet. I have to save us. For now, anyway.

"How did it happen?" Todd asks.

"Nobody knows for sure. It looks like he fell off the balcony."

"Wow, that's a good twenty feet," he says.

He's with me. We're like criminals.

"What do you mean, it looks like he fell?" I really want to know. It's all so weird. For a second it's like nothing happened before. Except when I catch Bruce's eyes, I don't like the look.

"Of course he fell," Elizabeth says, and I can see she's a little impatient with me. "But they don't know. I mean, it could have been one of those silent heart attacks or something. Who told you, anyway?"

"Out in the street," I say. "Everyone knows."

"It has to be Caroline." Elizabeth turns to Bruce. "Don't you think?"

Bruce nods in agreement, but he doesn't answer. He just watches us. Not good.

Elizabeth puts her arms out and we both, Todd and I, go to her.

I see Bruce leave.

"How about we catch a movie?" Now Todd was worrying about Jessica, pulling her out of the bad thoughts he knew she was having. They took turns worrying about each other.

"Sure," she said. "Whatever you want."

12
Sweet Valley

Liam had left for Los Angeles a couple of days earlier to see his parents. He and Elizabeth planned to meet up the afternoon of the party at LAX airport in Los Angeles and drive down to Sweet Valley together.

Elizabeth's plane was arriving at three thirty, which would leave enough time, even with delays, to change clothes in the ladies' room, drive down, and be at the club by seven for the dinner. Elizabeth had planned it so she and Liam would arrive after everyone else. Her parents knew she was coming, but she had asked them not to say anything to spoil the surprise for her grandmother, not to mention her sister and Todd.

This was all very devious for Elizabeth, but the circumstances called for taking any advantage she could get. After eight months and all that had happened it was beyond difficult.

Her parents wanted her to come enough that they agreed to keep her secret from Jessica, at least until the day of the party.

The six-hour plane trip passed quickly, so absorbed was Elizabeth in how she was going to handle everything from the trivial—her entrance—to the stomach-turning first sight of her loathsome betrayers. Eight months she'd spent with a wound that would never close, not even with the power of anger or revenge. Now she would see them for the first time since that day when the two people she loved most in the world had decimated her life.

How perfectly they had carried it off. Even at Winston's funeral. She remembered every moment of it.

he day of the funeral is gray and stays that way until the rain starts, around eleven o'clock in the morning. By twelve it's gone dark with sheets of driving rain. We all go together, the three of us, and arrive at the church just after noon, racing from our cars to avoid getting wet, but the wind catches the rain and blows it horizontally, sweeping it under even the biggest golf umbrellas. No one escapes a drenching.

By the time the people—and there are at least two hundred and fifty—arrive and shake off their umbrellas and take off their dripping raincoats, it's almost as wet inside as out.

"The only advantage of dying young is the big turnout you get at your funeral," says Jessica, looking around.

By the time the dampness combines with the natural mustiness and hollowness of the dark church, the event takes on the tragic feel it deserves. No matter how much people liked him or didn't like him, when a twenty-seven-year-old dies, there is a terrible sadness about it. The fact that it was an unnecessary accident only compounds the grief. According to the coroner's report, Winston fell from his twenty-foot balcony and died when he hit the unforgiving white marble floor below.

The high percentage of alcohol in his system more than certainly contributed to the accident.

People who didn't know him would have thought Winston was a winner, but we knew he was the model of a true loser. After making gobs of money in the dot-com venture with Bruce—and getting out just before it all crashed—Bruce was better than ever, but Winston was the classic spoiled-by-success story. He hardly had any friends and those were mostly hangers-on, a coterie of people who sucked up to him for whatever they could get.

I don't know what caused the transformation, but whatever it was, it was really sad because he'd been such a funny guy in school—goofy funny, who could really make me laugh. After, he morphed completely into an arrogant, self-centered rich man who flaunted his wealth. Because he was still single he was much sought after, despite the fact that his ears still stuck out and his Adam's apple jumped up and down on his long, skinny neck. More important, he treated women badly.

He was the perfect proof of my theory that you only see the truth of people when they're on top. Everyone's nice on the bottom when they need something.

Still, Winston's death is one of those tragic, wasteful accidents. Except to Caroline Pearce, who is already spreading a story that has nothing to do with an accident. Even at the funeral, she was whispering, "*Cherchez la femme,*" and because people like action, they're eating it up.

"Caroline has no boundaries," I whisper to Jessica, who is sitting next to me.

She nods, but it's like she's somewhere else.

I poke Todd, who's on my other side. "Thanks to Caroline, people are going to have a good time gossiping about Winston, aren't they?"

He barely nods. He seems very distracted, understandably. Even though they weren't close anymore, Winston had been his best friend in high school and Todd really feels the loss.

"I'm sorry. I shouldn't be talking like that," I say, taking his hand. Normally, he would squeeze my hand in response, but now he simply lets his rest, limp, in mine. I look at him to see if he's heard me, but like Jessica, he's somewhere else, too.

The minister, Reverend Archer, is a warm and kindly man in his fifties, and he's talking about Winston's place in the great hereafter. All I can think is that if all the beautiful stories about heaven are true, Winston will still have his awful pretentious white-and-gold house. And it won't ever get dirty.

Just that silly thought makes me tear up. He was an old friend, maybe not a friend anymore, but still someone who would always be part of my history, part of those indelible high school and college years. With his disappearance from the world, a small part of me disappears, too. When tears begin to slide down my face, they're for both of us.

And also for some strange, unnamed unhappiness I feel that has nothing to do with Winston or his death. I'm still holding Todd's hand, but I let it go, maybe too abruptly, and that wakes him from his daze. I guess he sees my tears, and he puts his arm around my shoulders and pulls me closer.

I feel Jessica's body move in against mine and we're joined.

"I know he turned out to be a real shit," Jessica says, "but maybe I had something to do with that."

"You?" I say. "How?"

"Because I was always turning him down. Like in high school, when he would ask me to some dance, I would like practically laugh at him. I should have been way more understanding. And it wasn't just me. All the girls he really liked treated him like that. I mean, he was goofy-looking and dorky, but that didn't stop him from having crazy crushes. Maybe that's why he was so cynical and nasty when he got rich and the A-list girls all started chasing him."

"So we should forgive his disgusting misogynistic behavior because he was rejected by cute girls in high school?"

"Actually, yes. It like scarred him."

"Maybe it did, but he still should have been better than that."

"I would forgive him. It's important to forgive."

Even though this is slightly out of character, I can see that Jessica is really sincere and that this does matter to her. Maybe my sister is finally maturing.

"I don't know," I say. "I suppose that rejection stuff could have had some effect on him."

"He couldn't help the way he felt. Sometimes people can't even stop if they know it's way wrong and it's going to hurt other people."

She knows how to get to me. "He really was such a nice kid in school, sweet and funny and all that, wasn't he, Todd?"

But Todd is barely paying attention. He's lost in his own thoughts and my question goes right past him. So I say it again.

"Yeah, he was a good kid," he says.

"We should have been way more understanding," Jessica says.

"You're right. We should have been more forgiving," I say, and hug my sister.

Now Jessica begins to cry and I hold her closer. And love her more.

The service goes on with Winston's father and a cousin getting up to speak. Mr. Egbert's reminiscences of his son's boyhood, and of how sweet and funny Winston could be, touch the audience. Despite the fact that most everyone knows what a bastard he became, I can hear the sniffles and see people reaching for their tissues.

Except not one old friend gets up to speak. Todd said he felt uncomfortable and considered saying something, but it seemed so dishonorable, considering that most people know he and Winston didn't like each other.

It must be worse for Bruce. There is no way he could get up and give an honest eulogy. Everyone knows how badly their partnership ended.

I see Bruce when we first come in and ask if he wants to sit with us, but he says, no, he's going to stay in the back.

Since Winston was cremated there will be no cemetery service. Instead, everyone is invited for a reception at Winston's home.

The crowd of two hundred and fifty seems to swell on the way back to the house. And as happens at these events, with the exception of a little staring at the balcony and the marble floor, the attitude might as well be Winston who? Mostly it feels like a school reunion.

Todd, Jessica, and I only stay long enough to give our condolences to Winston's father and relatives and then slip out.

Though we didn't eat at Winston's, none of us are hungry. We all make some excuse and go off to be alone, Todd to his office, Jessica to her bedroom, and me to my bedroom.

The house is painfully silent.

⸺

Elizabeth remembered it all. Looking back, she wondered why she didn't pick up on Jessica's out-of-character compassion for Winston. Even taking the blame, and offering her forgiveness.

"It's important to forgive," she'd said. Now, of course, Elizabeth knew why.

And then there was Todd's distraction. His unusual silence. He'd looked about as uncomfortable as she had ever seen him. But in her usual searching-for-the-best-part-of-people way, she'd worked everything into funeral sadness: the loss of someone who had been his best friend through all those school years.

In truth, it was just plain old shit guilt. Both of them.

13
Sweet Valley

"What do you think she'll do? Do you think she'll speak to me? To us?"

Jessica had already tried on five different outfits. And then mixed and matched pants and shirts and skirts and blouses. All in all there were about ten different looks that were basically the same, dressy but not cocktail. And she wasn't pleased with any of them. If only she could have asked Elizabeth. Elizabeth would know. Elizabeth knew everything about her and sometimes better than she knew herself. Not that Jessica always took the advice, but she needed to hear it.

That was almost the worst part—not hearing Elizabeth for these last eight months. And maybe never again. Sure, there would be a hello or good-bye, polite, impersonal words, but never again would they talk as sisters. Never as people who unquestionably loved each other.

A thousand times a day she needed Elizabeth, needed to see

her in a crowd and know she was hers, to touch her skin, to brush her hair, just to push up against her, so natural as to not even be noticed, to pluck a piece of lint off her skirt, wipe a crumb from her chin, to be able always to enter into that private space that everyone else holds around them, inviolable.

But not for them, not for twins.

Another thing she would never again feel, Elizabeth's arms around her, holding her. A feeling even more familiar than her mother's embrace.

There she was again, being Jessica, asking for everything when she didn't deserve anything.

Through all this, Todd was sitting on the bed, fully dressed in a blue blazer with beige pants and a blue-and-white-striped shirt, waiting. He was even wearing a tie, and he was watching her. She never asked him his opinion on any of the outfits.

This was the shallow side of Jessica. The Lila-like side that he worried about. But the truth was, even just watching her changing clothes, throwing rejects aside, studying herself in the mirror, grabbing another skirt, another blouse, working herself up to a small frenzy, he loved her. Why she should fascinate him so much, he didn't know. All he knew was that even through the pain and the guilt, this was the woman he wanted.

"You know what I think?" Jessica asked.

Todd shook his head.

"I think she's going to pretend we don't exist. Look right through me like the spot was empty. I remember once I had this thing with Caroline way back when we were in the seventh grade. She told everyone that I let A. J. Morgan touch my breast."

"And?"

"And what?"

"Did you?" Todd smiled.

"Of course, I did. That's way not funny. I was, like, furious that she told everyone and I didn't know how to get back at her. What was I going to say to her? And Elizabeth told me. Nothing, she said, just look right through Caroline like the spot was empty. That's what she's going to do to me tonight."

Jessica finally found the Betsey Johnson that looked a lot like the first outfit she'd tried on.

She sat down on the bed in the middle of the sprawling clothes and wept.

Todd took her in his arms and held her.

But nothing could quiet her deep unhappiness. And with it came that terrible day and the explosion that ended everything.

lizabeth's not back yet?" Todd asks. I can see he's not happy to run into me alone in the kitchen. He's been in his office with the door closed all morning and probably thought he'd heard Elizabeth come in.

"Not yet," I tell him. "Regan's coming here."

"Now?"

"Either that or tonight or tomorrow morning."

"What's he coming for?"

"I don't know. That's what scares me, that I don't know."

"What did he say when he called? How did he sound?"

"He didn't call. He texted me. And that's all it said: 'I'll be there within twenty-four hours.' That's like him not to give a time. It's like he has the advantage; he can jump out at me whenever. That's what makes me so totally panicked."

"Take it easy. I'm here. I'm not going to let anything happen to you."

"What should I do?"

"Nothing. Just wait. I mean, he's not violent. Is he?"

"Not so far, but . . ."

"What?"

"He can be very jealous."

"Of who?"

I shrug.

Now Todd asks another question, and I can see his interest isn't in Regan. "Does he have any reason to be?"

I just look at him. He shakes his head, turns, and goes back to his office.

We are so awkward together. But it's not like the anger of before, it's different now. Even harder.

I sit on the windowsill mostly hidden by the curtain, but I have a clear view of the driveway.

Elizabeth's been gone since early morning, so she doesn't know about Regan coming.

It's nearly twelve now. Todd is in his office working, but he checks on me every fifteen minutes or so. We don't say much. Mostly I just shake my head. In other words, no, he's not here yet.

I'm nervous, and the fourth cup of coffee hasn't helped, either. When I hold up my hands they're trembling ever so slightly. Watching them makes them tremble more.

When I'm being rational I say to myself, It's not like he's a nut case or something. Sure, he's angry that I walked out, or maybe even contrite, like, apologizing and begging me to come back.

No. His message didn't sound sorry. It was cryptic with a nasty feel about it.

So what? Todd's here. No one is going to mess with me with Todd around. Plus, Elizabeth will be home soon. It's not like it's a movie or anything; it's just a marriage that didn't work, that's all. Happens all the time. At least to me.

I make up my mind, no matter what Regan says it's *finito* and that's that. It was a stupid mistake anyway. And being here for these last two weeks has made it very clear just how wrong it was.

How come Elizabeth never makes these dumb mistakes?

At ten to twelve the blue Porsche pulls up in front of the house and my husband, Regan Wollman, steps out.

"Todd! He's here!"

Todd appears in the room like almost instantly, as if he's been waiting in the hall. Which he may have been.

Both Todd and I watch as Regan reaches into the car and takes out his jacket. With ultimate cool, no rush, he slips it on and looks around, sizing up the neighborhood. Which doesn't seem to impress him. I'd forgotten how handsome and elegant-looking he is, too city for this environment. Maybe too city for me, after all.

He closes the car door, hits the alarm lock, and starts up the front path. Now I'm really scared. He's too cool.

"Why am I so scared of this man?" I back away from the window and turn to face the front door.

I don't know why, but I am.

The bell rings.

"Do you want me to get it?" Todd asks.

"No. In fact, maybe you shouldn't even be here."

"No way. I'm here. And I'm staying. Unless you really want me to go."

I consider it for a moment, and then, thinking I can't do this anymore, say, "Stay with me."

Those three ordinary words take their own sweet time crossing the room. And when they do, they just hang there, heavy in the air, loaded.

The doorbell rings a second time. Like insistent now.

I go to the door, look once more at Todd, and open it. Instinctively, I stand back.

The entrance leads right into the living room, and when Regan steps in he sees Todd first. I can see he's confused for a moment, so I step forward.

"Hello, Regan."

But he's still looking at Todd, perplexed. Then recognition hits. "I know you. You're Elizabeth's friend, right?"

"Right."

By now I've moved to the center of the room, across from Regan, close to Todd, almost touching, within his protective shield.

Todd puts his arm out across my body, making a wall between Regan and me. His arm is resting against me.

Regan studies both of us. "Where is she?"

"Who?" Todd asks.

I still haven't said anything more than hello.

"Your girlfriend."

"She's out on a story. Why?"

Regan looks at me and then at Todd. He's taking his time, like he's studying us. Then he looks back to me. Slowly. "Why the fuck didn't you tell me? I wouldn't have wasted my time coming out here to get you."

Before I can answer, Todd says, "Take it easy, huh? Nobody asked you to come here."

"Look, asshole. She just happens to be my wife, you know." And then to me, "But it looks like maybe you forgot that little fact."

"Hey," I say. "Look . . . I'm, like, totally sorry for this whole thing. I really didn't—"

"Shut up." Regan spits the words at me.

That does it. That's the key that unlocks Todd's control. "Get out!" he says, and he starts toward the door, his hand out to open it. Before he gets there, Regan grabs his arm.

"You get out. I want to talk to my wife. Alone."

"No way. I'm not moving," Todd says, shaking loose of Regan's grip. "You have something to say to her, go on, say it. She doesn't mind if I'm here."

"I'll bet she doesn't. Though her sister might. If she wasn't out on a story. Or blind."

"What's that supposed to mean?" I'm pushed well past timid into confrontational.

"You sleeping with him?" Regan asks, moving in closer, paying no attention to my question. "Of course you are, but the real question is, how long has it been going on?"

Before Regan gets too close to me, Todd shoves him back. And like two bucks in the wilderness, they fall to it.

"Stop! Please stop!" I'm shouting, but I'm barely heard above the sounds of grunts and expletives, the scuffle of feet and the thud of fists against flesh, of bodies knocking furniture, a lamp crashing to the floor, of action too big for the room.

Just when it looks like nothing will stop them, from out of nowhere Elizabeth dives between them. I didn't even see her come in.

And recognizing something different has happened, both combatants jump apart.

"My God! What's going on?" Elizabeth shouts, one hand on the chest of each adversary. Todd and Regan are so stunned they don't even fight it.

Of course, neither heard her come in over their own commotion.

"Lizzie!" I rush to her and she throws her arms around me.

"I can't believe this," Elizabeth says. "This is totally crazy."

Both Todd and Regan retreat, embarrassed, chastised. Only Elizabeth could have that kind of power.

Regan recovers first. "You want to see crazy? Look what's happening here. Look at them."

Elizabeth shakes her head in confusion. "What?"

"He's nuts," I say. And then to Regan I say, "Get out of here. Now!"

But he's still talking to Elizabeth. "Look at them. I'm here two minutes and I can see it. What's with you? Don't you know what's going on right in front of your eyes? Or more likely, behind your back."

With an unreadable face, Elizabeth turns to look at Todd and me.

Regan makes an attempt to straighten his jacket. He takes a deep breath, and with his teeth clenched hisses at me, "I always knew you were a cheat. Don't waste your money on lawyers. That prenup is iron."

Lifting his shoulders and jutting out his chin, he shoots me one last nasty look and walks out the door. "Hey, I hope you two will be very happy. Actually, you three."

Then he's gone.

Nobody says anything. We just stand there, hoping for I don't know what. Maybe somehow Regan's words can be misinterpreted. Hoping. After all, he only insinuated. And he was in a fury and not exactly thinking rationally.

I'm working on that possibility, so I don't say anything. Todd, I can see, is like too sick at heart to do anything more, so he follows my lead.

"I don't even want to guess what he's talking about," Elizabeth says to us. "I want you to tell me."

Nothing has been misinterpreted.

I jump to the obvious defense. "Regan's crazy jealous all the time. That's one of the reasons I'm leaving him."

It hits silence.

Then Elizabeth turns to Todd. "You've been acting weird since my sister got here. Do you hate her that much?"

He answers Elizabeth, but he's looking at me. "Of course I don't hate her."

He keeps looking at me as if he's waiting for me to say something. Like I can save him. I can feel his eyes on me, but I can't take mine off Elizabeth. I leave him waiting.

There's an instant of stillness that holds all three of us in our own desperate positions.

Then I see the change on Elizabeth's face, the realization, and she breaks the frieze, takes a deep breath, and shakes her head. "Oh, my God, it's true. I must have been blind."

"No, Liz, it's not like that. . . ." Todd says.

"Was it funny, my stupidity? Did you laugh about it? Or were you just grateful?"

"Please, Lizzie . . ." I start toward her, but she puts up her hand to stop me.

"I take it back. I don't want to hear any of it. Go to hell, both of you!"

Grabbing her purse, she turns and, in a sweep of fury, marches to the door, opens it, and stops. Neither of us moves.

She takes a moment and then swings around and points to Todd. "I don't know when this started. Or how long it's been going on. I only know one thing: You're both despicable lowlifes!"

"Liz—" he starts, but she cuts him off.

"Liars! How could you do this to me?" Now the expression on her face is no longer fury. It has collapsed into total defeat, leaving her just enough strength to leave. Not even enough for a door slam. Only the smallest clicking sound as she pulls the door shut behind her.

I have just destroyed my dearest sister.

We both stare at the closed door, too paralyzed with horror to turn away. The only way to stop time is to keep looking. But Todd is stronger than I am. He turns first.

"What have we done."

Not a question, a condemnation.

Todd tries to take me in his arms. I can feel his love, but I move away. I can't bear the comfort now.

How can he love me?

14
Sweet Valley

It was only LAX, not Sweet Valley, but the proximity still made Elizabeth tremble. Just the sight of the palm trees and the bougainvillea almost turned her stomach. Why had she ever agreed to come?

It wasn't revenge. Will was so wrong about that. It was horrendous of him to accuse her like that. And insensitive, especially since they had the beginnings of a little relationship going. And it was so unlike Elizabeth to lose her temper like that. Maybe that was part of the problem. She was twenty-seven years old and this was the first person she'd ever told to go fuck himself. What was wrong with her?

If he hadn't attacked her like that she would have explained that there was no danger with Liam. To be fair, he couldn't know that if Liam wasn't attracted to her he certainly wasn't going to be attracted to her identical twin sister. Identical. If one doesn't turn him on, the exact same other isn't going to, either. Liam really was coming as a friend because he was a good guy, and he knew how hard it would be for Elizabeth to face everyone alone. When she'd invited him she hadn't known about Bruce, and besides, Liam had been planning to go out to L.A. anyway.

If Will had just given her a chance to explain instead of assuming the worst.

Yes, there was always the possibility of Jessica's attraction to Liam, but that would be the old Jessica. Elizabeth had to figure that the new Jessica really was in love with Todd. After all, look at what she'd sacrificed for him.

Additionally, it wasn't like old or new Jessica was going to live in a box for the rest of her life so that she would always be faithful to Todd. Anyway, that wasn't Elizabeth's problem. The only thing that counted was proving Will dead wrong. She wasn't purposely setting them up.

Of course, she wasn't.

Elizabeth played the possibilities of how to deal with them over and over in her head. In some she just ignored them completely, stared into empty spaces. In others she told them, quietly but viciously, so that no one heard, "Just stay far away from me." Although a little unrealistic at a small dinner, it nonetheless gave her more satisfaction than just pretending they weren't there. But nothing quenched the urgency of the payback she needed so desperately.

She needed something to wipe out the loser part of herself, the picture of that last day that would never leave her mind. She remembered every minute of it with stinging clarity.

She had left the house before eight that fateful morning planning to stop at the paper, turn in the story she was working on,
and go over to Winston's to help any way she could. There was a
whole house and a life to dispose of. And his entire family was
only his father. There were no real friends. The funeral was over,
the money had dried up, and the hangers-on had fled.

Only because she was Elizabeth, the do-gooder, would she
be involved in anything to do with Winston.

Just from the look at all the confusion when I walk into that big white-
and-gold McMansion, I know I'll be stuck there most of the day.

Around noon I tell Mr. Egbert that I have to go home for an hour or so
and see what's happening, but that I'll be back this afternoon to help him.

The man is in such a state that I'm not sure he hears me. Most of the
morning he just sits in a chair in the living room, dazed, staring into
space, trying to understand why his son, his only child, is not here.

I leave quietly. He doesn't move.

When I get to my house I can't pull into the driveway because it's
half blocked by a blue Porsche.

Regan. It has to be. And it's really not the day I feel like dealing with
this. I suppose no day really is.

Poor Jessica. She's been dreading this since she got home. Me, too.
I know he's not going to be easy; he never was. I just hope she doesn't
give in and go back with him. I think he's absolutely wrong for her. Right
from the first time I met him, I knew he was wrong for my precious sister.
It felt like she was running away—from what I don't know. Or just Jessica

on the move; always looking for something better, more exciting. That's one gene we don't seem to share.

Maybe I'm just selfish, but I want my other half near me, not traipsing off around the world or even just cross-country. But most of all I want her to be truly happy. I want her to find someone she can love the way I love Todd. And I don't think it's Regan. In fact, I *know* it isn't.

As soon as I open the car door I hear loud sounds and shouts coming from the house, and I leap out of the car and start running to the front door.

It's open!

I shove it wider and rush in. I can't believe my eyes. In a flash, a nano-second, I think some kind of robber has attacked my family. Then I see that it's not a stranger, it's Todd and Regan and they're fighting, pounding on each other.

I shout, "Stop!" But they don't, so I bend my head down, raise my hands in front of my face, and charge into them. I know they don't see me or even feel me until I shove them apart and then they look down at me, shocked.

"My God! What's going on?" I say.

They instantly step back.

"Lizzie!" Jessica shouts, and runs across the room and throws her arms around me.

"I can't believe this," I say. "This is totally crazy."

Everyone just stands there looking horribly embarrassed. I don't know what's going on.

"You want to see crazy?" Regan breaks the silence. "Look what's happening here. Look at them."

I'm totally confused. Jessica tries to tell me that he's nuts. And she shouts at him to get out of the house.

But he doesn't move.

"Look at them," he says. "I'm here two minutes and I can see it. What's with you? Don't you know what's going on right in front of your eyes? Or more likely, behind your back."

I look at them, Todd and Jessica, like he tells me, but I don't know what I'm looking for. It's Todd and my sister. What should I see?

Regan straightens his jacket, takes a deep breath, and turns on Jessica. And I mean turns on her, baring his teeth like an animal about to attack. "I always knew you were a cheat. Don't waste your money on lawyers. That prenup is iron."

I feel like I've stepped into some play where I missed the first act. I don't know what's happening. But I know it's very bad.

Regan sort of pulls himself straight, like he's trying to get back some of his lost dignity. He doesn't even look at any of us, just walks to the door. Then he turns. "Hey, I hope you two will be very happy. Actually, you three."

Then he's gone.

Nobody says anything.

I turn to look at Jessica. And I see something I never saw before. They are standing together, she and Todd. More than just near each other. Together.

It's not possible.

Not possible!

In that flash that slices through all reason and experience and history, right down to that instinct part of the brain, I know.

Just like that.

Blind? How about dumb and deaf, too?

They just stand there, silent, waiting for it to disappear. Waiting for fucking stupid Elizabeth to save them with some incredible rationalization. To find some reason for it all to go away.

Or maybe just for me to disappear.

"I don't even want to guess what he's talking about," I say. "I want you to tell me."

Jessica starts on how he's crazy jealous and that's why she's leaving him.

I turn to Todd and tell him he's been acting weird since she got here. "Do you hate her that much?"

He answers me, but he's looking at her. "Of course I don't hate her," he says.

It's like he's waiting for her to save him.

But she can't. Nobody can. Nobody can but me. And I'm not going to. Ever.

Regan's right. "It was right in front of my eyes and I didn't see it."

"It's not like that," Todd says, but I cut him off.

"Was it funny, my stupidity? Did you laugh about it? Or were you just grateful?"

Jessica starts to come toward me, but I put up my hand to stop her.

"I take it back. I don't want to hear any of it. Go to hell, both of you!"

I grab my purse and start toward the door in such a haze of fury that I barely see the door. I swing around to Todd, "I don't know when this started. Or how long it's been going on." Then I wave my finger at both of them. "I only know one thing: You're both despicable lowlifes!"

"Liz—" He starts to say something, but I cut him off. I don't want to hear anything from either of them.

"Liars! How could you do this to me?"

I sail to the door in a fury, my head screaming for me to slam it with enough force to break the wall.

But at the door my rage deserts me and collapses into defeat. I've lost everything. It's not possible that the most important things in my life are gone. Wiped out, just like that.

The shock of it turns my legs to rubber, and I barely have the strength to pull the door closed behind me. I hear the quiet click and I'm outside with my back pressed against the door, dizzy. Numb. With just enough strength left to propel me to the car.

Would that it were a nightmare! Please, let it be a nightmare that I can wake up from.

But it's not.

I get in the car and just sit there, stunned. My mind starts searching. I grab at all kinds of thoughts to explain this madness. When could this have happened? It can't be recent, Jessica hasn't been here. And not during the years she was in L.A. No, this is earlier. My mind focuses down on that weird time in college that I have never been able to explain. That thing with Todd and Winston. Somehow—I don't know how—I know it's got to be connected.

That would mean they have been betraying me for years. All the while pretending to love me.

I turn the key and press my foot down hard on the accelerator. It makes a roar.

And I roar.

Inside my car, with the windows closed, I roar in pain. Like a wounded animal.

I release the brake and put the car in drive, put my foot down, and screech away.

I'm not going to let them see me sitting in the car in front of the house.

I'm not going to let them ever see me again. Anywhere. I swear.

And now Elizabeth was going to be right there. And Jessica and Todd would see her again. No matter what she swore. Was she a fool to do this?

Liam pulled up at the curb outside the airport exit in his rented black Ford right on time.

"Yo, Liz. Over here!"

Like there was any way to miss this super handsome guy in a gorgeous pinstriped black suit, white shirt, and bright red tie.

"You look great," Elizabeth said, throwing her knapsack into the backseat. "Why are you leaving Hollywood? You're obviously movie-star material."

"Thank you. And you look fabulous. No way you just stepped off a six-hour plane ride."

"I cheated. I changed in the ladies' room."

They chatted comfortably for the hour and a half ride to Sweet Valley. Just before they arrived at the club, Liam asked, "Are you okay?"

"No."

"Can I help?"

"Only if we can change places, but I don't do red ties."

"Have you figured out your entrance?"

"Spoken like a true actor. I just did six hours of entrance practice cross-country. Five hundred different approaches and I still don't have it right. I don't know whether to pretend like nothing happened or ignore them. Spit in his face or rap her over the head with a turkey platter or just knee him in the groin. What do you think?"

"You have some nice choices there. But I think since it's your grandmother's party I would dump the action stuff. Play it cool, treat them like second cousins once removed you probably won't ever see again."

"I like the once-removed part."

"Feeling better?"

"Not at all. The only thing that keeps me sane is my dread theory."

"What's that?"

"It's simple and absolutely natural. If you dread something, I mean really dread it, right from the heart, it's going to turn out awesome, like, ninety percent of the time. The converse is that if you can't wait to get to that party, it's a sure bomb. But there's a hitch: It's got to be real. If you pretend the dread, it doesn't work."

"Well, this is a sort of party . . ."

"And I'm dreading it. Big time."

"It should work."

The country club was as all country clubs are: a sprawling club-house set in manicured, rolling green hills surrounded by a golf course and little else, but lovely in the seventy-degree, sunny Southern California weather.

Liam parked in the guest lot and they sat quietly in the car for nearly fifteen minutes until Elizabeth was relaxed enough to get out.

The minute she stood up, she began to tremble. "I love my grandmother, but this is probably a bad idea. I think it's too soon."

"Eight months? No. You wait too long and you lose your family. You become the outsider."

"I feel like I'm an outsider already." Just that terrible realization garnered Elizabeth's courage, and outrage. "Damn it, they're my family, too, and I'm not going to let them just take it away. Along with everything else they've stolen from me. I know it's ugly to feel this way about my own sister, but I really hate her. And him, too."

Elizabeth stopped just before the tears started. Liam put his hand on her shoulder. "You want me to punch him?"

"Yeah, except he's bigger than you are. A lot bigger, but it's nice of you to offer."

"How about her? That might be more my speed."

"I'm really glad you came with me."

"Just remember—keep dreading!"

Elizabeth reached into the backseat and took her grandmother's gift from her backpack. She smoothed the ribbons and tucked it under her arm. "Come on, I'm ready," she said, taking Liam's hand and heading for the clubhouse.

The gravel path up from the parking lot kept Elizabeth unsteady on her heels. As unsteady as she felt in her heart. How sheltered her life had been until now. There had been other times when she was scared and miserable, but because of a freak of nature, she'd never suffered them alone. Not like she was now.

She had run away from everyone and stayed away for the better part of a year. Even if she had their sympathy in the beginning, Jessica was a daughter, too, a sister and a granddaughter, family. They loved her and in these months they would have seen her suffering—she had to be suffering. They would have come to feel compassion for her. It would be natural.

Being there is an enormous advantage. Like teams playing on home territory.

In the beginning, they had sided with Elizabeth, the victim, but time had passed and everyone's lives had moved on. Maybe they saw how much Jessica and Todd loved each other and their hearts had opened.

The two of them had to love each other completely or they never could have done such a thing. Was there room in Elizabeth's heart to allow that love? To forgive it?

She would know when she saw them.

Jessica only found out that Elizabeth was coming that very afternoon when her mother called.

"Did you just find out today?" she asked.

"No, I've known since last week, but she wanted to keep it a surprise for Grandmommy."

"What about me? Like, how could you not tell me?"

Alice Wakefield knew this was going to be difficult. Twenty-seven years of her less-than-perfect—a lot less than perfect but extremely loveable—daughter had taught Alice how to avoid the deepest pitfalls. She had learned that the best way was to keep cool and loving. It wasn't always easy, but the alternative was tears and shouting and tantrums.

"Look, honey, I know this is hard for you. I understand that, but we're a family and it's time we started behaving like one.

Not like this angry, broken mess we've been. It's courageous of your sister to come. She's only doing it because she loves all of us."

"*You* maybe, but definitely not me. Between Steven and Elizabeth, everyone is going to hate me. I so can't go!"

It was at this point in every Jessica argument that Alice Wakefield cut to the chase. "It's your grandmother's eightieth birthday. You have to go." One couldn't hear the foot coming down, but it did.

"Todd is not going to be happy."

"Probably not, but it's your grandmother's happiness we're interested in right now."

"Are you like making me go?"

"Yes."

"That's the only reason I'm doing it, because you're making me," said the twenty-seven/thirteen-year-old. "I don't know what Todd is going to do."

"Act like a man, I hope. I expect you both at the club at six thirty." The conversation ended there, but Alice was certain Jessica and Todd would both be at the party.

Actually, Todd had been in the house the whole time. In fact, he was at his computer in the second bedroom turned office, and he heard enough to guess what was happening. As Jessica said, he wasn't happy.

Though he was desperately in love with Jessica, after the debacle eight months earlier he was suffering a deep, painful guilt for what he'd done to Elizabeth. Love was a lousy excuse. Even if Elizabeth were to buy it, he could never excuse himself. It was without question the worst thing he had ever done to anybody in his life. And to have done it to one of the best people he'd ever known was unforgivable.

In these last months, as the story spread, he found it harder and harder to be in Sweet Valley. But Jessica refused to move. She was deeply involved in her work. Sometimes he wasn't sure how much she was suffering, though she seemed to be. He hoped to God she really was, but he couldn't always tell and that bothered him.

After all these years, he didn't think he was deluding himself. He'd known Jessica Wakefield since grade school. Yes, she could be self-absorbed, yes, she could be a little selfish, but she was delightful, charming, smarter than most people knew, and utterly captivating. He never would really know her completely, and that mystery fascinated him. He'd never felt that way about any other woman. He couldn't get enough of her.

And she was in love with him. He was certain of that. She'd sacrificed her sister for him, a thought that tortured him when he couldn't sweep it out of his mind. But every day that he was with her was glorious despite the family troubles. Maybe he was a shit for feeling that way, but the heart wants what the heart wants. About the worst excuse you could ever conceive of. Until it's yours.

Walking up to the front entrance, something Elizabeth had done hundreds of times over the years her parents had belonged to the country club, was almost relaxing in its familiarity. She remembered with warmth that first time, just after her parents had joined when she was twelve, how her eyes had practically popped out of her head at the gorgeous pool and tennis courts and the clubhouse itself, with its extravagant bouquets of flowers in the lobby.

It had been spring and the apple blossoms and forsythia stood tall in their glass vases, almost like small trees. And she thought in her little-girl way, Wouldn't it be so fun to live here? Like this would be her home. She turned to poke Jessica to share her fantasy, but Jessica poked her first and pointed out a cute boy on the other side of the room. And Elizabeth forgot the flowers and the fantasy and went with her first reaction: He's not as cute as Todd.

Even then it was Todd.

What if she cried when she saw them today? Totally pathetic thinking for a twenty-seven-year-old. But no matter how she tried to rationalize the ways she should behave, the truth was that she was deeply wounded and still bleeding. Eight months of healing had been wiped out in an instant, and it was today's raw wound the minute she got off the plane.

As horrible as it would be, it would be better to shout at them than to cry. Anything would be better than tears.

"If this were a play," Liam said, "and I had to walk into this group and see the two people who had betrayed me, I would rev myself up to rage. Then I would put a lid on it but know the heat was always there, bubbling underneath. Like a weapon, ready to be used. That thought would fortify me enough to keep me from showing any kind of pain. Then I would say my lines, and maybe they'd be benign, but if I was good, really good, no one would miss the fury underneath."

"You have to be a trained actor for that."

"No, just hurt and angry."

"What are my benign lines?"

" 'Hi, everyone!' And then 'Happy birthday' to your grand-mother."

" 'Hi, everyone, including you asshole shitheads, you liar cheaters! Happy birthday, Grandmommy.' How's that?"

"You're letting a little too much of the bubbling stuff show."

By now they were at the front door, which was being held open by Jose, one of the staff who had been working at the club long enough that his son and daughter-in-law now ran the kitchen. His grandson, whom Elizabeth remembered as a small boy, spent his college vacations collecting balls from the driving range.

Too late to run.

"Is that you, Elizabeth? Or is it Jessica? Whichever, wel-come. Good to see you. They're all there in the small dining room."

"It's Elizabeth and thanks, Jose. It's good to see you, too."

Elizabeth directed Liam toward the small dining room on the far side of the lobby, which still looked as perfect as the first day she'd seen it. Only she was different, no longer that sweet little twelve-year-old, that nice little girl who didn't hate.

"I'm not an actor. I'm just going to do whatever hits me."

"That's the best. When in doubt, play it honest."

They walked across the lobby to the private dining room.

The double doors were closed, but they could hear the buzz of people inside. Elizabeth's people.

She was back to claim them.

Jessica kept glancing over to the door. She hadn't touched her champagne or the little salmon hors d'oeuvres. She could barely respond to Todd or anyone else who talked to her. All she could do was wait, watching the door for her sister. She couldn't ever remember being afraid of Elizabeth. But she was now.

She had decided that no matter what Elizabeth said, she would stay calm and say hello and try to look welcoming. That meant a small smile, not a big greeting, very subdued.

What if Elizabeth ignored her? She would still say hello.

Of course, everyone would get up to welcome Elizabeth, and there would be kisses and hugs and all that. Jessica had decided that she would hang back and let Elizabeth take the lead.

She and Todd hadn't really talked about it too much. It was too painful and so neither had told the other how they were going to handle this first meeting.

She could see that Todd was watching the door as intently as she was.

They weren't the only ones who were nervous. Her grandmother didn't know Elizabeth was coming, so she was cool, but her parents were keeping a sharp eye on her and the door. Darting back and forth. Jessica could see how nervous her dad was. He did a lot of tie straightening when he was nervous. Tonight he had straightened his tie so much it was halfway around his neck. Her mother was certainly just as nervous, but she knew she had to be the calm one, and so she forced herself to look the perfect hostess.

Even though it was her own family, Jessica felt as if she were in hostile territory. Steven still hadn't forgiven her for the business with Cara; his friend, Aaron Dallas, absolutely hated her; Bruce Patman, a close friend of Elizabeth's, certainly hated her, too.

Out of seven guests so far, she could only count on her parents and her grandmother, Marjorie Robertson, to be in her corner. And soon Elizabeth would come and that would add to the hate list. Her parents and grandmother loved her, of course. Or so she hoped. But the only one she knew truly loved her was Todd. And he was the most important. Without his love, she would have nothing left. Pretty bad for the girl who used to have everything; the one who always got the window seat.

Maybe her sister didn't hate her.

Why in hell not?

Then the double doors opened and Jessica could see instantly from Elizabeth's face, from the hard stretch of her mouth and the way she avoided looking in Jessica's direction, that it was going to be the worst scenario. Her sister did, indeed, detest her.

Eight months. The longest they had ever been separated. Elizabeth looked different, Jessica thought, older, more beautiful, with a sophistication she hadn't had before. A New York look—whatever that was. But it was a look. She wore a black empire dress that caught tight just under her breasts, shoestring straps slightly rounded to soften the neckline, which was a bit low for Elizabeth. Even her jewelry was black. Definitely not L.A. Not like Jessica's own Betsey Johnson little-girl pink. Elizabeth's hair was different. Shorter, with a center part giving way to a gentle sweep that cascaded along the sides of her face.

Weird, Jessica thought. Exactly the same cut as mine.

Jessica was so concentrated on Elizabeth that for the moment she didn't see the man behind her. And then she did, and he was gorgeous. He had to be Elizabeth's boyfriend. Who else would she bring all the way out here? If she had someone, maybe there was a chance. Maybe it wouldn't be so terrible.

For Bruce Patman, standing there with adoration in his eyes, it was terrible already. He and Elizabeth had never lost their closeness; they were on the phone all the time. In fact, he had flown to New York five times on some business excuse just to see Elizabeth. In all the conversations they'd had, she never mentioned another man—until the phone call the other day when she'd said she was bringing someone to the dinner.

"Someone you're dating?" Bruce had asked Elizabeth, digging for any information. But she was not forthcoming. Instead, she said it was a long story. He said he had time, but she wasn't talking. He practically hung up on her. And now, here he was, the boyfriend.

She was introducing him, and Bruce felt sick.

Elizabeth said to Liam, "I'd like you to meet my great friend, Bruce Patman. Bruce, this is Liam O'Connor."

They shook hands. Bruce wanted to know only one thing, but there was no way to ask, so he just backed away and made room for everyone else.

Elizabeth's grandmother, Marjorie Robertson, the only one who was truly surprised, let out a little yelp and fairly leaped from her chair, her arms outstretched, ready to hug Elizabeth.

"Oh, my darling, what a marvelous birthday gift! No one told me." She and Elizabeth hugged, and then Ned and Alice Wakefield greeted their daughter, and everyone else took turns hugging and kissing Elizabeth, simultaneously being introduced to her friend, Liam.

Jessica and Todd stood back, just outside the excited, fussing circle. It was obvious that everyone, save them, was delighted to see Elizabeth.

Despite her nervousness, her guilt and apprehension, there was a part deep inside Jessica that tingled with the thrill of seeing her sister again. It was an involuntary response deep in her DNA. But that thrill was well hidden; she didn't dare show even a hint of it.

Finally, the chattering, loving group began to drift back to the table, and then there was no one but Todd and Jessica left standing with Elizabeth and Liam.

Some of the awkwardness was deflected by the need to introduce Liam. Meeting a new person gave everyone a chance for a moment's normal behavior.

"Nice to meet you." Todd shook Liam's hand.

Elizabeth introduced Jessica without looking at her. In fact, she hadn't looked straight at her since she walked in the room. But when Jessica said, "Hi," and put out her hand to Liam, Elizabeth looked, watched to see her reaction. There was no noticeable Jessica response to this gorgeous man.

Relief washed over her. Jessica appeared to be passing the test. And that made Elizabeth's heart sink involuntarily, because it meant that maybe Jessica's love for Todd had changed her.

Okay, Will Connolly, you were wrong.

But when the gorgeous man, Liam, touched Jessica's hand, he almost lost his breath.

Elizabeth was stunned. For a moment it took her mind off the betrayers and a sick feeling greased around in her stomach. This was something she had never expected. It was not possible. Jessica was her identical twin. You're not turned on by one, you're certainly not turned on by the identical other. Right?

Wrong. Fortunately (or unfortunately), it didn't seem to register with Jessica, who smiled politely and backed off toward the table where the other guests, essentially the audience who had been silently watching the action and holding their breath, were able to turn back to the dinner table with an almost audible sigh of relief.

The twins' parents visibly relaxed, too. The first hurdle had been surmounted.

There was a little more awkward shuffling, and the four went to their assigned seats at the table. And well assigned they were, thanks to Alice Wakefield, who knew just how far apart to seat the principals—not easy with only ten people.

The easiest one, Liam, was between Steven and Aaron Dallas, Steven's now-accepted partner. Elizabeth was between her grandmother and Bruce. Jessica was tucked safely beside her father and her brother and Todd was on the other side of Alice Wakefield.

For a moment no one sat. Then Ned Wakefield held out the chair for his mother-in-law and everyone took his or her seat.

But when Elizabeth looked up at Liam, he had switched seats with Steven and was sitting next to Jessica.

Elizabeth looked away. Oh, shit.

It was a small dinner party, and the only way not to see each other was by purposely not looking. There was a lot of purposely not looking going on.

Oblivious, Marjorie Robertson took her granddaughter's hand and kissed it. "I couldn't be more delighted," she smiled. "I know they say time flies by when you're older, but these eight months away from you took forever. We all missed you terribly."

"I'm sorry, Grandmommy, but I had to get away. Had to get started on my life, and I think I did."

"Liam?"

"Oh no, he's just a friend who happened to be out in L.A. this week, so I invited him."

Jessica heard Elizabeth's words because her mind was programmed to pick up only Elizabeth's voice. Liam was only a friend. With those words her expectations collapsed. There wasn't going to be any easy way.

Todd too picked up on it and shared Jessica's disappointment.

But from across the table Bruce inhaled the information and suddenly the dinner was beautiful.

"Tell us about *Show Survey,* Elizabeth," Steven said. "We're dying to know."

"Well, it's really not that big a deal. I mean it's sort of a blog with a throwaway print component, kind of like Zagat for restaurants, only this is for the theater. Off Broadway mainly."

"Elizabeth is being modest," Liam said. "It's new, but it's catching on, and Elizabeth is the star writer. She's doing a piece on a new author whose play is opening next month."

"Who's that?" her grandmother asked.

"His name is Will Connolly. You don't know it now, but you will in about a month."

"Liz, that's awesome," said Bruce, still in the throes of delight from learning that Liam was not competition.

"I guess," said the slightly embarrassed Elizabeth. "But what's been happening here in Sweet Valley? That's what I want to know. What's the gossip?"

"Lila and Ken are kaput," said Steven. "My office is handling the divorce."

"What happened?" asked Elizabeth.

"He moved out," said Aaron, "and she didn't notice for two weeks."

"What about Enid? How's she?"

This time it was Bruce who answered. "Dr. Rollins, the eminent Aesculapian, is having a secret affair with A. J. Morgan."

"No way!"

"You're right," said Bruce. "No way it's secret in this town."

"Is he still the bad boy with that dirty long blond hair and the Mustang?"

"The hair is still long, still blond. Maybe a little blonder than before and not so dirty. But the Mustang? The one that used to look like a piece of junk? Now it's a classic. Outside of his doctor friend, that's his prize possession."

"What does he do?" Elizabeth was hungry for home talk.

"Works in the sporting-goods store in the mall right down the street from her office." Bruce couldn't resist. "Convenient for checkups."

"Isn't she a gynecologist?"

"Okay, everybody," Ned said, hands up for the stop signal. "Can we class this up a notch?"

"Oh, Daddy," Jessica said. "Gossip is the best part of Sweet Valley. If we don't dish, what are we going to talk about? Our opera company?"

"Sweet Valley has an opera company?" Elizabeth was truly surprised, and even though she hadn't planned on talking to Jessica, it just came out.

"Right, Don Giovanni does the mall."

And everyone, including Elizabeth, laughed. For an instant, they were family. There were possibilities.

The joy Jessica felt when Elizabeth laughed kept her going.

"Besides, Daddy, we have to entertain her. She's our guest, right?"

Elizabeth bristled. A guest? In her own family? Elizabeth responded quickly and just as Liam advised, the rage bubbled underneath her words.

"If you don't mind, I am not exactly a guest in my own family. In case you forgot, it is my family, too."

This was directed at Jessica, who was taken aback by the attack. She had only meant to be friendly. She used to be able to say anything to Elizabeth. Obviously not anymore.

For the first time Elizabeth looked directly at her sister. In that look she saw a difference. Older? No, but more mature. You could still see the sparkle, but there was something else. Something that she couldn't put her finger on.

Though Elizabeth never could really see the resemblance

between them, she could see the obvious. My God, she thought, She had her hair cut exactly like mine. How is that possible? She couldn't have known.

Lawyer Steven, exercising his newly honed negotiating skills, jumped in before Jessica could respond. "You're right, Dad. Let's class things up a little. How about Betsy Martin's Nobel?"

Betsy Martin was the wild loser sister of Steven's early love, Tricia.

"If I remember correctly . . ." Grandmother Marjorie started.

"You do, Mom." Alice nodded to her mother. "Perfectly."

"You mean there is no Nobel?" Elizabeth smiled, joining in with her brother. She was not going to let the real fight deteriorate over a dumb but trivial thing like Jessica calling her a guest. It didn't deserve any space when the true offense was a vile, premeditated treachery.

"Not unless you mean Sam Nobel." Bruce used his pleasure as an excuse to squeeze Elizabeth's hand affectionately, who smiled back at him.

At that moment the soup came and the conversation dropped to chatter between neighbors. Todd had not said a word, but now he was saying something to Jessica that seemed to relax her a bit.

Liam interrupted and asked Jessica a question that Elizabeth couldn't hear. Jessica gave a rather long answer. Maybe a little too long for Todd. And no wonder: one look at Liam's face as he listened to Jessica and his passion was obvious.

It made Elizabeth edgy, but she told herself it wasn't going anywhere. Dinner would be over in a couple of hours, and she and Liam would head back to the airport.

And again, why should she care if Liam acted like an ass? Only because she didn't want to be any part of it. It had nothing to do with her plan. This guy was screwing up everything, and she couldn't do anything to stop him. No matter whether Will was right or wrong, she couldn't have it happen on her time.

They had just finished the roast beef and things were comfortable enough. The wine was very good, a 2001 Amarone, and they were down to the bottom of their third bottle. Jessica and Elizabeth had managed to avoid each other with conversation split into twos and threes according to where people were sitting.

"Why are you hurrying back?" Bruce asked Elizabeth.

"I just took off a couple of days for my grandmother, but I have this piece I'm writing on the playwright that's due next week."

"And Liam, what about—"

Bruce's question was interrupted by a huge explosion. It being California, everyone jumped up in horror, then laughed with relief at the fireworks outside the dining room. The waiter told them it was a Sweet Sixteen party taking place in the large dining room.

The fireworks were brilliantly colored, no expense spared. Everyone stood and went to the window to watch.

Instead of the fireworks, Elizabeth watched Liam. Admittedly, she didn't know him very well, but he did seem a bit out of line, glued as he was to Jessica's side.

Steven and Aaron walked outside to the balcony to get a better view. Jessica followed, accompanied by Liam. But Todd stayed in the room.

Elizabeth was afraid that he would try to talk to her, so she walked out to the balcony, too, taking Bruce with her.

The evening was clear and the explosions covered the sky with lights like dripping bracelets and simulated palm trees. There was music playing, and the fireworks gracefully moved in the air in time to the sweet rhythms of "American Girl."

Truly, no expense had been spared. The fireworks, so extraordinary that they had to be watched, went on for almost fifteen minutes.

At some point Elizabeth caught sight of Liam and Jessica walking down the steps toward the putting green. Should she call out to Liam?

Out of the corner of her eye she could see Todd watching, too.

Jessica and Liam stood at the edge of the green, their figures silhouetted against the exploding sky, talking. Though Jessica seemed to be standing in a natural pose, Liam's body was almost devouring hers.

No, Elizabeth wasn't going to call Liam. I'm not my sister's keeper, she thought.

The bouquet, the grand finale of the fireworks where everything left goes up at once, was upon them. Now everyone else came out to watch. Elizabeth could see Jessica turn her face to the sky, but Liam never stopped looking at her.

The last notes of music followed the last lights as they slowly fell far out over the golf course in the distance. Everyone headed back to the table.

"If this is only a Sweet Sixteen, what are they going to do when she gets married?" Ned, a true father of the bride, asked.

"They'll have to go nuclear," Aaron said, and almost everyone laughed. It would take a lot more to make Todd laugh right now.

Elizabeth walked back to her seat, all the while sneaking glances at Todd. He wasn't aware of her, so intent was he on watching the French doors, waiting for Jessica to come back.

Finally she did. Jessica—and Liam.

As soon as Todd caught Jessica's eye, he spread his hands, palms up, and asked silently with his eyes and slightly open mouth, What was that?

Jessica, surprised and confused, shook her head and just as silently asked, Huh?

Todd made an annoyed gesture with his head and sat down a little too hard. Heads turned to see what had made that sound, and it was immediately obvious that a drama was building.

Alice Wakefield, who was on high alert, called for the birthday cake, and even though it wasn't there yet, announced, "Here it comes!"

That did it for the moment.

But the cake didn't show.

"What's your problem?" Jessica whispered to the sour-faced Todd. Everyone listened for his answer. Also whispered.

"Guess."

Elizabeth never meant to smile. In fact, she didn't even know she was doing it.

But Jessica did.

"You think something's funny?" she shot at her sister.

Elizabeth thought for a second and then said, "Well, yeah."

"Did you see that, Mom?" Jessica turned to Alice Wakefield, who was frantically motioning to the waiter.

"The cake! Bring the cake!"

One poke from Alice and Ned got up quickly and headed to the kitchen.

Steven, the negotiator, spoke. "Hey you guys, let's cool it, huh?"

"Why are you always sticking up for her?" Jessica's voice was no longer anything close to a whisper.

"I'm not. I'm just trying to cool things."

"It's okay, Steven," Elizabeth said. "There's nothing to cool."

"Well, I think there is." Jessica stood, poised for action. To Elizabeth she said, "I don't like your attitude."

Now Todd joined in. "Hey, Jess, that's enough," he said.

"Don't tell me what's enough. You started the whole thing with that nasty face. What was that about?"

Todd was losing his cool. "Well, I don't appreciate—"

"Who cares what you appreciate?" Jessica had already lost hers.

"You're out of control."

"Are you going to stick up for her, too?"

There was no way Elizabeth could let that pass. "I don't need anyone to stick up for me, and certainly not him!"

"Elizabeth . . . " Bruce tried the calm, quiet voice.

But it was too late. "It's okay. I can handle this."

Since his father was hunting the cake in the kitchen, Steven felt he had to exert his older brotherly position. "Jess, come on. This is a birthday party."

"You just mind your own business. I'm tired of you always blaming me."

"Like it's not your fault?" Steven shot back.

"You can go to hell!"

"Hey," Aaron said, more or less to both of them. "Take it easy."

Jessica turned on Aaron. "You shut up. This is family business."

"Don't talk to Aaron that way." Steven was no longer the negotiator. Jessica had stepped on his territory.

"Kids, everybody, please . . ." Alice tried, but Jessica couldn't be stopped.

"Then tell him not to butt in. It's not like he doesn't already hate me."

By now the shouts and insults were flying over the table. There were only two other groups in the small dining room, and there was no way they could pretend they weren't listening.

Everyone was in it now. Shut ups and stronger pejoratives were shooting back and forth. Everyone except the birthday girl, Grandmother Marjorie, whose sensible voice was lost in the shouting, was standing. And there were no attempts to lower voices.

Alice kept calling for quiet, but she couldn't break through. Even Liam, who by now had figured out why Todd and Jessica were fighting, tried to step in to defend Jessica and was one of the first recipients of a "Shut up!" Bruce didn't like the way Jessica was talking to Elizabeth and told her so and was rewarded with another "Shut up!"

"I think you're horrible to come back here and ruin Grandmommy's birthday!" Jessica said, looking straight at Elizabeth.

"Me! Who are you to talk about ruining anything? You betrayer! You liar! You horrible thief!" Looking right at Todd, Elizabeth let go a barrage of eight months' worth of fury.

"And you! All that time pretending to be so honorable. You're worse than she is. You're nothing but a miserable bastard, you . . ." There was nothing left to bubble underneath. ". . . shithead!"

Barriers had been crossed and it became a free-for-all. The well-mannered and normally courteous Wakefields were totally out of control, shouting at a decibel level that might well have been heard at the Sweet Sixteen party.

It continued with no sign of letup until Alice Wakefield threw down her napkin and louder than anyone, in a voice few had ever heard, stunned them all into silence.

"Ned!" she shouted. "Bring out the fucking cake!"

15
Sweet Valley

Silence, black and mean, as sharp as a slab of night ice, froze Todd's car. Jessica sat so far away from him that part of her back leaned against the door and her head was twisted uncomfortably toward her side window, staring out into the darkness.

Turning back to Todd, Jessica finally broke the silence. "I don't like what's happening." It was too dark for him to see her glare.

"And I'm supposed to like it?"

"What are you talking about?"

"The way you acted with that guy."

"How was that, exactly?" She bit out the words with fury.

"Flirting. In front of everybody."

"I think you mean talking."

"No, Jessica. I mean flirting."

"Excuse me, I didn't realize we were in the nineteenth century and I wasn't allowed to talk with an unmarried man."

"I've known you a long time, and I think I know what Jessica flirting looks like."

"I'm beginning to think you don't know what Jessica *anything* looks like. This isn't high school anymore, Todd."

"I sure as hell know that."

The frigid silence cut back in and stayed that way until Todd parked the car outside their town house.

This was the first time anything like this had happened between them, and Jessica didn't trust herself to say anything more because right now it looked like there was only one way to go, and she wasn't ready to leap onto that path just to win a good shot in an argument.

Except it wasn't about Liam. She was clean on that. Her defense was true and there was nothing to hide, but what about Michael Wilson, the almost mistake from her office? Of course, Todd didn't know about that. If she was truly open she would tell him the truth now, but that would just prove his point, and he wouldn't understand the revelation she had had and her sacrifice for him.

Truth can be deceptive.

Todd turned off the engine and, with the keys in one hand, used the other to open his door. Jessica was expecting more conversation, but it didn't happen.

She opened her door and got out. By then he was around to her side and without looking back, had started up the walk to their building. She waited an instant, but even though he must have been aware that there were no heel clicks behind him, he didn't turn back.

If he was going to play hardball, so was she.

Todd had the keys in his hand, so when they got to their apartment, Jessica let him open the door. He stood back and allowed her to enter first. Was this out of habit or a sign of some softening?

Well, she thought, she wasn't going to make it easy. This was a problem that impinged on the very foundation of their relationship. My God, it was shades of Regan Wollman. And that would never, ever happen to Jessica again.

Just the comparison to that unhappy time in her life fortified her. Jessica decided to let Todd make the first move.

But he didn't. Instead he went straight to his computer and started answering e-mails.

How could he concentrate on anything else when this catastrophe was threatening the most important thing in their lives?

Was this a strategy? Was he playing the "your move, my move" game and now it was her move? No way. Jessica had played too many games in her life, and it wasn't that she wasn't any good at it, because she was the best, but that was the very part of herself she'd vowed never to use again. She'd done it for too many years with boys and, more horribly, with Elizabeth. Even now the thought could make her nauseated, and at the first sign of the tactic she closed up, no matter what the cost of losing.

Maybe it was good to find out what this man she'd loved so painfully for so long, and for whom she had made so many sacrifices, was actually made of. Get a little trailer before she bought the movie.

Talk about reducing a catastrophe—he was e-mailing and she was buying movies. Would she ever stop being the old lightweight Jessica she'd come to hate?

Jessica changed into her old extra-large Sweet Valley U T-shirt that she still slept in. It was so far-out unsexy that it crossed the line and came back to sexy. Or that's what Todd always said, but that might have been because he thought whatever she wore was sexy.

He wouldn't tonight.

It was eleven thirty when Jessica got into bed and picked up the book she was reading. *War and Peace.* She'd lied for so many years about having read it that she'd decided finally to make it honest. Truth was, it was very heavy for bed reading and a lot harder than the movie and she might have to go back to lying.

Additionally, this was no night to lose herself in any book. Real life was tonight's novel.

Jessica stared at the same page, the same paragraph about Rostov spurring his Bedouin horse into galloping making less and less sense. She waited to hear Todd's footsteps in the hallway, but the wine and emotional exhaustion of the evening covered her in sleep before she heard anything.

Hours later, with the book still on her chest, the wine woke her just the way they say it does. Something about dehydration disturbing sleep. Todd was already in bed and asleep about as far away from her as a queen-sized bed would allow before he fell off the other side.

How easy it would be just to slide closer and put her arm around his body. He would be warm with sleep and she would feel his smooth skin covering the thick, hard muscles underneath and she would whisper to him, It's okay, we love each other. I trust you. . . . And what? I will allow you to control me?

Jessica resisted the urge to bury her foot in his back and shove him right over the side.

What was happening to them anyway? They were like drunk drivers who caused an accident, badly hurting someone very dear to them. Those culprits must think about their actions every day and find solace only in rearranging what happened so that it never happened. But it did. And at some point they understand that nothing will ever change that, and long after everyone else has moved on it will always be fresh in their minds. They'll never get over it.

Maybe she and Todd would never get over what they had done to Elizabeth. Eventually it would destroy them, as marriages are destroyed by a catastrophe like the death of a child.

Measure for measure: What was good about what they had? What was pure and untainted? Certainly not the beginning. And not these last eight months.

Where was the beauty of their love?

If beauty was the standard, then it wasn't even love, just two guilty people, trapped by their crime and forced to live with what they had paid for so dearly. They were isolated, with no one else but each other, so removed by the stories they had told themselves that they could no longer see the truth. Or they could see nothing but the truth.

Those first few months when love, that glorious euphoria filled with passion and happiness, was in total control, were gone. Now those uncomplicated days where they only marked time until they could be in each other's arms had become almost out of reach. The joy of being together was still powerful but no longer uncomplicated. And the delight of sharing and seeing everything brand-new with someone you adored was harder and harder to find. Only the very act of making love could erase reality and make the complications disappear, but only for those brief moments that were, more and more, becoming lost in the long days of reality.

It was rare that Jessica felt joy without the accompanying pain.

And tonight, instead of anger, she was overcome with a terrible sadness.

Would neither one of them be courageous enough to end this, to leave this agony?

As quietly as possible, Jessica lifted the covers and slid out of bed. She tiptoed, barefoot, across the room, opened the closet, and took out her shoes and her jeans. She would send for the rest later.

16
Sweet Valley

The ride back from Sweet Valley to LAX was ugly. Elizabeth had promised herself she wouldn't talk to Liam about what had happened. In fact, she wouldn't talk at all.

And she didn't for miles and miles of almost empty freeway. But Liam felt he had to explain.

"I admit, I found her very attractive. So I was talking to her. Big deal. I don't know why he went off the deep end like that. It couldn't have been just me. What was that about?"

"He was out of line, but so were you. I mean, come on. You weren't just talking; you were practically gobbling her up. And what's with changing seats?"

"Okay, I'm sorry. I guess I overdid it, but she just knocked me out."

"But you knew the problem. How could you? I think it was really shitty of you."

"I said I was sorry, but he shouldn't have made such a big deal of it."

"Just for the record, she's my identical twin. I mean, most people can't even tell us apart. So how come you . . ."

"I know. It's weird, isn't it? Pheromones, I guess."

There didn't seem to be anything more to say, so for the rest of the ride they listened to music in silence. A very uncomfortable silence.

Just before Liam dropped her off at the airport, he apologized again, but Elizabeth was too annoyed and upset to accept it graciously.

"Drop it, will you?"

"Hey," Liam said, trying for a little friendliness.

"What, hey," Elizabeth said, grabbing her backpack from the backseat.

"I would drop it, but I don't think you can."

"You're right; I can't."

Elizabeth flung the backpack over her shoulder and was about to close the door when Liam stopped her.

"Wait. Okay, I know it might not be the way you planned it, but you have to admit, it did sort of work out."

"Are you nuts?"

"Revenge? Remember?"

Every feature on her face was violent with fury. Without another word, Elizabeth slammed the door shut and walked off.

17
New York

The red eye landed in New York at 6:00 A.M. By seven thirty Elizabeth was back in her apartment. There were three messages on her machine: one from David Stephenson, her editor at the magazine, reminding her that the interview with Will was due Tuesday, and two from Bruce, just asking if she was all right. And to call him when she was ready.

Those messages gave her the first warm feeling she'd had since the beginning of her horrendous trip. Bruce could do that for her. The truth was, he was her best friend, had been for a long time now. With Jessica and Todd out of her life, she was closer to him than to anyone else. They spoke at least two or three times a week—long, honest conversations. She trusted him completely.

No phone call from Will. Not even a hang-up.

On the trip out to L.A. she had been busy agonizing over what would happen at the party. The way back gave her a chance to agonize over what had happened at the party. For once her dread theory didn't work, the exception that proved the rule.

Would she ever get that horrible, shouting, vicious picture out of her head? It had escalated so quickly no one could have stopped it. It was a match dropped on kerosene, and the whole family had exploded in a million pieces. Not just any family, her family. Her beautiful, loving family. And nothing could put them together again.

There was no one who wasn't to blame except maybe her grandmother. Even her parents were guilty. They should have known better than to throw everyone together without any preparation and just hope, like in a movie, that at the denouement it would all work out.

Well, they were wrong. It wasn't a movie.

Elizabeth hadn't slept on the plane in either direction. She had now been awake for twenty-four hours, the kind of awake that tortures every neuron in the brain until any thought is excruciating.

She was completely wiped out and could think only of sleep. But she had the Tuesday deadline hanging over her head. The way she figured it, she had the rest of the weekend—if she could stay awake—Monday, and most of Tuesday. A snap, if she had already gotten the interview.

Unfortunately, she hadn't. And the last time she saw Will, it was fuck-you ugly.

Either David would take her off the story or she would have to find a way to put things back together with Will. For one thing, she really wanted to do this story. She'd frozen her feet for weeks and spent whole days hiding in that frigid theater gathering some very good material. It wouldn't be a straight interview; it was more of a *New Yorker*–type piece, the anatomy of a writer's first show.

Whatever was going to happen with Will and their relationship, if there was one, couldn't happen now. She was too desperate for sleep to do any thinking. Elizabeth kicked off her shoes and crawled into bed fully clothed just as the phone rang.

Too tired to check the caller ID, she reached out and picked up the receiver.

"Elizabeth?"

Mistake. It was Will.

She didn't answer.

"You there?" he asked.

"Sort of."

"I know you just got back this morning. I figured I could catch you before you went to sleep. Could you meet me for a drink later? Like about six?"

No matter what had happened to their friendship or whatever you call it, she still had the interview to deal with.

"Okay."

"Across from the theater; you know, Liam's place."

"Not there."

There was a quick silence. Will didn't ask why; he just named a bar at Forty-seventh and Broadway. Sullivan's.

"Okay," Elizabeth said. "See you at six."

Elizabeth made a feeble attempt to think up a meeting plan, but before she got past the hello, she was greeting Will in a dream;

a soft and fluffy dream where she was flying over clouds, gloriously, without the plane.

A few hours later, it all crashed back with the alarm clock. Elizabeth had set it for five, leaving herself just enough time for a quick shower, a thrown-together sandwich of leftover chicken (six days won't kill you, she already knew from eating lots of week-old leftovers) from a doggie bag, slap on some jeans, and be out the door. Forty-seventh Street was a seven-minute walk from her apartment, which wasn't a lot of time for thinking but plenty if you had no ideas at all.

Sullivan's, another one of those ubiquitous faux Irish bars, was on the corner, and Elizabeth could see Will through the large front window. He was sitting at the bar reading a newspaper.

A tinge of excitement shivered through her, a tinge that could have been sexual, or just plain fear. With no other choice, Elizabeth decided to play it by ear.

"Hey," Will said when she pushed open the door. He stood up, smiling, welcoming.

Just what she didn't need. She could feel the apology bubbling up through his smile.

He was going to apologize for accusing her of just what had happened.

It would be worse than she'd expected. It smelled of moral decisions, no-win choices, and all the things that she should have considered earlier. How could she stop him?

"I'm really glad you aren't still angry at me—"

"Will, can we just keep this professional and finish the interview?"

"I'd feel better if we talked about it."

"Work, first. Okay?"

Was she turning into Jessica, the manipulator? Or had she always been this way, only cleverly disguised? From herself.

Pushing the thought away, Elizabeth jumped right into the safety of work. "How did you first get the idea for a play about Samuel Johnson?"

She really was Jessica.

And he bought it, the way everyone always bought whatever Jessica was selling. Additionally, she wanted him to talk about himself. That was hard for anyone to resist.

The interview went on very comfortably. Will was a good subject for the next hour, lubricated by some fairly decent Pinot Noir. When the questions stopped, they had moved on and something else was in the air.

And they were both feeling it.

It wasn't about dinner. Though Will did offer to make something easy, sandwiches, or to pick up a pizza to eat at his house.

"That's okay," Elizabeth said. "I'm not really hungry."

"Me, neither."

"So what are you?" It was a seduction scene and Elizabeth was the seductress and she was liking it.

Will tried not to let his surprise show, but he couldn't stop the delight. "Anything you want me to be. . . ."

"I have some ideas. . . ."

"You want to tell me? Or better still, show me?"

"Here?" Elizabeth was smiling. She really liked this guy.

"Not for what I have in mind."

"I'm really liking this interview."

"Me, too. Let's take it home."

As a journalist, Elizabeth insisted on paying. Rather than take the time to put it on her card, she left the cash and a tip on the table.

In the cab to Will's apartment, there wasn't much conversation because the unpleasant—especially for people who weren't at all hungry—odor of some spicy Middle Eastern dish the driver had probably just finished eating was so powerful that they were both hanging out their windows.

Even that didn't spoil the mood. Instead, it lent a humorous note that would have lightened any awkwardness, had there been awkwardness. Strangely enough, there wasn't. The Pinot Noir had done its job.

They could have gone back to Elizabeth's apartment, which was just a few blocks away, but Elizabeth needed a place where she could escape for all kinds of reasons, starting with cold feet and moving right on to the dreaded apology for what Will thought was an unjust accusation. An accusation that was, in truth, right on the mark. If only there was a way she could delay that talk forever.

For now, she had the perfect way.

Will fumbled a little with the key. Could he be as nervous as she was? Obviously not, as they were barely inside when he took her in his arms, kicked the door shut with his foot, and kissed her passionately.

The taste of his mouth, the warmth, the softness, sent a wave of passion that swamped her, pulled her out of everything but the feelings in her body.

Elizabeth responded with an urgency that surprised her. She wanted this guy more than she knew, and the body doesn't lie. She was going to go with it. All the way.

Will took her hand and, without a word, led her to his bedroom.

Any pretense at inhibition disappeared. Flinging clothes in all directions, they fumbled their way to the bed.

Once there, it all turned slow motion. They touched each other, the palms of their hands and tips of their fingers languidly caressing, exploring, like blind people, until there was nothing they didn't know of each other's bodies. This inch-by-inch build of passion created the aching need to join deeply, intimately, and overcame any trace of reality. The heat and sweat of their fervor combined to fling them onto their own trajectories and land them together at almost the same moment.

This time, there were no tears from Elizabeth. In fact, the wildness of the last half hour had wiped out all her anxieties. She lay content in Will's arms.

It was so different from being with Todd; even now it felt like a strange and disloyal thought but true. She tried to think of exactly how it was different. Yes, she and Todd had been together a fairly long time, had lived together for almost two years. That had to quiet passions. Or deepen them.

It had quieted theirs.

Elizabeth knew herself to be a commitment freak. When she made a promise, come hell or high water, she stayed with it. Long after the water had receded.

Will had drifted off to sleep, but he was still holding her. And she still liked his arms around her, liked it very much.

The respite gave her some introspective time, time without the bitterness that always accompanied any thoughts of her situation, known either as the Dumped Situation or the Betrayed Situation. Lest that belittle her circumstance, both came with all the accoutrements that attend such painful wounds.

In the last few months, the strongest longing she'd connected with Todd was for revenge, to hurt him as he had hurt her. Where was the quiet ache of a broken heart? That dreaming of the happiness they had once shared? That longing for a missed love that crushes the spirit and leaves a dark pit of loneliness?

Not one had a chance against her fury.

Would she want Todd's arms around her now?

Absolutely not.

But was that lack of love or too much anger?

Suppose it wasn't love that had broken her heart. Suppose it was rejection and duplicity.

Maybe that's what she would have needed to end it. Something catastrophic. She could never have ended it by falling out of love. She never would have known that she had; she cared too much. She was the commitment freak.

Will stirred, opened his eyes. He smiled at her and held her closer.

Elizabeth smiled back and kissed his cheek lightly.

That was enough to rekindle the embers, and the heat took them back to where they'd left off.

Sometime around 2:00 A.M., without time out for dinner, Elizabeth pled her deadline and left.

It was a good leaving—no promises. They both had some interesting thinking to do.

18

New York

Elizabeth was back at her apartment in less than ten minutes. That can happen in the city in those rare times between breaths when there is no traffic. Nothing is really that far away. It just seems that way when you're trying to go crosstown during rush hour. And in New York, it's always rush hour for someone.

"How're you doing, George?" Elizabeth flung a wave to the doorman as she passed. The tenants always joked about how the doorman job would be perfect for the wheelchair-bound since, save one, not any of the doormen ever got up from behind the desk to open the door or help with a package. It was a marginal West Side building with marginal doormen. The one exception was a new man who came from an East Side apartment house and hadn't yet learned lethargy. But that wasn't George. George was a sitter.

"That was fast," said George from his usual perch. "Really fast."

"I guess," Elizabeth answered, not having any idea what was fast and not wanting to ask and get ten minutes of the latest tenant gossip.

The mailboxes were in the back of the lobby. She could hear George going on about how he didn't even see her leave.

"And I was right here. All the time," he said.

"Relax. I'm in for the night," Elizabeth said, holding her mail and slipping quickly into the elevator. "See you, George."

"It's not possible . . ." The elevator door closed off the rest of his response.

The mail was as expected, bills and advertisements, and no invites to marvelous New York parties. In her eight months here, no one had invited Elizabeth to a marvelous party—or any kind of party. Part of it was her own fault; she never hooked up with any women her own age. The only way singles can move around in a city like New York is in clusters, and Elizabeth didn't have a cluster. In fact, with the exception of a woman she ran into occasionally when she was doing laundry in the basement, she didn't know any other women her age. The only woman in her office was married and in her fifties.

Lots of excuses, but the truth was, she hadn't tried. In fact, she'd discouraged any attempts at friendship. She was too busy suffering.

But now, that might be over.

The elevator stopped at the seventh floor and Elizabeth got out just as her neighbor, the one right next door without a name, stepped in. They both said hi and smiled. Two o'clock in the morning and she's just going out? New York neighbors are very interesting.

The smile was still on Elizabeth's face when she turned the corner toward her apartment, but it froze when she saw who was sitting on the floor outside her door.

Poor George. Now Elizabeth understood what had confused him. In front of her door, in a sleeping heap, surrounded by a sequined backpack and a Prada bag, was her twin sister.

It was a shock to see Jessica here in New York. More shocking still was the pounding reverberating in Elizabeth's heart, an involuntary combination of excitement and, if she didn't know better, happiness. But that lasted only an instant. The reverse quickly took over and she even considered carefully and quietly opening the door and, without waking Jessica, stepping over her and slipping into the apartment.

That option was lost when Jessica opened her eyes. There was a dazed nanosecond of disorientation before she readjusted and jumped to her feet. The movement could have continued forward toward her sister, but Elizabeth imperceptibly pulled back and Jessica stopped.

"Can you ever forgive me?" Then, without waiting for a response, she said, "I left him."

Elizabeth paused to take in the news and swallowed it, choking a little on her possible involvement. Had Liam triggered this? It was too complicated a thought to deal with now.

Without a word or a sign of any sort, Elizabeth unlocked the door and pushed it open. She stood back and, with a small nod of her head, motioned Jessica to step in.

Jessica scooped up her things and entered.

This was the first time Jessica had been in this kind of New York apartment. That time during spring break Alice's friend's building had been brand new and very grand, and with Regan, of course, they'd always stayed in chic, modern penthouses or hotels. Additionally, this was old and looked it, and so completely different from Sweet Valley that it seemed more like Europe to her. Since it was already furnished, there was nothing of her sister's she recognized. And it wasn't even Elizabeth neat; there were clothes thrown on the chairs and a half-eaten sandwich on the kitchen counter, which was actually a piece of kitchen in the living room.

Maybe she wouldn't know how to deal with this new Elizabeth. She'd already deviated from her plan and lost any advantage she could have had by not being awake to see Elizabeth's first reaction and judge what kind of chance she had.

Somehow, when Jessica had made the decision to come to New York and throw herself on her sister's mercy, she'd pictured it differently. Though she planned to be true and honest, not to spare herself any blame, her explanation would be couched in a gentle, loving, apologetic but hopeful manner. Instead, she had blurted out everything in two sentences and Elizabeth hadn't responded. Were they so far apart that nothing would ever heal the rift?

"What are you doing here?" Elizabeth asked evenly, calmly picking up her clothes from the couch.

"Didn't you hear what I said? I left Todd."

"That has nothing to do with me." Her response was so cold, Elizabeth couldn't even look at her sister when she said it.

That's why she didn't see Jessica sink to the couch and put her face in her hands, but she did hear the sobs.

Jessica had had many unhappy times in the last eight months, and though there were many tears, she'd never broken down and wept like this.

It was the sound of irretrievable loss. It was almost a wail.

It cut through to Elizabeth's heart. After years of conditioning, of always being the one responsible for answering her sister's needs, her response was involuntary, and it was excruciating not to be able to take Jessica in her arms and comfort her the way she had done countless times in their lives.

But she couldn't. Right now, it seemed she would never be able to love her sister again. It was inconceivable to think that part of her life was over, but it was.

"I swear I didn't see it coming. I mean, with Todd all that time ago." Jessica forced the words through her tears. "But once it did, I was shocked. It was the ugliest thing I had ever done in my life. And I couldn't stop myself."

"That's your excuse? 'I couldn't stop myself'? Well, you should have."

"But I never have. I know it sounds crazy, but you were the one who always stopped me. You were my fail-safe. You shouldn't have been, but you were."

"So actually, it was my fault?"

Jessica had stopped crying. She had an expression on her face that Elizabeth had never seen before. It was too serious, too knowing for Jessica. At least for her Jessica.

"No, of course, it wasn't your fault." Again, the tears. "I love you so much, and I've ruined your life." The words were mangled between sobs. "And I've lost you forever."

At those unbearable words, Elizabeth's resolve almost weakened, but then she found the steel of anger to hold it together.

"I want you to leave."

"Please." Jessica came toward Elizabeth, her arms extended. "Just let me hold you once before I go. I know I can't have your forgiveness, but just let me feel one more time that other part of me that I can never have again."

The sight of her sister, her face torn with the love and need, and Elizabeth's own longing defeated her resolve. Was any man worth losing this most precious thing in her life?

Elizabeth reached out and took her Jessica in her arms.

Even when Jessica felt her sister's arms around her, she couldn't stop sobbing. In fact, feeling that familiar body, almost an extension of her own, only escalated her loss.

For Elizabeth, holding Jessica was more than holding a sister. It was what she would feel had it been her child, and she understood now that short of the ultimate separation, she could never let go of Jessica. And she never wanted to. They would have to find a way.

Would Elizabeth ever learn and change and see the unfairness of the relationship? No. Love is not fair. Just undeniable.

Still, maybe there was a little difference.

"I love you, too, Jess, and my life is not ruined."

And just like that, with those few words, they were on their way to healing.

Jessica turned to her sister and returned the embrace. Together they sat on the couch and held each other until they calmed down enough to giggle, sitting there hugging as if, had they let go, they would have fallen into space.

Finally, Elizabeth did let go. "Do you want some tea or coffee?" she asked, smiling. "On second thought, I'm actually down to only air and water in the house and you can have either. Or there's a six-day-old half-eaten chicken sandwich, if you like."

"Thanks, but I have everything I want."

"Me, too."

Jessica began to talk to her sister as she had always done, but it was different this time. They were equals. She told her about the last eight months with Todd and what guilt was doing to their relationship.

As Jessica talked, Elizabeth found herself less interested in her own part. In fact, she wished herself away from it. Hers was the dead part, and even her anger had quieted. She found that she could almost remove herself and concentrate on what was still alive for Jessica.

And she sensed that it was still very much alive for Jessica. That maybe she had underestimated her sister's ability to love.

Elizabeth decided she was owed a small advantage, a payback for a lot of tough Jessica years. She decided to take it and not own up to her hand—or accidental hand—in the Liam incident.

"Was Todd right?" Elizabeth had to know. "Were you flirting with Liam?"

"No way," Jessica said. "Liam. I like didn't even remember his name, but whatever it was, he was hanging all over me, and actually, it was getting annoying. I didn't feel any kind of response— which I know is weird for me, but it wasn't the first time. I know it's hard for you to understand, but I *so* don't have any interest in other guys. I'm not even sure why."

"Because you're in love."

"In that case, maybe I was never in love before."

"Maybe you weren't."

"I thought I was like lots of times, but it was *so* never like this."

There was no point in chickening out now. Jessica had to ask. "Are you still in love with Todd?"

Elizabeth wanted to be honest, but it was a terrible question. Lost love was not the first thing that came to her mind when she thought of Todd. Just the fact that she couldn't answer an immediate yes made her think either she was falling back into the pattern of taking care of Jessica or she really didn't know how she felt about Todd. Well, she did know the anger, but she hadn't looked beyond that in a long time. Now she did, and she answered.

"I don't think so. I think if it hadn't ended like a car crash, it would have faded gently, dropping into one of those well-worn friendships."

"You wouldn't have married him?"

"I don't think Todd would have gone through with it. But I know now that I would have needed him to stop it."

Jessica couldn't hide the hope in her face.

"In fact, okay, so I'm not in love with him, but you are, and I want to help you put it together again."

"The old Jessica would have sat back and let you do it all, but I'm *so* the new Jessica and I'm doing it myself. In fact, I'm getting back on that plane first thing tomorrow morning and straightening it all out. Just the way my sister would."

"Hey," Elizabeth said, happier than she had been in months.

"Okay," Jessica said, "now tell me how I should do it."

Elizabeth hugged her sister and together they crept into bed just the way they had done thousands of times before. And it felt right and good.

19
New York

As promised, Jessica left at the first light of dawn, kissing her sister and borrowing her new suede jacket. But Elizabeth's euphoria could not be diminished.

As Jessica passed the hopelessly confused doorman still on duty, she waved and wished him good morning and stepped out into the clean, fresh, early New York morning.

The street that had been jammed with people and cars when she'd arrived last night was empty. She started out to the curb to hail a cab when she saw a young man leaning against a parked car.

As sometimes happens, in the picosecond before recognition, you see the unvarnished reality. This passing flash for Jessica was of a man, young but not a boy, his face kind and gentle, staring at her.

Then she saw that it was Todd.

He smiled, shrugged, and put out his arms to her.

She went to him, and the first words from both of them were "I'm sorry." Then, "I love you."

"Let's go home," Jessica said.

Todd hailed a cab and the doorman watched the couple get in and was happy that nice lady in 7C who always looked so unhappy had finally found someone in her life. He could see they were very much in love.

Then he went off duty and, just as well, didn't get to see the nice lady come out later that morning. Alone. But not unhappy.

Will called before nine, but Elizabeth said she couldn't see him until she finished the piece. They arranged to have dinner Tuesday night after rehearsal, and Elizabeth knew exactly what she had to do. It was truth time.

When she walked into the small Italian restaurant a couple of blocks west of the theater, Will was already at the table. He had on jeans, of course, but had dressed up a bit with a blazer, especially for her. She was pleased. He had long since stopped looking like Todd, but he was that kind of traditional magazine handsome that she liked. It wasn't the only thing she liked about him, but it didn't hurt.

It was good to see him, very good, but not over-the-top. Maybe she had forgotten what over-the-top felt like. She was definitely attracted to this guy, but . . .

"First thing," Elizabeth started, barely sitting down. "A confession . . ."

"Your plan with Liam worked."

"Liam told you?"

He nodded.

"It wasn't a plan," she continued. "At least not a conscious plan. You're right, it did work and in the most horrible way. Even though it was the opposite of what I expected—Liam was knocked out by my sister and she didn't even care. That's what made it horrible; she really is in love, but what I did was enough to ruin everything."

"You talked to her?"

Elizabeth told him about Jessica's visit and the rapprochement and how she spared herself a confession.

"I still don't think that kind of cruelty was what I had in mind. Do you believe that?" Elizabeth asked.

"Yes. Consciously you didn't, but it was in there someplace. You admit that?"

"Yes. I guess it was. But it was so deep inside, so powerful, that longing to hurt them, that I let myself be fooled. Is that possible or am I just rationalizing?"

"A little of both, but I understand. And for what it's worth, I think that makes you human. Now what happens?"

She told him what had happened and how the new Jessica, the in-love Jessica, had taken over and was going to work it out. How she called from the airport and told Elizabeth that before she could do anything, Todd had showed up in New York to take her home. According to Jessica, they had a most way-perfect movie meeting right outside the apartment.

"I still don't know the details, but the wedding is back on, and I'm going. And I take back the fuck you."

"Well . . ."

"Don't go cheap on me."

They both laughed, and the dinner was delightful, so delightful that they went back to her apartment afterward because she didn't need an escape.

Maybe it didn't need to be over-the-top. Maybe it was just a nice New York experience that people have when they like each other.

Friends with benefits.

She'd always thought that was only a cute joke. She was surprised at how well it fit.

20
New York

Elizabeth's interview with Will was a success. Instead of cutting her story, David, the editor, let it run fifteen hundred words and everybody loved it. In fact, he wanted her to do a follow-up after the show opened.

She received compliments left and right. Especially from Will and the producers. When she walked into rehearsals the next day, it was worse. She was a star and had to sit down front with them.

And there was more good news. Right after the piece came out, she was contacted by *Time Out,* a slick magazine for events in New York. They were offering a freelance job that guaranteed at least two articles per month for an amount much closer to real money than Elizabeth had been making at *Show Survey*. The best part? It wouldn't interfere with her work there. She said yes immediately.

Now she would be able to afford to stay in New York as a writer. Maybe even a journalist.

Elizabeth also included the piece in a letter she sent out to half a dozen New York media sites asking if there were any openings for a job. Though she hadn't heard from any of them yet, she was hopeful.

Actually, for the first time in many months, she was all-around hopeful.

And that's the way she was when she started to get dressed for Will's opening. She hadn't seen him in the last week because he was at the theater all the time now, every night for previews, plus rehearsals in the daytime. Elizabeth had stopped going to the rehearsals since the next article was about opening night and reviews.

It was a very different relationship from any she had ever had before. Of course, so much of her dating life had been spent with Todd that she really didn't know how relationships evolved. Fundamentally, she was still thinking teenage. Even worse, going steady.

The first nice thing about her relationship with Will was that there was no need for excuses. They talked on the phone and texted, and it was very comfortable, without the intensity of constant communication.

She wasn't sure it was love. The wasn't sure part made her pretty sure it wasn't. She didn't think it was for him, either, and she hoped she wasn't misleading him.

After fifteen minutes, her bed, every chair, the dresser, and the radiator were covered in rejected opening-night outfits. When she finally decided on one, it was her little black dress. She and Jessica had always laughed when their mother talked about her little black dress, but in New York, you needed one. It was always safe.

In some ways she would always be the same Elizabeth, but in a bow to her new persona, she'd had her little black dress made littler.

It was a cool, dry, late August night that could easily have been mistaken for fall. The plan was to meet Will outside the theater. He was there when she arrived, pacing like an expectant father.

A play is like a new baby except that with a baby, no matter how ugly it is, no one dares to comment. Whereas with a play, reviewers delight in telling you and the world what a little monster you spawned. The uglier, the better.

"Will!" Elizabeth called out.

He heard her and turned to look but almost without recognition, so frantic was he.

She smiled and walked over to him. "How about a little Valium?"

"Or a truckload. You may have to sit alone. I don't think I can make it through sitting in one place. I need to pace."

He dug in all his pockets before he came up with her ticket.

"Not to worry," Elizabeth said. "What about your parents? Do you think they're coming?"

"I don't know. I sent them the information, but I haven't heard."

"I hope they do."

"I don't know. They're pretty angry."

"I'm going to sit down so you can pace in peace." Will stood still long enough for Elizabeth to give him a quick kiss. "See you at intermission."

That felt natural, she thought, a kiss on the cheek. Without noticing, they had drifted into a warm and caring friendship, but maybe not an intimate one anymore. She didn't know how she knew that, but it was okay.

Elizabeth went into the theater with fingers crossed for her friend.

The audience seemed to like the play: They laughed in the right places and kept a respectful silence in the serious moments. Elizabeth could feel their involvement, which was all for the good. It was working.

If she had to make a criticism, it would be that the Boswell character and Mrs. Thrale weren't sexy enough together. Maybe it was something she felt knowing that offstage, the actors despised each other. The audience might not have realized that; they were both professional actors, after all, but the audience would miss the warmth between them and blame the play. That could hurt Will.

In the intermission she looked for Will, but he was nowhere to be found. She asked an usher, who told her that Will had left before the end of the first act. Fled, more likely.

Elizabeth searched the crowd, looking for his parents. Not that she knew what they looked like, but she thought she might see people with a resemblance to Will. She didn't. And she didn't hear any conversation about the play, either. The people milling around in the lobby talked only about how much the M&M's cost and all kinds of unrelated subjects. The closest she heard to a comment was that it was too cold in the theater—her own constant complaint.

The lights flashed, warning that the intermission was nearly over. Still no Will.

Elizabeth went back to her seat. And there he was, sitting in the seat beside hers.

"It's good," she said. "Are you okay with it?"

"No, but then I never am. I think the audience is okay, though. What do you think?"

"Definitely with it. Did you look for your parents?"

"No, I was backstage. I could have asked at the box office, but I didn't want to know."

The second act sped by. The audience was truly enraptured. Second acts used to be a weak point when they were middled, but now with only two acts, all the preparation was done in the first act and the second act was the payoff. And in a good play, it was very satisfying.

Will's play was good. Maybe not perfect, but very good.

Good enough to get a standing ovation, which for a straight play might happen only on opening night and not all the time. Musicals almost always got standing ovations, Elizabeth thought, but it was special for a straight play. Elizabeth could see Will's pleasure.

Before the applause stopped, he slipped out.

"See you in the lobby," he said as he left.

The crowd slowly exited, jamming the aisles. By the time

Elizabeth got to the lobby, Will was surrounded by well-wishers. She noticed three people waiting just outside the group around Will. She could actually see the resemblance. But not on the third person, a young woman she knew in her heart had to be Wendy.

Elizabeth watched, waiting for Will to notice them. And then he saw the older couple, and the happiness on his face was wonderful. But what happened to his face when he saw Wendy said it all.

It certainly explained why she and Will could never have been more than friends. Well, she thought, there go the benefits. But it didn't hurt. Something had been missing, though she wasn't really aware of what it was, probably because she didn't need it. For that reason she felt nothing but joy when she saw the love in his face for Wendy. And Wendy's face matched his in delight.

Will was wrong. He did love Wendy.

At that moment, Elizabeth decided that no one needed the convoluted explanations, as harmless as they would be, about who she was.

She would call Will first thing in the morning. Tonight she would get as many reviews as she could and start to put her story together. Even before she started, she had her ending: Wendy and Will into the sunset.

Will called Elizabeth before eight the next morning.

"What happened? I looked all over for you. My parents came."

"I saw."

"And they brought Wendy."

"I saw her. She was standing by herself and just from the way she was looking at you I knew it had to be Wendy."

"You should have stayed."

"There'll be lots of time for our friendship."

"I'm taking that as a commitment, and I know how sick you are about keeping commitments."

"So what did your parents think?"

"My father was impressed. I don't know what he thought I was doing all this time, but now that he sees my work, his attitude is different. He's beginning to take me seriously. They all seemed to like it. My mother had a few suggestions on how to improve the play. Fortunately, I was too happy to rap her in the teeth."

"So what about the reviews? The two I heard on television were pretty good. I saw the *Times* and *News* online. Brantley liked the play, but he didn't like Mrs. Thrale so much. He wrote he thought you were a talent to watch. That's pretty good, huh?"

"Yeah. But some of the others were a little mixed. A couple of raves would have been nice."

"I thought it was wonderful, especially the second act. It was so powerful. You really are talented. The audience was mesmerized. Will it run?"

"It's only a six-week engagement, so it will certainly do the six weeks. After that I don't know. But the best news was totally unexpected."

"What?"

"Universal wants to option it for a movie."

"You're kidding!"

"And with me writing it. I'll have to go out to L.A."

"My country. And Wendy?"

"She's going to go with me."

"Why am I not surprised? I saw your face when you first spotted her."

"Weird, huh? When you and I first met and you asked me about her, I was being honest. I really didn't think I loved her enough. But when I saw her last night . . . How can that be?"

"I don't know. Maybe you just had to get away. From everyone. Even the ones you loved."

"Maybe it was the same for you."

"Maybe."

"We're okay, aren't we?"

"Better than that. I'm really happy for you."

"It's looking up for both of us, isn't it?"

"Yes. I got a freelance job with *Time Out*."

"Fantastic! Tell me."

"I can't. I'm rushing out. I leave for Sweet Valley at noon. I'm the maid of honor, you know."

"How do you feel about that?"

"I'm doing it, aren't I?"

"Will you call me? And don't worry about the time. I want to hear everything."

"I will. *Now* can I say good luck?"

"Right on. And for you, too."

"Thanks. Bye."

Elizabeth hung the phone up. Surprisingly, even to herself, she really did feel the way she'd said.

But she still wasn't ready to open Todd's letter.

21
Sweet Valley

On the twenty-fourth of August, the day after Will's opening and the day before Jessica's wedding, Elizabeth flew out to L.A. She arrived at two in the afternoon, and Bruce picked her up at LAX and drove her to her parents' house.

"I know most of what's happened in the last two weeks, but maybe, being on site, you know more. So, tell me," she said.

"Do you want Caroline Pearce's story or the truth? Fair warning: The truth is not nearly as interesting."

"I'll start with the truth."

"Well, first of all, Todd went nuts when he found out that Jessica'd left him. You know how cool he can be? This time he just lost it. He wouldn't consider anything but getting on the first plane to New York. Whatever happened in New York, he wasn't going to talk about it, but whatever it was, they came back here together.

"All he would say was that they both had changed. I know it

sounds impossible, but everyone could see something was different. Jessica was calmer and happier. Even your brother and Aaron had to admit it, and that's saying a lot. However you did it, she and Todd came out better than ever. The question everyone wants to ask is, What kind of magic did you perform?"

"None. It really was all Jessica . . ."

"Whatever you say."

". . . and Todd, too. They just let love take over. Don't ask me to explain. It's like hope, you can't explain it."

Bruce turned onto Calico Drive and pulled up at the Wakefield house. "Look," he said, "I've got a problem and I need your help."

"Sure, anything. Tell me."

"I can't now. Meet me tonight at my house about seven. Can you do that? And by the way, it's not bad news."

"Done. I'll be at there at seven." Elizabeth got out of the car, but before she closed the door, said, "Bruce?"

"What?"

"You're in love, you're getting married, you're moving to Europe, you're—"

"Enough." He cut her off. "Tonight at seven."

"Thanks. Love ya." She smiled and closed the door.

At three in the afternoon, her parents came back from their respective offices. Steven and Aaron came over and so did her grandmother. It was a glorious welcome home. Just the way her family had always been. Around five, Jessica and Todd arrived.

It was harder with Todd, and awkward. But Elizabeth didn't

feel the hostility she expected. In fact, it was strangely anticlimactic. Was it possible that there really was no other feeling behind the anger, and once that was quieted, it was really over?

Perhaps they were both adapting, though they managed not to look at each other, even when the conversation called for it. Maybe it would never be perfectly comfortable, and that would have to be good enough. Lots of rooms had elephants in them.

After an hour or so it was a little easier. And seeing how much Jessica and Todd loved each other softened Elizabeth's heart somewhat.

"I want to do something," Elizabeth said, and took off her lavaliere. "I want you to wear mine, with my initial on it. And I'll wear yours and then, no matter what, we'll always be joined."

Elizabeth held out her hand with the little gold-and-aquamarine lavaliere with an *E* written on the back.

One look and Jessica burst into tears. Todd reached out to her and then stopped and allowed the sisters to hold each other. He realized he was in for a lifetime of that. It would never change again.

Jessica wiped her tears and, reaching behind her neck, took off her lavaliere and handed it to her sister.

It was like a beautiful ceremony, the exchange.

"Don't worry, Jess, I'm ready." And then to Todd Elizabeth said, "Really, it's going to be all right."

"I want it so much to be all right, Lizzie." Jessica took her sister's hand. "I know I want more, but I'll wait."

"Me, too, Liz," Todd said. "You know you'll always be special to me."

Elizabeth knew he meant it, but she also knew it would take

time. Loving her sister as she did, though, would make the wait worthwhile.

Later, as they were leaving, Elizabeth was able to kiss Todd good-bye on the cheek. It was weird, but she made up her mind to get used to it. Turned out that along with Jessica, Elizabeth had changed, too.

Enough that she was also able to take her suede jacket right off the new Jessica's back.

And she knew she was ready to open Todd's letter.

The contents of the letter would mean little now, but her readiness to open it meant everything.

Jessica and Todd walked out of the house holding hands. Todd stopped and turned to Jessica.

"You are truly fantastic. How you ever accomplished that, I mean with Elizabeth, I'll never know. You are brilliant and amazing and beautiful and I love you. Forever."

"And I love you, too," Jessica said, smiling, "and I want to live here always."

"Sweet Valley?"

"No." She hugged him. "In the eyes of the beholder."

Todd laughed. "You got it."

And arm and arm they walked into the sun, which just happened to be setting.

Bruce's house was twenty minutes outside of Sweet Valley. Just before seven, Elizabeth borrowed Alice's car and drove there.

Bruce had built the house four years earlier and though he hadn't mentioned anything to her, Steven told her that he'd just sold the house a couple of weeks ago and was moving at the end of the month. Where, Steven didn't know.

That was so strange, Bruce not mentioning anything to her. Despite Bruce's assurances that whatever he had to say wasn't bad news, Elizabeth was concerned. He was, after all, her best friend. Why hadn't he told her about the house or anything else lately? All their conversations had been about her problems.

For a long time now, at least since the debacle, he was the only person Elizabeth had confided in. She was very open with him, though for some reason, she had held back on the details of her relationship with Will.

Elizabeth felt terrible about being so self-involved that she hadn't even noticed big changes were happening in Bruce's life. Some friend, huh?

But why was he intentionally keeping it from her?

By the time she arrived at Bruce's house, she was a cross between upset and worried.

Bruce's house was too well furnished to have been done by a single man with very little interest in decorating. Fortunately, he had money and the good taste to hire a professional. The result was an impeccable home done in primary colors, always the favorite of bachelors, and good enough to be featured in a style magazine.

Bruce did have an interest in art, and it showed in his choice of paintings and sculptures. Most of the work was traditional, with some ventures into abstract in the sculptures.

The well-maintained look had more to do with Clara, who had worked for the Patmans since Bruce was a boy, than with any innate neatness.

There were so many things Elizabeth liked about Bruce. In fact, they were very much alike in myriad ways; they liked the same books, movies, plays, and politics. Best of all, they didn't like the same people, which gave them lots of fun conversations and private jokes.

More important, they felt the same way about serious issues like family and loyalty and love. Both surprisingly square and homey, almost old-fashioned. They were romantics.

Then it came to Elizabeth. She knew what Bruce's secret was—he was in love.

For an instant there was the delight of knowing, of guessing right, because she knew she was right, but that lasted only a few seconds before another much darker emotion bubbled up.

She would lose him.

The thought took her breath away.

Bruce must have heard her car pulling up, because he opened the door before she could ring the doorbell.

Given a choice, she would have run and not had to hear anything about this mystery woman, about how he adored her and how she was everything in his life.

"No!" The word escaped her lips.

"What's wrong?" Bruce was alarmed.

The devastation had turned Elizabeth sheet white. Her eyes opened so wide, they stung. Or was it the beginning of tears?

Bruce reached out, gently brought her into the house, and led her to the couch.

"My God, what happened?" he asked as she collapsed on the cushions. "Are you all right?"

"It's okay. I'm okay," Elizabeth said, struggling to collect herself. "I'm sorry. I just . . . I tripped. That's it. I lost my balance. But I'm okay now."

She tried a smile to reassure him, but no smile came, only a twisted grimace, the harbinger of tears.

Bruce was concerned. "Did you fall? Is that it? Are you hurt?"

"No. I didn't fall, I didn't even trip." She was uncomfortable with the lie, but she couldn't really tell him the truth because she wasn't sure of it herself. Why did his possible happiness crush her so? He was her dearest friend; she loved him. She should be overjoyed.

"It's just been too overwhelming. Everything."

"I know." He poured two glasses of wine, a Pommard, her favorite, and handed her one. "Let's relax. Not talk about anything important."

"But you want to tell me . . ."

"It can wait. Come on, take your glass and I'll show you the new flowers I put in next to the deck. The *I,* of course, is actually Frederico, the guy who does my garden."

"But you sold the house."

"Who told you that?"

"It's true, isn't it?"

Bruce was caught. "Yes. Caroline?"

"No, my brother. But why the secret? And why did you keep it from me?"

"I'll tell you everything, but first I need some fortification."

Bruce downed his wine, refilled his glass, and topped off Elizabeth's.

"How many people are they expecting at the wedding?" he asked, stalling.

"A hundred and fifty or so. Todd has a million cousins."

"Who from Sweet Valley is coming?"

"It looks like our whole high school class."

They continued with the safe conversation for a couple of minutes. Both were uncomfortable about moving on.

Elizabeth was dreading the big revelation, but she couldn't help trying to guess who it was. Maybe it was someone from Sweet Valley. What if it was someone like Lila? Lila was separated, that made her available.

No way, Elizabeth told herself. That little fling they'd had in college was nothing. According to Bruce it had disappeared without a trace.

She quickly went through other possibilities while Bruce told her about how he'd sold the house to people who lived someplace, Elizabeth didn't hear where. She was too busy with the list of potential brides and beginning to feel more nauseated with every new candidate.

It turned out to be a whole long story about how the broker made a mistake on the price and they actually were going to pay ten thousand more than he was asking until he owned up.

Elizabeth studied Bruce's face while he spoke. He had the longest lashes for a man. They were almost pretty, but the blue eyes were dark and his expression was very masculine, strong, and honest.

Bruce had been pronounced gorgeous since high school, and he was. Since the time his parents had died, Elizabeth had been his closest friend and had stopped seeing his appearance; their psyches were so deeply connected she hardly ever noticed the surface. But looking at him now, aside from the gorgeous part, there was a warmth and even a sexiness. . . .

Sexiness? Bruce, her friend? Well, there it was.

She couldn't wait any longer. "Okay, so who is it?"

"What do you mean?"

"I know you too well. You're in love. So who is it?"

Even as she said the words and tried to make them sound light and fun, she dreaded the answer.

"How do you know I'm in love?"

"I can feel it."

"Describe it."

"Look at you. You're practically oozing love. You're almost electric in your warmth. No, make that hot—dare I say—passionate? You're on fire."

"That sounds like the writer talking."

"No. It's just what I feel."

"You feel?"

"Well, I feel you feel."

"You're right."

Now she wanted to run. It was okay up to this point, but when he named this woman, that would be the end of them together. Oh, yes, he would say he and Elizabeth would always be friends, but just from the look of him, she knew there would be no room for her. Or for anyone else.

Suddenly Elizabeth knew she didn't want to lose Bruce.

Her reaction was so startling, she didn't even know how to explain it.

It was far beyond just the selfishness of keeping her friend to herself, but any other reason was too weird.

She chickened out. "Okay, I don't want to know who it is. Just tell me where you're moving."

"To New York."

"Wow! How come? Is she there?"

He nodded.

Elizabeth poured herself another glass of wine. She'd need it for this. He would be living in New York, practically her neighbor, and she would have to pretend to be whomever's friend. Well, she would. Because she really loved this guy.

"Enough." Bruce sounded almost angry. "How can you be so dense? You're supposed to know me so well. Can't you see? It's you. I'm in love with you."

Elizabeth gasped. That was all she could do.

"And it's been you since that horrendous time in the hospital with my father. You took my hand. Dumb high school thing, but that was it. I've been struggling through your life for the last ten years and I can't do it anymore. At least not quietly."

It was like a huge wave hitting Elizabeth, knocking her down and burying her under a sea of water. Now she really had to gasp for breath.

"Me? You love me?" Her voice was so small it was barely a whisper. Certain she had misheard, she winced, expecting the embarrassing correction.

"Yes." Bruce moved closer. Close enough for her to feel the aura of heat emanating from his body.

Elizabeth let herself be drawn in. There was nothing she could think to say. In fact, there was no thinking, only feeling. An awesome, overpowering feeling.

Then he kissed her. Bruce Patman kissed her! That had never happened before. Not while she was conscious anyway, but that's a long story.

All those years of being so close emotionally but never touching, always keeping that little distance. He was the one who kept it, not she. She loved her friend and would have been warmer and more affectionate, but there was always that slight awayness.

It wasn't that Bruce wasn't appealing, because he was. In fact, he was very sexy, but absolutely off-limits.

For one thing, those were mostly the Todd years. Even the other brief relationships, like with Tom Watts and Sam Burgess, always had the shadow of Todd clouding them. Besides, the possibility of Elizabeth Wakefield cheating on anything or anyone was near impossible. That was her reputation and, truth is, it was deserved. Dummy that she was. But perhaps more important, it would have been a betrayal of their friendship. In those terrible years of loss, Bruce needed her. Taking advantage of that vulnerability would have been dishonorable.

Additionally, he certainly never showed any signs of liking her as anything but a friend. Although there were times when she thought she felt . . . stared at. Mostly when she wasn't looking. And when she turned around, it was gone. But she felt it all the same, then dismissed it and chalked it up to silly teenage romantic nonsense.

But this kiss was no silly romantic nonsense. It was real! And it was wild!

It reverberated right through her whole body. Before she knew it, Elizabeth threw her arms around Bruce as if she had just returned from a million years away from the man she loved.

At last Bruce had the love of his life in his arms, the unattainable woman he had adored for ten years, the woman he watched loving someone else. He'd known their love was wrong, but he couldn't tell her the truth because he cared too much.

They were both overcome, out of breath. Bruce stood up and held out his hand. And as she did ten years ago in that hospital waiting room, Elizabeth slipped her hand into his. Together they walked up the steps to his bedroom.

Once there, they just held each other. Then Bruce put his hands on her shoulders and moved her back slightly, only far enough to see her completely. To make certain she was absolutely there.

Gently, he unbuttoned her silk blouse. She didn't move. He slid it down over her shoulders, deftly unhooking her bra and allowing her breasts, with their taut nipples, to be free. He just stared at her, drinking in the sight of the flesh and blood of years of longing. Still she didn't move, waiting for him to slip her skirt and thong down over her hips and reveal her total nakedness to him.

With the excitement of standing in front of this man whom she had known so long from the distance of friendship, of being completely exposed to him, it took all her willpower to keep from closing the space between them and feeling the heat of his body against hers.

But now it was her turn. Elizabeth reached out and began to unbutton Bruce's shirt. She moved her hands to his belt, unzipped his pants, and with a gentle push, allowed them to drop to the floor, exposing his smooth, almost sculpted body and his desire for her.

Bruce let his shirt drop from his arms, kicked his legs free of the clothes, and took his love in his arms, pressing so hard he feared he would break her, but he couldn't stop himself and she didn't break. Together, they fell to the bed.

When they made love, it was completely loving, full of such deep tenderness that the passion almost played second to the adoration.

But the passion was there, and once the love had been established, the excitement took over and spun them out into the wild reaches of the glorious.

At last Elizabeth knew the splendid, the marvelous, the amazing, the spectacular!

The over the top!

EPILOGUE

For All Sweet Valley Fans of Old

They all came, from far and wide, to the Wakefield wedding, people who hadn't seen each other since high school at least ten years earlier. There were all kinds of whoops of delight, shrieks, hugs, and kisses along with some silent snubs, glares, and outright snaps.

Of course, it was at the Wakefields' country club, whose rooms were transformed into gardens of orchids, roses, peonies, and long branches of nascent cherry blossoms, all in blush tones with barely a hint of pink. The tables were draped in blanc cassé—colored soft voile with borders of tiny live roses. The cocktail room was done in deep pink and light pink peonies interrupted only by tall, fragrant eucalyptus branches, their silver leaves shimmering in the candlelight.

The procession started with two little flower girls, Todd's six-year-old cousins, flinging petals to the tune of "Sing" from *Sesame*

Street. They were followed by bridesmaids in soft cream-colored gowns. Elizabeth, the maid of honor, dressed in deep blush and carrying matching flowers, was escorted by Bruce Patman, a last-minute (only this morning) usher addition. Both looked radiant. They walked to a mélange of Beatles' music. Next the bride's mother, also in shades of cream highlighted with subtle threads of beige, followed by Todd, the groom, with his father in an electric blue tuxedo and his mother in a matching blue gown. Just a reminder that even in the most perfect wedding, there's aggravation.

And for the pièce de résistance, Ned Wakefield with his daughter Jessica, the bride, on his arm. She was dressed in a strapless sequined gown. Together they walked to the strains of "All I Ask of You" from *The Phantom of the Opera.*

Jessica said she'd had enough with "Here Comes the Bride" the last time around.

It was a fun wedding. Not a whole lot different from any Sweet Valley High dance, which, as everyone knows, is not a whole lot different from real life.

Plus ça change, plus ça change pas.

Bill Chase drove up from San Diego. He's still great-looking, with his signature long blond hair and blue eyes, very handsome in his tuxedo. In Sweet Valley High, he dated Dee Dee Gordon, but that ended when she went off to college in Maryland.

As a teenager Bill was an incredible swimmer and surfer. He broke all the records at Sweet Valley and went on to win All-State medals. Three years ago when he was competing in a triathlon in Australia he was attacked by a shark and lost his right leg below the knee. Today, he teaches surfing to handicapped teenagers and is involved in the Special Olympics. He married his longtime girlfriend, Lianne Kane, an almost six-foot-tall Sweet Valley basketball star whom he wooed away from Jim Regis.

After college Lianne played briefly in the national woman's basketball league, but gave it up to travel with her husband, a sacrifice she has never let Bill forget.

Lianne spent too much of the wedding ogling the bridegroom, Todd, the ex-basketball player she always had a crush on, and flirting with her ex-boyfriend Jim. It turned out to be too much for Bill. They left before the cake.

Roger Collins, known only as Mr. Collins the Robert Redford double, was there. Elizabeth was delighted to see her favorite high school English teacher and faculty adviser for *The Oracle,* the high school newspaper.

While he was teaching at Sweet Valley, he had a near-disastrous experience with Suzanne Devlin, who had been a houseguest of the Wakefields, and had accused him of sexual molestation. He was completely innocent.

After that incident, he felt too uncomfortable being a teacher, and he left to become a nonfiction writer. After four biographies, his latest effort is a memoir called *Lies,* about his teaching experiences. It's his most successful book so far, hitting the bestseller list and staying there for fourteen weeks.

Mr. Collins hasn't remarried and has lived with the same woman for the last eight years. He met her when she was a senior at Sweet Valley High, though not in his class. His son, Sam, now nineteen, is finishing his junior year at UCLA.

Of course, **Aaron Dallas** was there. He's never going to love Jessica, but since he might be his sister-in-law (California laws permitting), he has settled into a fairly comfortable, if distant (a room's length is usually best, but a table length will do) relationship with her.

All of his former classmates who still live in Sweet Valley are well aware of his new life, but the out-of-towners were knocked out when they learned he and Steven Wakefield have been living together for almost a year. They couldn't stop talking about it. Indeed, word spread so fast through the seated audience that some of them forgot to look at the bride—and don't think Jessica didn't notice.

Lila Fowler, still Jessica's best friend (and sometimes worst enemy), looked fabulous despite the bridesmaid gown. She wore her blond-streaked brunette hair loose with a center part separating the cascading waves that framed her lovely face. Of course, she still had brown eyes, but now they were disguised as green thanks to new contacts. She and Ken Matthews have been separated (a most unusual separation that changes as the wind blows) for almost six months, and her date for the wedding was Jeffrey French.

Jeffrey French moved to Sweet Valley from Oregon with his father and attended Sweet Valley High in his junior year. Lila and Enid Rollins competed for him, but it was Elizabeth who won. Lila's not really wild about Jeffrey, but having lost him to Elizabeth all those years ago, coming with him to the wedding made things a little spicier. Added to that, flirting with Ken, her ex-husband, made it even more spicy. Just like all the high school proms.

Somewhere after the soup course, Lila lost interest in Jeffrey. Still unmarried and unattached and now a practicing dentist, Jeffrey had a grand time dancing with Dee Dee Gordon and showing her around the grounds for a good forty-five minutes. Her fiancé had to work that night.

Dee Dee Gordon, as cute and petite as ever, and a talented working artist, dated Bill Chase in high school and still has a bit of a thing for him. She was able to sublimate it nicely with Jeffrey.

Charlie Markus, a truly nice guy, came with his wife, Annie Whitman, aka Easy Annie, the girl he saved in high school by teaching her to have self-respect. Charlie writes for an automobile magazine and hates it. His ambition is to publish a novel. He's written four, but so far he's had no luck in selling them. He just finished his latest novel with Annie as the protagonist. She's okay with it except for the title—*Easy Annie*.

Betsey Martin, dear, good Tricia Martin's older sister, was the traditional bad girl, a high school dropout who took drugs and slept around. She's off drugs, has switched to alcohol, and can't be counted on for anything important after five in the afternoon. She's still sleeping around, but thanks to the martinis, most of the time she doesn't remember with whom. Of course, she had a great time at the wedding, an inordinate amount of which she spent in the cloakroom.

Ken Matthews, Todd's best man, was captain and star quarterback of Sweet Valley High's football team, the Gladiators. He's still a football player, now for the NFL, but he hasn't played this season due to a knee injury. He's a local celebrity and in his off time, the host of a popular sports program. Even at the wedding he had fans bugging him for his autograph, another un-welcome distraction from the bride.

About two years ago he married Lila Fowler; six months ago, they separated. For no reason anyone can understand, he still likes her. A lot. Caroline Pearce, gossip supreme, says he has proposed to Lila again.

A. J. Morgan was another of the bad boys from high school. Why are bad boys always so gorgeous? After high school he was in college for about a week, but decided it wasn't for him and drifted. He's ended up selling sneakers at the Nike store in the mall. Caro-line Pearce has outrageous gossip about him and Dr. Enid Rollins that everyone finds hard to believe. But, of course, they do. Espe-cially since Enid went out of her way to ignore A.J. at the wedding.

Roger Barrett Patman, Bruce's late-found cousin, is the illegitimate son of Bruce's uncle. Not nearly as handsome as Bruce, Roger was a champion runner in high school and hasn't gained a pound since. He looks pretty much today as he did then, boyish, with friendly gray eyes somewhat obscured by thick-framed glasses that keep slipping down his nose. He was so poor in high school that he couldn't afford to take the regular bus. There were no school buses in his neighborhood. He had to walk—except he didn't, he ran. That's how he became a track star. At twenty-one, he inherited part of the Patman fortune. He now works as a pro-ducer in Hollywood and has had a few minor hits.

He brought his wife, **Zoe Jones,** a talented rock singer just starting her career. It promises to be a big one. She was the sec-ond celebrity at the wedding. All important parties need at least one, and the Wakefield wedding had two.

At one point, Zoe did a number from her new album that

Jessica managed to miss, not being in the mood for that kind of competition.

Bruce Patman was, as always, Bruce Patman, except today he was the happiest Bruce Patman anyone had ever seen. He could barely stop smiling. Even during the most serious part of the ceremony, he couldn't keep the smile down.

He never left Elizabeth's side and she didn't leave his, either. Though they didn't tell anyone, with a little help from Caroline Pearce, everyone knew that they were the hot new couple.

Most people were delighted because they loved Elizabeth and were thrilled to see her happy again. In the last few years they'd learned to love Bruce, too. He'd changed that much. Now they understood why.

Caroline Pearce has put on a few pounds but essentially looks the same as she did in high school: nosy. Unfortunately, Caroline has had to battle cancer. She underwent a year of chemo and radiation and has been in remission for a while now. As the star real estate agent of Sweet Valley Heights, she has keys to everyone's home. She uses them too often, but because she has so much information on everyone—and a potentially terminal illness—everyone tolerates her uninvited visits.

This was a wedding she was not about to miss, despite Jessica's attack at Lila's the week before. She needed the wedding for her gossip blog, which she puts out six days a week to the tune of five hundred hits a day. Tomorrow's blog might be more fun than the wedding.

Enid Rollins was Elizabeth's best friend from grade school, but hasn't been so for a long time. Enid looked cute as always (she hated that description) with her curly shoulder-length brown hair, green eyes, and a Betsey Johnson dress. She was always very intelligent and put those smarts to good use. The teenage years were a little hard on her. Too much drinking led to a dependency, but she licked that and became a doctor, a gynecologist. She keeps an office in downtown Sweet Valley right across from the very same Nike store in the mall where A.J. works, when he works.

One would think her background might have made her more understanding of vulnerability, but unfortunately, it hasn't. In fact, Enid has turned arrogant and extremely right-wing. She is totally enthralled with her own accomplishments and has great plans for herself.

Except for the tiny problem of the affair with A. J. Morgan, sneaker salesman supreme. It's secret because Enid is planning to run for city council, and an unsuccessful shoe salesman is not what she would consider the right partner. But she can't keep away from him.

She refused to come to the wedding with A.J. and made him sit at another table—where he ended up having a great time with an adorable cousin of Todd's from L.A.

Enid was beyond pissed off.

Nicky Shepard was wild in high school. He drove an old Mustang and hung out at the Shady Lady. He was always pretty much a loner, smoking cigarettes before anyone else and into alcohol and drugs. Jessica, during one of her wild periods, considered running away to San Francisco with him.

About two years ago, he bottomed out. Now he lives in Utah teaching at an AA recovery center. Skinny as he was in high school, mostly from drugs, he's close to roly-poly now, clean and content. He brought a date who is also a recovering alcoholic three years clean. They spent the wedding proselytizing anyone with a drink in hand. Everyone tried to escape.

Cara Walker, ex-wife of Steven, came. A cheerleader at Sweet Valley High, she still has the figure, but she looks different now, more serious. Actually, she looks more like what she is now, a math student supporting herself by baking her way to a master's degree.

Recently she began dating an accountant and CFO of a chain of diet centers, whom she brought to the wedding. She and Mr. and Mrs. Wakefield are on good terms. She forgave Steven and even speaks to Jessica now.

Annie Whitman, aka Easy Annie, so called because of her promiscuity in high school, married Charlie Markus, the boy who saved her. She is still beautiful, with dark curly hair, green eyes, and a flawless complexion that looked even more lovely against the cream and beige satin of her gown. Jessica thought it edged a little too close to white but let it pass.

Annie and Charlie, who live in San Diego, are the parents of a two-year-old boy they brought to the wedding. That Jessica didn't let pass.

Annie is a lawyer and, by way of compensating for all the high school years lost in shyness and insecurity, has become an unstoppable talker. Still one of Elizabeth's good friends, she spent most of the wedding giving Elizabeth and Bruce a condensed law 101 course. But they barely noticed.

Robin Wilson was once very overweight, but she lost the excess pounds to join the PBA sorority. Once she was slim and beautiful and therefore acceptable, she saw how shallow the sorority sisters were and turned them down. Since then she has put on a bit of the weight because of her work as a senior editor of the West Coast *Bon Appétit* and owner of The Smart Cookie catering company. In fact, she catered Jessica's wedding. Everyone said the food was great.

Robin had a wonderful time dancing with her new husband, Dan Kane, a lawyer from Steven Wakefield's office. She was delighted to see her old high school boyfriend, **George Warren,** who came in from England, where he represents a Silicon Valley company.

Todd Wilkins, the groom. Who would have guessed? The high school basketball star, now a sports columnist for the *Sweet Valley News,* was elegantly dressed in a Hugo Boss tuxedo, and as adorable and charming as ever. He looked happy and nervous. And for good reason. Marriage to Jessica Wakefield is not likely to be a walk in the park. But from the joy and love on his face, he looks ready.

Of course, there were those people who weren't there for the obvious reason.

Winston Egbert had died earlier that year.

Regina Morrow was the wonderful girl loved by everyone, who overcame a hearing disability only to die at sixteen from a bad combination of a heart murmur and a party drug.

Tricia Martin was Steven's first love, a lovely girl from a terrible family who died bravely of leukemia.

Suzanne Devlin, who had stayed in Sweet Valley for a nightmare month as a guest of the Wakefields, is also dead. Years ago she had caused a terrible scandal involving a sexual molestation charge that almost cost Roger Collins his career. In the nick of time, Elizabeth revealed Suzanne's mendacity and saved the school's favorite teacher.

Suzanne was forced to leave Sweet Valley but returned six years later a changed person; unfortunately, she was ill with multiple sclerosis. She apologized to everyone, then crashed her specially equipped car after taking medication with champagne.

And, of course, there were our stars, the Wakefields.

Ned and Alice Wakefield are the proud parents of Jessica, the bride, of Elizabeth, the maid of honor, and Steven, Todd's usher.

Ned walked his beautiful daughter down the aisle for the third time, but this time, everyone agreed, it felt right.

Ned's position as a senior partner in the biggest and most successful law firm in Sweet Valley meant most of the important people from Sweet Valley, the mayor included, came to the wedding. It was the social event of the season, just the way Jessica liked things.

And lucky, too, that both Wakefields were so successful because, from Jessica and Todd's initial impulse, "Let's just run off and get married," the wedding turned into a many-thousand-dollar country-club extravaganza.

Alice still looked like an older version of the twins with her blond hair, blue eyes, and a figure trim enough to wear a body-hugging cream silk Mandarin-style gown. Three years ago she opened her own interior design office in the new mall in Sweet

Valley, and it's been successful enough that she was able to kick in for part of the bill.

These last few years haven't been easy for Alice. Just before she opened the new office, she was diagnosed with breast cancer. She underwent a lumpectomy and a year of radiation, which slowed her down but didn't stop her; she's been very successful designing lobbies for new office buildings. And there are lots of them. Sweet Valley has burgeoned from a small town to a thriving city.

Both she and Ned are very happy with their new son-in-law, Todd, but are holding their breath about their much-married daughter, Jessica.

They have been holding their breath about Jessica for twenty-seven years now.

Steven Wakefield was slim, dark, and handsome in his tuxedo. He served as an usher, as did his lover, Aaron Dallas. Steven was happy for his baby sister, for the moment. But he has no illusions. Maybe being truly in love will make a difference for Jessica. It certainly did with him. Since he found Aaron, Steven has never been happier. With any luck, and some good California politics, the Wakefields will end up with three sons-in-law.

Elizabeth Wakefield was the maid of honor for her little sister (four minutes younger), Jessica. She's glowing. The eternal "good girl" had a wild night with her new lover, Bruce Patman, and from the glorious happiness beaming on her face, a face that has been without joy for too long, she might really be in love.

In fact, she is.

All through the ceremony, she and her lover looked at each other with such passion that it was hard to know who was getting married.

Jessica Wakefield, even in her sequined cream strapless wedding gown, still looks exactly like her twin, especially today, with her matching glow. Jessica, like her sister, Elizabeth, is truly in love.

Actually, being the bride, with that ethereal quality that only brides have, she's a hair more exquisite than her sister.

She, too, without being blameless, has suffered these last months, and now she is shining with happiness.

Happily, still Jessica, the one without the watch who always says that nothing starts until she gets there, is absolutely right today. The entire wedding party waited an extra fifteen minutes for the bride to appear.

She was well worth the wait.

THE POWER OF READING

Visit the Random House website and get connected with information on all our books and authors

EXTRACTS from our recently published books and selected backlist titles

COMPETITIONS AND PRIZE DRAWS Win signed books, audiobooks and more

AUTHOR EVENTS Find out which of our authors are on tour and where you can meet them

LATEST NEWS on bestsellers, awards and new publications

MINISITES with exclusive special features dedicated to our authors and their titles

READING GROUPS Reading guides, special features and all the information you need for your reading group

LISTEN to extracts from the latest audiobook publications

WATCH video clips of interviews and readings with our authors

RANDOM HOUSE INFORMATION including advice for writers, job vacancies and all your general queries answered

Come home to Random House
www.rbooks.co.uk